I0570821

INTO THE

YELLOW

AND OTHER STORIES

BARBARA DAVIES

Mindancer Press
Bedazzled Ink Publishing Company * Fairfield, California

© 2013 Barbara Davies

All rights reserved. No part of this publication may be reproduced
or transmitted in any means, electronic ormechanical, without
permission in writing from the publisher.

978-1-939562-18-0 paperback
978-1-934452-16-5 ebook

First published 2006

2nd edition 2013

cover
by
C. A. Casey

"Cordie and the Merman" by Barbara Davies. Copyright © 2002 by Barbara
Davies. First published in *Andromeda Spaceways Inflight Magazine*, Vol. 1/Issue 4,
Dec 2002. Reprinted by permission of the author.
"Journey to Niskor" by Barbara Davies. Copyright © 2000 by Barbara Davies. First
published in *Spaceways Weekly,* Issue number 132, March 10, 2000). Reprinted by
permission of the author.
"Time and the Maid" by Barbara Davies. Copyright © 2003 by Barbara Davies.
First published in in *Alternate Species Print Magazine,* Issue 2, Feb 2003.
Reprinted by permission of the author.
"Dog and Kat" by Barbara Davies. Copyright © 2000 by Barbara Davies. First
published in *Noesis,* Issue 6, March 2000. Reprinted by permission of the author.

Mindancer Press
a division of
Bedazzled Ink Publishing Company
Fairfield, California
http://www.bedazzledink.com

For Joyce,
who has shared my love of Fantasy and Science Fiction since
we were tiny tots hoping fairies lived at the bottom of our
garden.

ACKNOWLEDGMENT

I'd like to thank Casey and Claudia for all their encouragement and hard work. A big thank you also goes to those writers in the BSFA Orbiter and Critters Online workshops who "critted" some of these stories.

TABLE OF CONTENTS

FOREWORD

Patience is part of the writing life. It's the norm for several years to elapse between a story being accepted for publication and its appearance in print. In July 2006, though, came the straw that broke this patient camel's back and which led directly to the collection of short stories you hold in your hand. Four different anthologies folded, all at the same time, and stories that I had thought sold years ago came boomeranging back to me.

Rejection is also part of the writing life. I'm no stranger to rejection slips; some of my best stories have only made it into print after being rejected twenty times. Some stories richly deserve rejection, and I put them out of their misery and move on. Others I keep sending out. Let's just say my conviction is that it's a matter of taste (the editor's) and belief (mine)—belief that a particular story has merit and that someone, somewhere, will enjoy reading it.

In July 2006, though, I confess, my frustration at not being able to get some of my favourite stories out there so they can simply be read finally reached boiling point. So when my publisher, Bedazzled Ink, asked what book I would like to publish next, I suggested a collection of short speculative fiction. They agreed, and I couldn't be more delighted.

This collection contains 15 short stories—four previously published (in magazines few readers will have had access to), seven unpublished (because the magazines that accepted them folded), the remaining four brand new. Here are tales of Fantasy and Science Fiction that range from ancient Rome to the far flung future, featuring zombies and vampires, lunar settlements and alien worlds, mermen and dragons, spacemen and canal boatwomen, nano technology, time machines, and demons. I hope you find something in these pages to enjoy.

Best wishes,
Barbara Davies
December 2006

INTO THE YELLOW

"KESHO . . . KESHO, WHERE are you?" The familiar voice came drifting up the rise. "You promised to help me get ready for tonight."

From her hiding place, Kesho watched Mother turn downslope and sighed with relief. She'd been cooped up for the last two days, but it had been drizzling anyway. Today the weather was fine and still, and the urge to escape from the endless preparations for her brother's betrothal party had proved irresistible.

She had grabbed her knife and haversack as she left the cave, and now she strapped the knife belt on, and slung the sack from her shoulder. The base of her tail itched, and she twisted and nibbled the creamy skin until the irritation subsided. Decisions, decisions. Her best friend, Buki, would be cloudskimming—should she go down and join him? But there would also be a good view from the top today—maybe even as far as Batian Mountain. On an impulse she turned upslope.

A twinge of guilt at her desertion nagged Kesho. I'll take back some glimmer-flies for the party, she decided. Buki liked them too, and there were usually plenty on the glacier—they thrived in the thin air. Her mind easier, she began to climb.

THE HIGHER SHE climbed, the hotter it became, and Kesho was having to pause often for breath. Morning sunlight had melted the night's ice crystals but not yet baked the liquefied soil into a crust. This was the worst bit, she thought, stirring a mud puddle with her toes while she waited for her aching lungs to ease.

Sunlight glinted off the ribbon of ice above. A heat haze hung over the glacier, and Kesho knew it would be cooler up there. She took a deep breath and scrambled the remaining distance. The ice soothed her tired and overheated paws, but it wouldn't be long before the pleasant coolness became a debilitating chill, in spite of the sun's rays. She eased herself over to her favourite dirt patch and, now insulated from the cold, lay on her belly. Perfect.

In spite of the haze, the view was breathtaking. To the north, Batian Mountain's distinctive double peak looked closer than ever.

Kesho flicked out her tongue and tasted the moisture-laden air. Not as pleasant as the stream by the cave, but not bad. She sighed with contentment and basked in the sun. A shadow flitted over her and she looked up. It was only a bone-bird, cruising the rising air currents, looking for food. She watched its beady eyes assess and dismiss her, then turned back to the distant mountain, which jutted like an island above the yellow cloud sea. How far away was it really? And how high?

Today the Yellow was calm, with barely a billow or eddy. Kesho could just make out the moving dots of bone-birds diving as near to its surface as they dared. Only once had she and Buki seen one fly too low, and then it had been mere seconds before the choking cloud took effect. The bird's carcass had floated for days before rotting and sinking from sight, a potent warning to foolhardy younglings. It didn't stop Buki and the others from cloudskimming for long though.

An inquisitive glimmer-fly hovered in front of Kesho. She flicked out her tongue, reeled it in, and crunched it between her gums. Its sharp tang was delicious. As she spat out the fly's inedible core, she remembered her earlier resolution. One eye scanned the glacier ahead while the other looked behind.

There. Iridescent insect bodies caught the sunlight as they batted to and fro. Kesho raised herself off the grit patch and inched closer to the shimmering cloud. She took a deep breath.

Snicker. Her tongue snagged the nearest glimmer-fly and in one practised movement banged it on the ice, crushing its tiny body like a bone-bird would a bone. Crack. She released the corpse and started again. Snicker. Crack . . . She had caught and killed twenty of the dull-witted insects before they realized their danger and vanished. A satisfying haul, she thought, stowing the catch in her haversack.

"WHERE HAVE YOU been?" Mother's tail was mauve with annoyance and her eyes glittered in their protuberant sockets. "I've been looking for you all morning. You know tonight is important. I've even invited the Storyteller."

"I brought you these," said Kesho. She emptied the haversack onto the cave floor.

The mauve tint faded at once. "Glimmer-flies—what a treat!" Then one eye swivelled towards her. "You've been to the glacier again?"

Kesho gazed at the floor and said nothing.

"When are you going to settle down and take your responsibilities seriously, Kesho?" Mother sighed and began to collect the food. "It won't be long before it's your own betrothal party." She bustled to the back of the cave and began to core the flies.

Kesho grunted and sat on her favourite rock. Her brother was marrying his cousin, a female he'd known since they were younglings. How could he think of her in that way? It baffled Kesho. My turn next, she thought. And her heart sank as she considered Buki. What sort of a mate would he make? Oh, he was a good friend, and handsome enough, she supposed—his skin was attractively mottled, not streaked like some of the other males. And at least he was healthy, no sign of the deformities increasingly occurring among the tribe. Their younglings would probably be normal. But they had grown up together, and she felt no physical attraction to him at all. Mother had assured her that it would come in time—hadn't that been the way with her father, after all?—but Kesho was still doubtful. Why couldn't things just stay as they were?

"Mother," yelled Ngojea, pulling into the cave a leaf piled high with large crimson spheres. His tail was turquoise with pride. "I've managed to get some crush-berries from old Tomar."

An appetizing smell wafted over and Kesho sniffed appreciatively. Crush-berry juice was much prized—she wondered what her brother had promised in exchange. It looked like tonight was going to be a real celebration. No wonder Mother was so flustered. She sighed and hunkered down even further on her rock.

"Sulking because it's not your party, little sister?" jeered Ngojea on his way out again.

She didn't deign to reply.

"ONCE, THE PEOPLE lived all over the earth, even on the surface now hidden deep beneath the Yellow—because once there was no Yellow."

The Storyteller paced up and down, his heavy tail leaving drag marks in the cave floor's soil. Such was the old one's control, he could change colour at will, signalling what emotions his audience should feel. It was an impressive sight, thought Kesho, watching the tail change from orange to turquoise and back again.

"Once, we were many tribes," he continued, gesticulating with the two digits of a forepaw. "Some had colourful crests, some fierce horns deadly in battle . . ."

She let her mind drift at the familiar words.

". . . then the Yellow came, and we were forced to flee its suffocating fumes. Steadily, relentlessly, it rose. Our ancestors climbed higher—those who stayed behind died . . ."

Just lately Kesho had begun to wonder about the ritual chant. Was it myth, or could it mean that People had once lived on Batian Mountain, were perhaps still living there? If only she could find out for certain. But nobody had ever travelled there and survived—though some had tried. The last attempt had been five years ago, when Grofor, since renamed "the mad one," had taken a cloudskimmer and oars and set off alone into the Yellow. He had never returned.

The Storyteller's chant ended, and Buki passed her a beaker of crush-berry juice. "Cheer up, Kesho," he whispered, mistaking the reason for her solemnity. "Soon be our turn."

She took a gulp, feeling the warm glow burn down her gullet. Our turn. That's part of the problem, she thought glumly.

FROST CRYSTALS ENCRUSTED the ground when Kesho crawled out to the basking stone. The first to wake, she emerged through a cave strewn with leftover food and dirty utensils, and the bodies of still comatose guests.

She stretched as the sun's warmth penetrated her hide and quickened her sluggish blood. It was a fine, clear morning, no sign of rain. A good day for cloudskimming.

Kesho had slept fitfully, her stomach churning with too many glimmer-flies, her mind awash with images of handsome males with crests and horns. But there had been that other dream too, the one that came more and more often lately. It returned now, as she lazed in the sun.

She was riding a cloudskimmer, the huge green leaf floating on the surface of the Yellow. The toxic cloud stretched featureless on all sides, and it seemed that she was adrift without oars on some desolate sea covered with nothing but trailing banks of fog. She felt surprisingly calm, given the circumstances—unperturbed by the skimmer's aimless drifting. Then came movement overhead, and she looked up. Spiralling lazily down towards her was a huge bone-bird.

The beady gaze met hers, and Kesho wondered for a moment if it were waiting for her to die so it could feast on her bones. Instead, it began to circle the skimmer—once, twice, three times—and then it set off away from her in a straight line. The skimmer, its means of propulsion a mystery, began to follow the bird.

The gliding motion had lulled her almost to sleep when she realized that the bird had alighted on something up ahead. At this distance, it was hard to make it out—a tree, a rock? In the middle of nowhere? And then the fog bank rolled away, and the unmistakable forked outline of Batian Mountain materialized. As her skimmer crunched onto its lower slopes, the bone-bird stared down at her from its branch, and gave a single loud croak.

Batian Mountain dissolved like smoke before the wind, and a confused Kesho watched the Storyteller approach her with his measured tread.

"Hello, young Kesho," he wheezed, and she became aware of the basking rock, hard beneath her belly and knew she was awake.

She yawned, dispelling the remnants of the rapidly receding dream, and made room for him, shifting another inch when his bony knee dug into her side.

"Did you enjoy yourself last night?" he asked. She gave a non-committal grunt, and his nearer eye swivelled towards her. "You are healthy, and loved, Kesho. And it won't be long before you marry Buki and have younglings of your own. Why should you be unhappy?"

She fidgeted, uncomfortable under his piercing stare. "I don't know what's wrong with me, Storyteller. I'm so restless these days. And there's this recurring dream."

"Tell me."

So she did. "What does it mean?"

He considered for several moments and tasted the air with his warty tongue before answering. "You're not the first to feel this way, Kesho. Some years ago, Grofor became obsessed with Batian Mountain and felt compelled to journey there, in spite of the dangers. I advised against it, but there was no stopping him." He gazed sadly at Kesho. "Fight against these yearnings, if you can."

A shadow blocked the sun, and Kesho glanced up.

Ngojea loomed over her. "You've basked long enough, little sister. It's my turn now."

With an apologetic glance at the Storyteller, Kesho rose and went back to the cave.

THE YELLOW OFF Skimmer Point was full of cloudskimmers performing intricate manoeuvres, the sort of daredevil activity that made the Elders hiss with disapproval. It wasn't unknown for collisions to throw riders from their green craft into the toxic cloud— one of Kesho's childhood playmates had been killed that way.

"Are you coming in, Kesho?" yelled Buki, skimming along the shoreline in front of her.

She nodded, placed the huge skimmer leaf on the Yellow, grabbed her four oars, and stepped carefully aboard. After sinking onto her belly, she grasped a paddle in each paw then dug them in deep. The cloudskimmer shot forward with a whoosh.

"Coming through." Buki swooped in front of her then steered his skimmer in a tight curve until they were running side by side. He grinned at her, displaying his gums.

Kesho concentrated on her rowing, until the rhythm of the oars and the swish of the two skimmers had induced an almost trancelike state. The excited shouts of the other riders faded into the background. Back and forth she and Buki zigzagged, each sweep taking them further from shore. From time to time they exchanged companionable glances, but neither spoke. The sun was warm overhead, and a cool breeze feathered her skin. Later would come the headache, caused by proximity to the Yellow, but for now . . . a feeling of contentment stole over her.

She had no idea how long they had been skimming when the light seemed to darken and the breeze to strengthen. She glanced up and noticed that the sky had turned a sickly beige.

"Buki," she shouted. "The weather's changing. Better head back."

He signalled his agreement, and they turned the cloudskimmers back towards Skimmer Point. Had they really drifted that far out?— the other craft were mere dots. Alarmed, Kesho began to power towards the Point. Buki followed close behind.

Before they had reached half way, the smooth surface of the Yellow began to break up, the choppy surges sending wisps of vapour into the air. Kesho steered round the stinging plumes. She could hear the faint encouraging cries of the other riders, now disembarked on the shore and waving to her. "Hurry up, Kesho . . . Buki."

She glanced back.

"Keep going," called Buki.

Kesho took another deep breath and dug in once more. Already her joints ached. Then a wisp of Yellow trailed over her left foot, and she gasped as it burned, instinct making her retract her toes. The oar bobbed away before she had time to grab it again. Damn! Buki's craft caught up with hers as she lost momentum.

"Are you all right?"

She grimaced and rubbed her stinging foot. "I'm fine, Buki. Lost an oar, that's all. Go on. I'll follow."

She glanced towards the shoreline again. The crowds had deserted the Yellow's edge and dark blobs now milled about on the higher ground above the Point. What on earth were they doing? She strained to see, the wind howling past her and almost upsetting her balance. The wind. It must be nearly gale force, and blowing directly towards the shore. She turned to see what was causing it.

Kesho's heart almost stopped with terror. A wall of Yellow was thundering towards her and Buki. She had heard stories of such cloud waves, but never seen one. It would reach her before she could regain the safety of the shore. With his four oars, however, Buki might just make it.

"Buki," she yelled. "Get ashore, quick!"

His tail had whitened with shock as he too saw the wave, and for a moment he remained frozen. Then he turned towards her, his mouth twisting with anguish and indecision. He doesn't want to leave me, she realized.

"Get going, stupid! No sense in both of us getting killed."

Buki gave a slow nod, while inside Kesho screamed at him to hurry. Then he began to paddle, with increasing desperation, and the distance between the two skimmers lengthened.

A numb Kesho stared at the giant wave, feeling the wind of its coming on her snout, and tried to remember what she had been taught about the afterlife. Yet even as she resigned herself to death, part of her refused to give up. If only she could somehow harness the wind . . . But all she had was three paddles and the knife in her belt.

An idea skimmed the surface of her mind, leaving a ripple of hope, and her pulse began to race. It was a crazy idea. But if she didn't do something, she was going to die—choked and burned by the noxious fumes. She pulled out her knife.

Over and over Kesho scored the blade's edge across the width of the cloudskimmer. The leaf's thick membrane was tough, and she had to saw vigorously to make any impression at all. Twice she glanced up to gauge the wave's progress before returning with even more urgency to her task.

It was almost on her, the wind nearly tearing her from her perch, when she decided the cut was deep enough. Yellow stung her paws as she gripped the leaf's farthest edge, braced herself, and tugged. For a moment, the leaf refused to budge. Then, so suddenly she almost lost her balance, the hinge gave, and half of the huge leaf swung upwards. And as it did so, the vertical portion caught the full blast of the wind, and the skimmer was propelled forwards with the speed of a tongue catching a glimmer-fly.

Kesho's now winddriven skimmer flashed past Buki's wallowing craft. He gaped at her and waved one exhausted paw in what she swore later was a gesture of farewell, but could equally have been a plea for help. She had time only to yell his name once, before he had disappeared behind her. Beneath the choking wave.

BUKI'S BODY BOBBED near Skimmer Point during a week of stormy, gloom-ridden days, and garish sunsets, as though even the weather were marking his passing. Then the skies cleared once more, the Yellow calmed, and the retrieval party managed to launch a skimmer.

While the Elders performed the funeral rites, and the Storyteller told of the better place to which Buki had now gone, Kesho felt frozen, both physically and mentally. From time to time she shivered, and was dimly aware of her mother's concerned glance. It could not be real, she felt. They were mourning someone other than her childhood friend. Buki was only late as usual. He would turn up soon, apologetic and breathless. The feeling was so intense, she had to fight to keep from looking round, searching for him.

After the ceremony, when they had buried the body beneath a cairn in the graveyard, Mother took her home.

MONTHS PASSED, AND Kesho tried hard to get on with her life. Then, one morning, the Elders summoned her and Mother to their deliberations.

The oldest member of the Seven pinned her with a sharp gaze from his one good eye. "The tribe needs more younglings, so you must choose a mate."

Outrage surged through Kesho, so hot and strong she could almost taste it. Unable to speak, she gazed at the floor, letting the mauve of her tailskin speak for her.

"Buki was to be her betrothed," blurted Mother.

"Buki is dead. She must choose another."

Choose another. Kesho was overcome with repulsion. Did they really think she could mate with any of the other eligible males: arrogant Voket, for example, the most handsome of his peers but also the most cruel; or Sregan, with his timid manner, strange odour, and withered paw? Or what about Krepa, with his disgusting habits? Unable to stop herself, she began to weep.

"Shhh," soothed her mother. Then, to the council: "My daughter has barely recovered from the shock of Buki's death. She needs time to consider."

The Seven gave reluctant grunts of agreement. "Very well. She shall have a month. Then she must choose."

Mother helped Kesho from the council cave.

"I CAN'T, MOTHER," she sobbed. "I'd rather die than marry any of them."

"I know, dear. But what choice is there?"

"I'll run away. Find others of the People. Maybe I can marry one of them instead?"

"Don't be foolish." Her mother sighed. "There are no others of the People."

But Kesho, hoping her mother was wrong, began to lay her secret plans. She had a month, after all.

IT WAS A still morning with the promise of fine weather to come—the first such morning for two weeks. Kesho thought she would probably never trust the weather again; even so, she eased her skimmer out onto the Yellow, climbed on board, and began to paddle.

Beside her lay a pile of glimmer-flies and sweet-fruit bulbs, sneaked from the larder yesterday while Mother was preoccupied with Ngojea's newly pregnant wife. The food and drink should last three days—plenty of time in which to reach Batian Mountain.

Kesho had scored the skimmer leaf across its middle and attached twine to the far portion so she could hoist it like a sail, but there was no breeze. She began to row, steering the craft towards the forked mountain on the horizon.

"Kesho," came a plaintive cry.

She turned. Mother was waving at her from the shore.

"Be careful, Kesho. And be happy."

Her mother must have found the farewell note already. But instead of the expected alarm and panic, instead of pleading with her to stay, she seemed to have accepted her daughter's decision. A bubble of love swelled in Kesho's gullet and threatened to burst into her mouth. She swallowed it with difficulty.

"I'll bring my younglings back to visit you, Mother."

Mother nodded, then turned and plodded back upslope towards their cave. Kesho gazed at the suddenly old and frail figure through blurred eyes until it disappeared. Then she turned towards her destination and dug in the oars.

KESHO ATE A glimmer-fly wing, swallowed some sweet-fruit juice, and gazed at Batian Mountain. A morning's hard rowing, yet it seemed no closer. Suppose she hadn't brought enough food and drink for the journey after all? Was that what had happened to Grofor? Had his rotting carcass provided a feast for bone-birds, spread invitingly on his skimmer like a meal on a platter? For a moment, she trembled at the image, then she grew angry with herself. This won't do. It's foolish to expect any change in the mountain's profile so soon. She pushed the fear aside and picked up the oars once more.

A little later, the sun came out, and a stiff breeze sprang up, blowing towards the twin peaks. Kesho raised the sail; at once the craft picked up speed, and her spirits began to rise. This is more like it, she thought. I'll be there in no time. For the rest of the day, progress was swift, then twilight fell, the wind dropped, and the craft was becalmed. To her dismay, the temperature began to dip.

Kesho had never slept out in the open before, and the unexpected severity of the cold almost sent her into hibernation. She struggled to remain conscious, counting the stars, which sparkled like frost crystals in the clear night sky. Several shivering hours later, wisps of cloud began to block out the stars one by one. And when dawn came, it brought only watery sunlight.

Kesho began to panic. The new layer of cloud cover was preventing the sun's rays from reaching her, and she desperately needed warmth. Until her blood temperature reached a certain level, she could barely stand let alone row. Another fit of shivering overtook her and she forced herself to eat a glimmer-fly, aware that her body must be consuming energy at a frightening rate in its attempts to keep warm.

As Kesho chewed, she gazed at the forked mountain and was puzzled to notice it drifting to the north. Was something dragging the skimmer off course? She struggled to the side and peered over. A stream of Yellow about a yard wide was coursing through its surroundings, wisps of disturbed vapour marking its edges.

The current that had caught the skimmer was weak, but so was Kesho. She lay helpless in the middle of the boat, almost weeping with tiredness and frustration, and watched the mountain drift farther and farther to the north. It was midday before she finally felt strong enough to bring the skimmer back on course. There was still no breeze, so she had no option but to row. At this rate, she would have no energy left to survive the rigours of the coming night.

Fortunately, the low cloud made the night warmer, or Kesho would surely have succumbed to the deep winter sleep, which in these circumstances meant certain death. The morning sunshine, when it finally came, was more powerful too. Although she now had a fierce headache, from being on the Yellow for so long, she felt stronger. She was even able to row for a while before making the most of a barely perceptible breeze.

During the afternoon, she finished the last of her food and drink. Batian Mountain looked at least two days away still—she wondered if she could keep going without nourishment. Already her skin felt loose; her fat reserves must be depleted. But what choice did she have? Grimly, she plied the oars.

Kesho found she could row and let her thoughts wander—

providing she surfaced occasionally to check the course, and to correct any discrepancies. More and more her thoughts drifted into the past, recalling days when Father had been alive, days when she and Buki had played truant and gone cloudskimming off Skimmer Point. Each time she returned to the present, it seemed harder to remain.

Then the fog bank rolled in, coating her skin with a clammy dew. It was not one of the Yellow's manifestations, or she would have been dead in minutes. Gratefully, she licked the slick layer of water vapour, savouring the moisture on her parched tongue and throat. At least she wouldn't die of thirst. But when she had finished lapping, she realized that the fog was as much a curse as a blessing. For the familiar beckoning outline of Batian Mountain had disappeared.

Despair filled the pit of her stomach, then worked its way upwards. Had the last sighting of the forked peak been over here . . . or there? She peered through the wet, drifting fog, but it only made her headache worse. She could just as easily be rowing away from the mountain as towards it. Eventually, she was forced to admit defeat. She curled up in the centre of the skimmer, as though back in her egg, and waited for the fog to thin.

Kesho was wondering what the Storyteller would tell the young-lings about her journey—would it be coupled with that of Grofor?—when the sky above her seemed to darken even further and she looked up. Something blacker and more substantial than the fog was circling above the skimmer, descending in a lazy curve. After a moment she recognized the huge white head and pointed beak, the broad sweep of brown wings.

A bone-bird's unwinking, orange eye was fixed on her. She sat up and waved, to scare it away. "I'm not dead yet." Her voice was hoarse from disuse. "Go away."

The bird spiralled closer.

Surely bone-birds liked dead prey? Kesho had never heard of one attacking the living. But perhaps in the middle of the Yellow, where prey was scarce . . . Her heart thumped in panic. The bird's beak was as large as her forearm. She imagined it tearing into her, ripping huge chunks of flesh from the bone . . .

"Leave me alone . . . Haiya!" She grabbed an oar and waved it at the bird.

It made another sweeping arc around the skimmer, as though

satisfying itself that there were no titbits to be had, then to Kesho's relief it turned and flew away.

Something about this is familiar, she thought. Now why is that? Then she remembered. My dream! Perhaps if I follow . . . She picked up the oars and with what little remained of her strength began to paddle after the disappearing bone-bird.

Constant hard rowing left Kesho panting. The bird had long out-stripped her, but she continued blindly in the same direction. Then, as she lapped more droplets of water vapour from her skin, the skimmer cleared the fog bank, and the welcome outline of Batian Mountain appeared directly ahead.

For a moment, she remained motionless, stunned at the sight, then huge, uncontrollable sobs of relief shook her. She had made it. Batian Mountain was so close she could almost reach out and touch it. Within the hour she had beached the skimmer on the gravel of its lower slopes.

KESHO WAS FEEDING on the fleshy bulbs of a sweet-fruit bush when she realized she was being observed. Movement gave away the watcher's position in the dense shrubs to one side of the clearing. At first she thought she must be mistaken, for it blended perfectly with the grey, green, and brown of its surroundings. Then it moved again. There. An eye blinking, she realized with a start.

She spat out the sweet-fruit pips. "I see you," she called, heart pounding with a mixture of fear and excitement. "Come out."

The male who emerged sheepishly into the open was larger than males of her own tribe. But what struck her at once, and took her breath away, was the spiky crest that started on the top of the stranger's head, followed the line of his neck, then tapered to nothing on his broad shoulders. She gaped at him, her nostrils flaring at his unfamiliar scent.

"Hello," he said. "My name's Rethic." His accent was peculiar, but she could understand his words. And in spite of his size, he was only young. Perhaps her own age, thought Kesho.

His skin was resuming its normal coloration—a mottled pink and green, totally unlike her own. He returned her fascinated gaze.

"Kesho," she said after the silence seemed to have lasted longer than was polite.

"Have you been injured?"

His question took her by surprise, and she frowned. "No. Why?"

He pointed to his crest.

"Oh." Comprehension washed over her. "My tribe doesn't have crests."

His earholes widened. "Your . . . tribe?"

Kesho hunkered down and began to explain.

KESHO WAS THE first uncrested person the Batian Mountain People had ever seen, she learned over the next few weeks. They had developed in much the same way as her own people, but were larger, with different coloration, and they spoke with a strange singsong intonation. Their younglings too were afflicted with an increasing number of deformities—minor as yet, but enough to worry the Elders.

Unlike her own tribe, some of the Elders were scientists, fascinated by everything. They asked her questions for what seemed like hours. The deformities were probably caused by inbreeding, they said. Their own Storyteller had often chanted of the days before the Yellow, when People covered the earth, but this was the first evidence of its underlying truth. Excitement coloured their tails red as they realized that others of their kind existed, even if they were on the far side of the Yellow. Research into a safe method of travel began in earnest, the scientists examining and dismantling Kesho's cloudskimmer, and proposing improvements in size and safety modifications.

Hopeful males followed Kesho's every step, vying to impress her with their strength and health, Rethic prominent among them, but none attracted her as she had hoped. Eventually she tired of the, at first, gratifying attention. She needed to be by herself. So one morning, a month after she had beached her skimmer on the shores of Batian Mountain, she set off upslope. Perhaps they have a glacier at the top too, she thought.

At first, the more persistent suitors accompanied her, but when they realized the effort involved, and that she resented their presence, they dropped away. She climbed on regardless of the aches and pains of unused muscles, until the twin peaks came in sight. Both were topped with the white glint of ice. She turned towards the leftmost, slightly taller, peak.

After the constant hubbub, the glacier's peace and quiet was a blessed relief. Kesho found a suitable grit patch, dropped onto her belly, and gazed out across the Yellow. It was strange to see the single peak of her birthplace, after so long spent staring at Batian Mountain's fork. It was even harder to picture herself on the glacier there. A pang of homesickness overwhelmed her, and she rested her snout on her front paws and began to snuffle in misery. Perhaps when the scientists had perfected a method of travel . . .

She had lost track of time when she heard the sound of gravel sliding. A male, a few years older than her, scrabbled up onto the glacier. She had seen him around the settlement once or twice, but they had never met. He stopped, startled, when he saw her, and had turned to go, when on impulse Kesho called out, "I'm sorry if I've taken your favourite spot. Please don't go. Stay and talk to me."

The male looked uncertain, so she moved over and patted the space beside her. He nodded, and hobbled to join her. His front paw was crippled, she realized—twisted back on itself. It must have taken great determination and effort to climb the mountain.

As he settled stiffly beside her, he seemed aware of her gaze, but said nothing.

"Your paw," she said, choosing her words with care. "Does it hurt?"

One eye swivelled to observe her, then turned back to the view. "Sometimes." His voice was self-conscious, braced for rejection. "It was crushed when I was a baby. Wouldn't heal properly."

"That happened to a friend of mine. His back paw, though," she said. An almost palpable feeling of relief flowed from him at the matter-of-fact comment.

They basked in the morning sun in companionable silence for a while, then he gave her a shy glance. "My name's Frenet," he said. "And you're Kesho—from the far mountain." He pointed at the distant peak, now beginning to be obscured by cloud.

"Yes."

Something in her voice must have alerted him. "You wish you were back there?"

"Yes . . . No . . . I don't know."

"I understand," he continued. "You left your family behind."

He pronounced "family" wistfully, and she turned her full attention on him for the first time. Apart from the paw, he was quite handsome, she thought. His crest was at least as good as Rethic's, but his smell was different from the other males. Theirs seemed acrid, unpleasant, whereas his was sweet with undertones of musk. With a start, she realized that a small thread of attraction was running up and down her spine and making her limbs tingle.

"What about your family?" she asked, trying to collect herself.

"Dead. In the rock slide that crushed my paw."

The breeze wafted her scent towards him, and she saw his nostrils flare. She shuffled closer and noticed with satisfaction that he didn't move away. The last shreds of her homesickness evaporated, and more pressing questions surfaced. If they were to mate, would their younglings be healthy? Would they have crests or not? And would Mother like him?

She gave him a wide smile, and for a moment he looked taken aback, then a spark of answering interest gleamed in his eyes.

"Tell me, Frenet," asked Kesho. "Would you like to be part of a family again? And have you ever considered going on a journey—into the Yellow, perhaps?" Eagerly she waited for his reply.

AFTERWORD

Watching a BBC wildlife documentary one day, I was struck by the image of Mount Kenya's glacier-strewn summit rising above a sea of cloud. Up there, chameleons experience winter each night and summer each day. It didn't take much of a creative leap to propel Mount Kenya into the future and make the cloud sea real. Then to ask myself: How could the chameleons, now evolved, cross the lethal sea? And what would they find if they did?

LONE WOLF

ONLY ONE PASSENGER, a woman in a brown leather jacket, had disembarked from the last park-and-ride bus of the night. Tarian watched the woman clutch her shopping bag closer to her chest. Her instincts must be warning her that something bad was lurking in the poorly lit carpark. The question was, would she listen? Most humans didn't.

Tarian turned to regard the man crouching by the crumbling wall. Though moonlight cast the scene in deep shadows, to her it appeared as bright as day. He sensed her regard and returned her look with a challenging one of his own. *Mine*, it said, as clearly as if he had spoken aloud. *Keep away.*

She knew he had been aware of her since she started following him, the best part of two hours ago. But her scent was close enough to his that he discounted her as a threat.

Wrong.

She resisted the urge to draw her bow, though her fingers itched. His scent identified him as the killer from last night, but she needed to be sure. Burdon and the Professor were fussy about things like that.

The shopper took a deep breath, lowered her head, and charged towards her Volkswagen, her hand delving feverishly in her jacket pocket for her keys. The lurker's "change" took mere seconds, then he was loping across the tarmac after her.

Tarian reached inside her open trench coat, slipping the tiny, loaded, double crossbow free of the hook in the coat's lining. Her actions attracted the attention of the thing with the shaggy wolf's head and upper body. It paused and looked back at her.

"Mine." It was part speech, part growl.

"OK." She aimed the crossbow at its left eye and pressed the first trigger. The bolt loosed with a soft twang. Her target ducked, evading the projectile, then, prey apparently forgotten, launched itself at her.

A car door slammed shut, and an engine started up. Headlamps flicked on, bathing Tarian and the thing bounding towards her in bright light. She registered the look of shock on the face behind the windscreen. Then a scraping of gears split the night, and with a screech of tyres, the Volkswagen reversed at high speed towards the car park exit.

Tarian pressed the second trigger. The bolt hit the werewolf in the right shoulder. It yelped but didn't slow.

Shit!

She dropped the now useless bow and tried to dodge . . . not quickly enough. Its mass and momentum toppled her backwards, and she hit the back of her head on the tarmac, momentarily streaking her vision with dots of white.

Something was smothering her, a mass of rank, stinking grey fur. She tried to push it away.

"Betrayer," came a distorted growl. It reared up above her and opened powerful jaws. Spittle spattered her cheek.

Tarian was tough, but even she could not survive having her jugular ripped out. She grabbed the narrow muzzle with both hands, forcing the lethal teeth away from her, inch by painful inch. An ordinary human would have been dead meat by now. She changed to a one-handed grip and reached for the knife in her belt.

The snout twisted violently, shaking her off, and once more the beast tried to savage her. Once more, she forced the head back, her wrists aching from the effort. This time she managed to retrieve her knife, and the blade slid home, its silver-tipped point driving smoothly through the yellow eye and into the brain.

The werewolf howled once, stiffened, then collapsed on top of her.

Tarian took a moment to get her breath back, then heaved the corpse off and got to her feet. Wearily, she brushed the dirt from her trench coat and turned to look at the thing she had killed. It had already reverted to human form. For a moment she simply studied the young man, then she crouched and tugged her knife from his eye socket.

She was wiping the blade on his jeans when headlights attracted her attention. Half expecting to see the woman in the Volkswagen returning to check what she had seen, she straightened. A familiar white transit van cruised into the carpark. It drew to a halt next to her, its engine still running. A door opened and the driver got out.

"You found it then," said Burdon.

"Yeah." She rehung the crossbow inside her coat, then looked round for the bolts she had discharged. "I'm running low on ammo. Got any more?"

"I didn't bother restocking." The man in the pinstriped suit frowned. "I thought this was your last job for a few days."

"There are more out there. I can smell their scent on him. Must be the pack he runs with." She retrieved one silver-tipped bolt with a satisfied grunt, then set about scanning the tarmac for the other. While she did so, Burdon pulled his mobile phone from a jacket pocket and began to speak.

"Cleanup crew. Just the one." He scanned the scene carefully. "There's a small complication. Surveillance cameras. We'll need to get the video tapes." He listened intently then nodded. "OK." He snapped the phone closed and looked at her.

"I'm serious, Tarian. You know the Professor's rules. Two days off either side, just to be sure."

"Can't. More people will die." She turned away and sniffed the night air, searching for the scent of werewolves but finding none. She'd have to quarter the surrounding district until she found the pack.

"It's stupid to risk it."

"Tell that to the grieving families. Besides, one more night won't hurt." She strode across the carpark, aware that the moon, only two days from full, was making her a little reckless, but finding it hard to care.

He made to follow her, then stopped. "Don't be an idiot, Tarian! Come back."

She laughed, feeling the thrill of the hunt come on her. "One more night, Burdon," she called. "And next time we meet, make sure you have plenty of ammo with you!"

Then she was running, into the dark.

THE STREET DOOR opened, jangling the bell above it. Peter looked up from the second-hand paperbacks he was pricing.

The woman in the trench coat was tall, very tall. And too young, surely, for that mane of silvery-grey hair to be natural. From his basket near the rear of the shop, Rory growled.

"Quiet, boy," said Peter absently. "Can I help you?"

Glacial blue eyes gave him the once over. Her nostrils dilated, and he had the distinct impression she was sniffing him. Or maybe it was his shop. Bookshops always had that musty smell to them; he had got used to it.

"Just browsing." The voice was a deep contralto.

Something brushed past his calf, and he looked down as his dog, hackles raised, placed itself between Peter and the woman and growled deep in its throat.

"What's up with you today?" He gave the woman an embarrassed look. "I'm sorry. Rory isn't usually like this. But lately . . ." Only that morning, the normally placid cocker spaniel had almost taken a bite out of a customer. He wondered if the dog was sickening for something.

She shrugged, crouched, and matter-of-factly held out her hand to the dog. For a moment, Peter feared Rory was going to bite the long fingers, but, to his relief, the dog sniffed them, then licked them. After a long thoughtful pause, Rory's hackles smoothed and his tail began to wag.

The tall woman gave a satisfied nod and straightened up. She turned to go.

"Are you sure I can't get you anything?" asked Peter.

She paused, considering. "I'm looking for someone. They were in here today, or maybe it was yesterday." Her nostrils flared. "Woollen coat, probably wet. Wellingtons, with cowshit on them."

How on earth did she know that? "Yes. This morning. Rory almost took a bite out of him too."

The ice-blue gaze sharpened. "Him?"

"One of the hippies from the commune . . ." She raised an eyebrow and he hastened to elaborate. "They moved into the Old Farmhouse in Blackberry Lane last week."

"How many of them?"

"Seven, eight. I'm not sure."

"Where's Blackberry Lane?"

"Not far from here. The southern edge of the village. Near the church."

"Thanks."

She turned to go, and he glanced past her through the glass of the front door and noticed that dusk was drawing in.

"Be careful," he blurted. "Some strange things have been happening at night. They think there's a pack of feral dogs on the loose."

The woman eyed him coolly. "I can take care of myself."

"Of course." Embarrassed, he busied himself patting Rory.

"But thanks for the warning anyway."

He looked up. She was standing in the open doorway looking back at him, the light from the interior illuminating the sharp planes of her face. Her expression unnerved him; there was something almost wild, untamed about it. Then she smiled, and the disconcerting impression vanished.

"You're welcome."

She nodded and walked away, her open trench coat flapping in the evening breeze.

AS TARIAN LEFT the bookshop, a familiar hunger began to overtake her. She looked up, searching. As she had suspected, an almost full moon was rising in the eastern sky. Perhaps Burdon was right and she was cutting it too close.

At the end of the street was a little restaurant, lights burning in its window. With relief she headed towards it. Inside, she chose a table for one and ordered, "Steak, as bloody as you can make it." Half an hour later, hunger temporarily sated by the almost raw beef and feeling a lot less edgy, she paid and asked the friendly waitress for directions to Blackberry Lane . . .

She was nearing the edge of the village, had spotted the crossroads she had been told to look for, when she picked up the trail. Though it was stale and faint—this morning's heavy downpour had seen to that—it belonged unmistakably to the werewolf who had been in the little bookshop. She grinned and broke into a jog.

The trail led her across open fields towards some rambling old farm buildings, the "commune" presumably. She was halfway there when the wind shifted. She stopped dead in the long grass, then closed her eyes and inhaled, rotating until the fresh scents were at their strongest. A pack of werewolves, out hunting their supper, she decided. It took her only a moment to separate out the individuals. Six, no seven of them, including the one she had been tracking. She opened her eyes and found herself facing a hill; on its summit was a church with a steeple . . .

Tarian had stopped to catch her breath near the church when a noise from inside the adjoining walled graveyard attracted her attention. It sounded like digging. Moments later came the noise of wood splintering. She pulled out her bow, slotted two bolts into the twin grooves, and nocked them. Then, keeping low, she crept towards the wall and peered over it.

Chaos met her gaze. A gravestone leaned at a crazy angle, and a ruined coffin lay open amidst sods and dirt torn from a recent grave. Something was kneeling by the coffin, its grey furred back towards her, its head bent. Powerful shoulder muscles flexed, then came the dull sound of something tearing. A shaggy head reared up, a chunk of flesh dangling from powerful jaws. Tarian grimaced. This one obviously liked its food a little gamy.

The werewolf turned, saw her, and froze.

In one practised movement, she aimed and pressed the trigger. The bolt took the beast through the left eye, killing it instantly. It toppled over backwards, crashing into the coffin and splintering it even more.

She checked there were no other werewolves lurking, then vaulted over the wall and made her way between the graves and headstones. The beast had "changed" by the time she reached it, into a fleshy, middle-aged woman with long grey hair.

Tarian was stooping to retrieve her bolt when a dog barked somewhere nearby. She straightened. The bark became a pained yelp that ended abruptly. A man cried out, then came the sound of wolves howling.

She checked her inner pockets. Six bolts in total. Plus the one in her hand. For a moment she hesitated. Then she heard the man's voice again, this time raised in fear. It sounded familiar. She inhaled deeply, tasting and categorising the scent traces wafting towards her. Cursing, she began to run.

The six werewolves were in the lane that ran along the far side of the church. Two of the younger ones were playing with a headless bundle of brown fur and bloody flesh, their tongues lolling, lips drawn back in open-mouthed grins. The others were gazing intently up at an ancient oak tree, their eyes wide and ears erect.

Something moved, high up in one of its branches. Tarian caught a glimpse of a man's terrified face.

At her approach, shaggy wolf heads turned her way. Yellow eyes appraised her and muzzles lifted to catch her scent. The pack leader, a big Siberian white, glared at her, raising its hackles and puckering its lips. It gave a low growl of warning, then came the distorted words, "Leave now."

A surge of recklessness came over her. She raised her bow and pressed the second trigger, then, without waiting to see if she had hit her target, launched herself towards the oak tree.

Something large, heavy, and rank smelling hit her from the right, bowling her over. She rolled with her attacker—not the pack leader, but a massive red werewolf—before coming back to her feet, bow-stock in one hand, knife in the other. A quick slash with the silvered blade made the beast draw back with a snarl, then she was standing beneath the tree, looking up.

Quickly, Tarian sheathed the knife, hung the crossbow from its hook, and leaped. She grabbed the lowest branch and pulled herself up from limb to limb. The bookseller's eyes were wide as she made herself comfortable on the branch next to him.

"Hello again," she said.

"What are you doing here?"

"I might ask you the same thing."

"I was walking my dog." His mouth trembled and she saw the tear tracks on his cheeks. "Who *are* you?"

"A friend."

She peered through the leaves. The bolt had entered the ear canal of the smallest grey werewolf. It was lying on its back, eyes unseeing, limbs twitching. Not dead yet, but it soon would be. Its companions slunk towards the tree trunk and began to circle it. Outraged yellow eyes gazed balefully up at her.

"What in God's name are they?"

Tarian didn't answer but concentrated on reloading her crossbow. She took aim and fired. A bolt sprouted from the eye of a white werewolf that was almost as large as the leader; it jerked violently and fell over backwards. As it turned back to human form, the man sitting next to her stiffened.

"It's a woman!"

"Not really." She loosed the second bolt, but the werewolves had got wise to her now, and it only succeeded in spearing a small grey in the shoulder. The silver tip burned it like acid, and it whimpered and writhed, trying to pull out the bolt and failing. Eventually, one of its companions took pity on it and helped. Blood gushed black in the moonlight. She pursed her lips. The wound wasn't fatal but it would slow it down.

The clouds parted, allowing bright moonlight to illuminate the lane. The members of the pack looked up at it and howled. Tarian clenched her jaw and pushed the cravings down.

"Are you all right?" The bookseller was looking at her. "You're sweating."

"You don't look too good yourself."

He grunted.

She checked her watch. Ten o'clock. Burdon would be coming for her eventually. If she could hold out until then . . .

She glanced down. The werewolves had formed a huddle by the wall, and from it emerged soft barks, growls, and more human-sounding noises. Every now and then, yellow eyes turned assessingly their way. Tarian didn't like the look of that. Perhaps they would be safer in the church.

"When I say 'go,'" she said quietly, "run for it."

"Are you crazy? After what they did to Rory? They can't climb. It's safer here."

"If they 'change' back, they'll be able to. And I'm pretty sure that's what they are planning."

"What? But I thought they had to keep this shape until dawn."

"Not quite. As long as it's night, they can change at will." Tarian ignored the bookseller's horrified look, raised the crossbow, and sighted along it. "Head for the church. I'll be right behind you. Go!"

She reached out a hand and pushed him off the branch.

PETER RAN ALONG the path as though the Devil himself were after him. It was a distinct possibility. The thought of Rory's last moments made him want to cry. *Brutes!*

It was only the woman's crossbow that had got them this far. He had landed awkwardly beneath the oak tree, jarring his ankle on a root, and was still off balance when two of the creatures tried to slash his belly open. A couple of crossbow bolts changed their minds. She killed one of them, wounded the other.

A distant howl made him glance back. Silhouettes moving in the distance hitched his heart up into his throat. He squinted, and the one closest to him resolved itself into a running figure, trench coat flapping out on either side like a cloak. His anxiety eased a notch.

He faced front once more and ran on. The sound of his own panting was loud in his ears, the thudding of his feet loud enough to wake the dead. He shuddered. Mustn't think about things like that in a graveyard!

The church porch came into view and he pounded over the grass towards it. What if Reverend Brown had locked the door? They had been having problems with tramps sleeping on the pews, and the Vicar was worried about the church silver . . .

He took hold of the handle. For a heart-stopping moment the stiff lock resisted his efforts, then the handle turned. The door swung open. *Thank God!*

He pushed his way into the small porch, then on through the inner doors into the church itself, switching on the lights as he went. Once past the stone font, he turned right and headed up the aisle towards the altar. Maybe the creatures, whatever they were, wouldn't be able to enter a holy place. He sank to his knees on the steps in front of the altar and crossed himself.

A heavy door thudded closed, and he heard the sound of a lock turning and bolts slamming shut. He twisted round, in time to see the tall woman in the trench coat entering the church. She strode past the font, her pale blue eyes scanning her surroundings.

He turned to follow her frowning gaze up to the stained glass windows that the parish had spent ten years raising the funds for. "What's wrong?"

"No shutters." Brushing past him, she headed for the altar. She stopped in front of it and reached for the silver cross that stood on the clean, white cloth.

"But you can't—"

But she had already grabbed it. She swivelled on one booted heel, her coat billowing out as she did so, and headed back towards the porch, on the way grabbing one of the loose, wooden chairs that had been brought in to swell the seating for a recent wedding.

"Come on. And bring that." She pointed at a candlesnuffer propped against the wall nearby. Peter opened his mouth to ask why, then closed it again and did as she asked.

After he had followed her into the porch, she closed and locked the inner door behind him, leaned the chair against it and jammed its back under the handle for good measure. Then she sat cross-legged on the carpet runner, pulled out a wickedly sharp penknife, and started to whittle the top of the silver cross.

He perched on one of the wooden chests that ran the length of the small windowless room and doubled as benches. "What now?" he asked.

"We wait."

Peter chewed his thumbnail.

From inside the church came the sound of glass shattering and wood splintering. Then something thudded into the inner door, bowing it slightly, pushing against the chair jammed hard against it. The chair held, and his companion gave a half smile.

He swallowed. So they could enter holy places after all. "Wait for what?"

Another unidentifiable thump made the door judder.

"Reinforcements or dawn. Whichever comes first."

"But no one knows we're here."

She shrugged. "I've got a tracking device. In time, a friend will come looking for me."

He gaped at her. Tracking device? Then a brilliant idea struck him, and he stood up, patting his jacket pocket. She looked up at him, one eyebrow raised in query.

"My phone! We can call the police." His hand faltered as he registered that the mobile's usual bulge was missing. "Oh no. I must have lost it." He slumped onto the chest once more, on the edge of despair.

It had gone deathly quiet inside the church, and the woman with the silver-grey hair stood up, crossed to the inner door and pressed an ear to it.

"Are they—?"

She raised a hand for silence and he subsided. "No one there. Must have gone outside again."

As though in confirmation, something cannoned into the exterior door. Though the lock held, around the hinges the ancient wood showed signs of splintering. Peter stared at it in horror. The woman noticed his concern.

"It'll hold them for a while," she said.

"I hope so. You didn't see what they did to my dog. If only I—" He suppressed a sob. "Why are they after us?"

She rotated the cross through ninety degrees and resumed her whittling. "You taste good."

Was she serious? He decided he didn't really want to know. Something she had said earlier came back to him. "What happens at dawn?"

"They can't hold their wolf shape in daylight. Should make the odds a lot more even."

He checked his watch. "That's four hours away. Can't you just kill them?" He gestured at the bow, loaded with two bolts, which was lying next to her on the carpet runner beside a growing pile of silver shavings.

She shrugged and rotated the cross once more. "That's all the ammo I've got. And there are more than two of them."

"Christ!" He put his head in his hands.

A satisfied grunt made him look up. The cross now sported a sharp point on its top.

"That'll do. Here." She handed it to him. "Pass me the candle snuffer." Baffled, he did as she asked.

"Use that if they get close," she told him, gesturing at the cross then picking up her penknife and beginning to work on the silver portion of the snuffer. "Stab the point in an eye, if you can manage it; if not, go for the throat, or stick it in an ear. Failing that, go for the balls."

He gaped at her.

"The silver hurts them," she explained. "But it's only fatal if you stab them in the brain with it."

"I see." But he didn't see at all. How did she know all this? And who was she? If she was aware of his scrutiny and doubts, she showed no sign of it, simply concentrated on her damned whittling.

The constant thudding against the porch door was getting on his nerves, and more worryingly producing a shower of dust and splinters. Was there really nothing they could do except wait? He had no desire to face those snarling, snapping teeth once more, but . . .

A flashback of those creatures tearing Rory's head off made Peter feel sick. He punched the wall hard enough to scrape his knuckles, then sucked them ruefully.

"Feel any better?" Amusement coloured the tall woman's gaze.

"No. I need to *do* something!"

A fierce buffet shook the outer door, sprinkling them with flakes of rust and splinters. Frowning, she got to her feet and began to examine its hinges. He followed her gaze. One of the metal hinges was bending, he saw with concern, and the rotten wood surrounding it was failing fast.

As he watched, another blow from outside popped a screw right out of a hinge and it swung free. The door lurched inwards, hanging at a crazy angle, and a shaggy muzzle poked round the gap. Peter cried out and reached for the cross.

The woman jabbed the snarling snout with the snuffer, which now sported a wicked point, and reached for the bow with her other hand. "Looks like you're about to get your wish."

THERE WERE FOUR werewolves waiting for them, Tarian saw, as she wrenched aside the now useless door and stepped out into the moonlight. The larger red werewolf's chest bore the marks of her knife, the grey's shoulder was still bleeding sluggishly, and the smaller red's snout was cut. Only the white pack leader was unscathed. He was already big, and with his hackles raised he seemed twice the size.

She bared her teeth. Then, candlesnuffer in one hand, crossbow in the other (fingers resting lightly on the triggers), she pressed her back to the church's stone wall and edged along it. Yellow eyes watched her.

The bookseller edged after her, swinging the cross in a clumsy arc whenever one of the beasts got too close. He had been reluctant to leave the porch, until she pointed out that, with the door breached, it was more prison than haven. So far so good.

The pull of the moon was strong, and in spite of herself, Tarian glanced up and stared at it in wonder. Something sharp raked across her left forearm. Stinging pain followed numbness, and she dropped the snuffer. It clattered on the paving slabs and rolled out of reach. Instinctively, she pressed a trigger. The bolt took the large red werewolf attacking her in the middle of its forehead. It howled and fell over backwards, stone dead.

She ignored the thing transforming at her feet and examined her wound. Four long gashes; not too deep, fortunately.

"Are you all right?" called the bookseller.

"Another good coat ruined."

She had come to the end of the wall and now faced a gravelled carpark. A drive led from it to a lane, which in turn led towards the main road at the bottom of the hill. Headlights gleamed momentarily in the distance before disappearing. Tarian blinked. There they were again. She smiled.

"Bookseller," she hissed. "Stand back to back with me."

When his shoulder blades were pressed against hers, they began a crablike shuffle across the carpark. The beast with the injured muzzle lumbered towards the bookseller, but a swipe from the cross drew blood from its shoulder and made it think again.

"What next?" came her companion's shaking voice.

She could hear the sound of a diesel engine labouring up the hill. "I'm expecting company."

The bookseller's hearing wasn't as acute. "Who?"

Twin beams speared the heavens like searchlights, before tilting back to earth once more as the white transit van topped the hill. The searchlights wavered then swung towards them, pinning humans and werewolves alike in a brilliant glare.

Tarian took advantage of the diversion to shoot her last bolt, killing the grey werewolf with the wounded shoulder outright. Then she reached for the knife at her belt. But before she could grasp it, the two remaining beasts were leaping at her.

"Watch out!" yelled the bookseller.

A mass of stinking fur landed on top of her, bringing her crashing to earth. The sharp gravel grazed her hands and face. She rolled over and gripped the throat of the white werewolf with one hand, forcing its snapping jaws away, then turned to deal with the other beast. Razor-sharp teeth sank into her calf.

She cried out. As if in response, there came a pained yelp, and the agonising bite disappeared. Digging her fingers into the throat she still held, she twisted round, wondering what had happened. The bookseller, teeth bared in an unconscious snarl, was bashing the werewolf with the silver cross.

"Use the point," she yelled, before the ferocious thing on top of her reclaimed her attention. A terrible dying howl told her he had taken her advice.

The pack leader broke her grip and went for her throat once more. Tarian twisted, curling into a ball and tucking her head in. Its breath was hot on her neck as it searched for a hold, and something warm— saliva?—dripped on her. She jack-knifed, catching the werewolf by surprise and managing to roll free.

"Tarian. Catch," came a familiar and very welcome voice.

She shielded her eyes against headlights—the van had come to a halt not far from her. A pinstriped man was running towards her, clutching something in his hand. He threw and she reached out . . .

Something landed hard on top of her, squashing her flat. Grimly, she reached a hand towards the bundle, which had landed a mere foot away. If she could just . . . Got it!

She detached a bolt and flipped it over, pointed end outwards. As the huge white werewolf reared back then lunged for her throat, it impaled its chest on the silver-tipped bolt. It howled, gave a mighty shudder, then tried to pull back. She shoved the bolt in deeper.

"Why?" The muzzle distorted the words. "Sister?" Its yellow gaze was full of pain and confusion.

"Because your kind has no place here any more." By feel, she grabbed another bolt and stabbed it cleanly through the eye. "Go now."

With a great sigh, it collapsed on top of her and lay still.

For a moment, she simply lay there, feeling a sense of sadness. Then she shook off such morbid feelings, took a deep breath, and pushed the thing off her. He had been a handsome man, she saw, as she struggled to her knees. Tawny-haired, muscled . . .

The bookseller limped towards her and held out his hand. She used it to pull herself to her feet, then became aware that he was staring at the man she had killed.

"He was in my shop just yesterday," he said. "Bought some Horror paperbacks. We joked about it."

Tarian shrugged. "Takes all sorts." She started to brush the muck off her trench coat then decided it was a lost cause.

Burdon was lounging against his van, smoking.

"You took your time," she called.

He gave her a lazy wave. "You're welcome." He exhaled a lungful of blue fumes, then added, "Oh. Cleanup squad's on the way."

She grunted, stooped to pick up the bundle of bolts, and slipped them into her trench coat's inner pocket. Then she re-hung the bow from its hanger.

"What did he mean: 'Sister'?" The bookseller was regarding her curiously.

She shrugged. "More like distant cousin, twice removed." She turned her face towards the moon and closed her eyes, bathing in its rays. Its call was strong now. It was almost time. "Only the Professor knows the exact relationship."

He was regarding her nervously, and she realised her smile was more like bared teeth. She patted him on the arm. "Burdon's colleagues will want to talk to you. When it's over, go home, forget about it. It's for the best."

Burdon had come up beside her, and now he took her gently by the arm. "It's time to go, Tarian." She could have easily shaken him off but she didn't.

"Yeah. It is." She let him lead her round to the back of the van, then clambered wearily inside. It had been a tough assignment, closer odds than she liked. She wouldn't make the same mistakes again.

After Burdon had closed the door on her, hiding the bookseller's goggling face from view, she made herself comfortable on the little mattress then snapped the restraints closed around her wrists and ankles. It was always best to play safe.

"All set?" came Burdon's muffled voice.

Tarian banged twice on the van's side. "All set," she called. As the vehicle began to move, she closed her eyes and gave herself up to the change . . .

AFTERWORD

In the action-packed anime "Blood: The Last Vampire" a mysterious, violent woman defends humans against vampires with her katana. I wondered if I could do something similar but with werewolves and crossbows, and combined it with an image I had of a woman striding through the night, her trench coat flapping. Incidentally, Tarian is Welsh for "shield."

MORRIS DANCING

IT WAS THE terrified bleating that signalled something was wrong. Morris of Worcester stopped playing and eyed his recorder, but the musical instrument wasn't the source of the din. On all sides, the formerly placid sheep were fleeing, some racing for the wooded valley bottom, others for the shelter of a nearby outcrop of rock.

He put down the recorder and rose stiffly, using his pilgrim's staff for leverage. Something blocked out the sun, and he shaded his eyes and looked up.

A black dot was hurtling towards him, growing larger and more distinct by the second. At first he thought it must be an eagle; England had its fair share of birds of prey, some with a marked partiality for lamb chops. Then his jaw dropped. The creature was winged all right—but its wingspan must be every inch of twenty feet. And its barrel-like body was huge and green—the dark green of foreign seas clogged with seaweed.

As he gaped at the four massive legs tipped with cruel talons, at the barbed tail streaming behind, his knees gave way, toppling him onto the grass next to his half-eaten lunch of bread and ale.

A firedrake!

"God save me. It's Satan himself!" Morris squeezed his eyes shut, crossed himself, and began to pray, expecting a rush of hot flame at any moment. "Into your hands, O Lord, I commend my spirit."

The ground shook as something massive landed nearby, and he steeled himself for the slash of dagger-sharp claws.

Nothing happened.

Morris cracked open an eyelid. The firedrake was glaring at him.

"Help me, St Michael and your angels," he croaked. And then, since one could never have too much divine intervention, he added, "St George and St Margaret, lend me your aid."

Still nothing happened.

He took another peek and wished he hadn't. The firedrake's wide-open jaws seemed to block out the heavens; a scrap of wool was snagged on one wicked-looking, yellow tooth. The breeze changed direction, and he almost fainted at the stench coming from the terrible maw.

By Our Lord! He covered his nose with one hand. The smell was worse than the stink aboard *The Weary Traveller*! And that had been disgusting, the stench from its cargo of fish far outweighed by that from the twenty pilgrims, who, without benefit of washing facilities, had been cooped up with him for the entire voyage back from the Holy Land.

Which reminded Morris of something. *The holy relics.* If anything could banish Satan, surely they could. With shaking fingers, he reached for his knapsack.

DIDN'T THE PREY know it was meant to run away, screaming, like the sheep?

Bright Star glared at it; this was no sport at all. But the long flight over the ocean had left the young dragon too tired to be bothered correcting the manners of prey ignorant of lunch etiquette, of rules which had existed since time began. He yawned again.

The human in the ankle-length, shabby robes looked up then resumed rummaging through its belongings. After a moment, it let out a triumphant cry and held up a small square of off-white cloth.

The reaction puzzled Bright Star. It should be almost catatonic with terror by now. So he was new at this, but what had gone wrong? He thought back over his recent lessons. If one's presence failed to scare the prey, Mother had told him, try something more forceful. *Right.*

He inhaled, then sent out a jet of fire. The human's facial whiskers sizzled, and a thin layer of soot blurred its features. The square of flimsy material disappeared with a *whump* and an odour of singed wool that made Bright Star's nostrils flare with distaste. A diet of nothing but sheep, sheep, and more sheep had left him craving something different.

Knowing his luck, the human would also taste of sheep. Still, he had started; now etiquette demanded that he finish.

MORRIS WAS CLOSE to tears. His irreplaceable piece of St Veronica's handkerchief—gone. Just like that! And with it, those precious drops of Our Lord's sweat which the saint had wiped from

His brow. A wisp of smoke curled from his sleeves, and he patted the smouldering worsted until it stopped.

Something else was different—some sensation he couldn't quite put his finger on. Realisation dawned. He could feel the breeze on his face. He ran a hand over what had once been a magnificent beard, the result of years of cultivation, and felt the unfamiliar sensation of bare skin. *Damn it!*

"'The serpent I will trample underfoot'!" he roared. "Psalm 91, verse 13."

A horrible thought struck him, and he opened the blackened flap of his knapsack and peered inside. *The Lord be praised!* His sacred stones, gleaned from the hill of Tabor and the holy cave of Bethlehem, had survived the intense heat of the firedrake's breath. Alas. His prized collection of pilgrim badges had fared less well. In disbelief, he reached for the emblems of Wolsingham and Canterbury, of Assisi and Cologne. It was hard to tell the distorted clumps apart, and the hot metal burned his hand.

This was going too far. Anger spurted energy through his trembling frame. "If you're going to kill me, get on with it!" he shouted. Then he braced himself and brandished his staff.

HOW PECULIAR! THE prey was waving a stick at him.

Bright Star belched out a tiny puff of smoke. Mother had warned him pickings in England would be lean—something to do with a plague recently wiping out half the human population—but you'd think those surviving would play by the rules.

And this uncooperative specimen was looking more and more unappetising, never mind the smell of singed wool, which was beginning to get on Bright Star's nerves. He had a sneaking suspicion that, beneath the voluminous brown robes, the human was mere gristle and bone—not much more than a snack.

Rumbling his dissatisfaction deep in his throat, he took a step forward. Instead of retreating as expected, the human whacked him hard on the nose.

MORRIS TOOK A firmer grip on his staff and hit Satan on the snout again. The solid wooden knob connected with a thwack, the jolt almost dislocating his shoulder.

" 'The Lord takes vengeance on his adversaries.' The Book of Nahum, Chapter 1, verse 2!"

To his surprise, the firedrake backed away.

Success made him reckless, and he chased after his foe, yelling and waving his staff. At first it continued to retreat, step by ground-juddering step, then a mean look came into its eyes and it stopped. Almost before Morris could draw breath, the reptilian head snaked forward and snatched the staff from his hands.

He watched, trembling, as the massive jaws ground the solid oak staff, his support throughout five long years of wandering, into splinters, showing far more relish for the task than was strictly necessary.

Whoops!

Morris picked up the hem of his robes and ran.

BRIGHT STAR SPAT out the last of the sawdust and roared, "It'll take more than that!"

All the same, it was embarrassing. Just for a moment, the prey had gained the upper hand. Thank the Fiery Mountain his mother hadn't witnessed it. The thought made his ears and tail droop.

He was back in charge now, at any rate. His stomach rumbled. Lunch! it demanded. No more playing around. Feed me.

Bright Star lurched after the fleeing human, and was about to grab it in his teeth, when a horrible sound smote his ears and made him cringe.

What on earth was it? It seemed to be coming from something the human was holding to its lips. A hollow twig of some kind.

He wished there was some way he could stop up his ears. The dissonance was making his teeth hurt. This really wasn't fair! How could he be expected to eat his lunch with that racket going on?

MORRIS CHANGED HIS fingering and blew into the recorder's mouthpiece once more. He couldn't quite remember the exact melody. *Did it go like this?* He tried an experimental trill. It had sounded much better when the snake charmer in the Holy Land bazaar played it. But it was close, he was sure of it. Maybe it would still do the trick.

It was a long shot. But Satan was "the ancient serpent" according

to the Scriptures, and serpents could be charmed, couldn't they? He
blew another random combination of notes.

It was certainly having an effect. The firedrake was trying to put its
front paws over its ears. It writhed once more then sprang into the air
and sped off.

By Our Lord! Joy washed over Morris. Satan had been defeated.

BRIGHT STAR SWOOPED, grabbed a bleating animal in his
talons, and with an expert twist, wrung its neck. He tore off and
gulped down a sizeable mouthful of flesh, then cracked a bone
between his teeth and swallowed the marrow.

Sheep again. He spat out a gobbet of wool. Ah well. It was better
than going hungry, and Mother would be sure to have caught something nice for dinner tonight. The important thing was to be out of
range of that awful din at last.

Casting a resentful glance back in the direction of his abortive
lunch, he almost fell out of the sky with surprise. The human seemed
to be dancing! Celebrating its deliverance, no doubt.

With a head full of questions, Bright Star recovered his height and
momentum and flew on towards the ocean and home.

MORRIS'S SANDALED FEET almost lost their purchase on the
lichen-covered rock, and he stretched out the arm holding the recorder
for balance. An angry hiss greeted the movement, and he recoiled.

Not that way either.

He leaped back to his former perch, and looked round. Everywhere
small grey snakes with broad black zigzags along their backs fixed
him with their cold gaze and hissed their disapproval.

Hubris, he thought sadly. *God's way of teaching me humility. I was
too proud of overcoming Satan, and look where it got me. Still, how
was I supposed to know that a nearby nest of adders would be
attracted by the snake charmer's music?*

Morris hitched up his long robes and leaped for a different rock.
There, he placed the recorder to his lips and tried another selection of
notes. It had no effect on the adders whatsoever.

At this rate, he thought, sighing, *it's going to be a very long day
indeed.*

AFTERWORD

A newspaper clipping sparked Morris of Worcester. Human remains were discovered under Worcester Cathedral beside a staff and a cockle shell, leading archaeologists to believe they'd found a 15th century pilgrim. I set out to write a series of humorous stories in which my religious pilgrim encounters otherworldly beings. In the end I wrote just three. "Morris and the Mermaid" and "Morris and the Unicorn" have been published, but the very first story never made it into print (the magazine that bought it folded before publication). It's nice to be able to remedy that.

CORDIE AND THE MERMAN

CORDIE HAD BEEN hauling line for two hours, and was looking forward to a hot pizza breakfast, when she saw the leaping grey shapes up ahead. She squinted through the early morning fog. Porpoises were meant to be good luck, but—

"What's up, Cap?" Geary was stretching the kinks out of his lower back.

She pointed. "Too close to the line."

Cordie had once found a baby porpoise, its tail snagged in the longline. The mother had stayed with it all night, helping it to the surface to breathe. When Cordie had cut the baby loose, the exhausted pair had circled the boat several times, as though thanking her, before finally swimming away. She hoped nothing similar had happened.

"It's their funeral." The *Eva Larsen*'s butcher stooped once more, and, with a few practiced strokes of the meat saw, removed the disappointingly small swordfish's bill, fins, and head.

"Gee, Geary," she called. "You're all heart."

He grinned nastily and flung the bloody entrails over the side, where a storm petrel swooped on them.

Cordie edged the boat forward, following the string of orange floats, keeping one gloved hand on the remote helm's throttle and the other on the line being spooled onto the drum.

Yesterday, it had been brilliant sunshine, and one hundred pound swords had been almost throwing themselves onto the *Eva Larsen*'s white-painted deck. Today they had only caught two sickly-looking thirty pounders.

Should've known better than to think this trip was a slammer. I jinxed it. Either that or the blip on the radar, whatever it was, had scared the bigger swords away.

A change in line tension alerted her. The next hook was hanging heavy; she hoped it wasn't a mako shark.

She eased the boat to a stop and slowed the drum speed to a crawl. "Start hauling, guys."

Harlan leaned over the rail and began hauling up the line, hand over hand. Geary and Johnny, who at nineteen years old was the youngest, each grabbed a sixteen-foot-long gaff and stood either side of their lanky crewmate.

First the lime-green lightstick came into view, then the swordfish neared the surface. The familiar shades of purple, blue, and silver were absent, noted Cordie in dismay. Actually, it looked more flesh coloured. *What the—?*

"Shit!" yelled Harlan, almost dropping the line in shock. "It's a man!"

The drum continued to turn, hoisting the man slowly towards the rail. Now everyone could see the hook embedded deep in his side, and the blood-streaked water streaming off him.

No one in the fleet has reported a man overboard.

While the three men rushed to pull him aboard, Cordie shut off the drum, grabbed a six inch ripper knife, and hurried forward . . . just in time to hear something hit the deck with a loud, wet *slap*. She gaped at the speckled, blue-green fish tail.

"Jesus!" Bobby, her first mate, had left off removing lightsticks and uneaten squid from the line, and had come up beside her. "I don't believe it!"

"Is it a merman?" asked Gene, who had been helping Bobby.

A prickle of unease ran up Cordie's spine. God knows she had encountered enough oddities at sea over the years, including deep-sea creatures that belonged in a horror novel—but still, a merman! She struggled to remain calm. If she lost it, so would the crew.

"Whatever he is," Cordie told the little cook, "he's gonna bleed to death unless I get that hook out fast." She knelt on the sopping wet deck and tried to ignore the painful gasping—the merman was reacting like a stranded fish. She assessed the hook, then took a deep breath and dug her knife deep into his side.

The merman's eyes opened—his irises were a very pale green she noticed—and he hissed and writhed and fought to throw her off. Blood spattered her lucky orange T-shirt—human looking blood, she noticed absently—and she stifled a curse. "Someone hold him still."

Bobby and Johnny volunteered, and were soundly slapped by the muscular tail before they got him pinned down.

Cordie resumed her excavations. *Hook's caught on a rib. He's not cartilaginous, then.*

Geary loomed over her. "Cap. We can't risk having him on board. He's bad luck and you know it."

Sailor's lore was full of mermaids bringing bad weather or enticing men to their deaths, mused Cordie. But some tales portrayed them as kindly creatures who offered advice or even granted wishes. Who was to say which, if any, were true?

She held Geary's gaze. "They used to say women were bad luck too. They were wrong."

His jaw worked. "The boss ain't gonna like it."

The owner of the *Eva Larsen* was Geary's cousin . . . as the big man loved reminding her. *Roll on the day I've finally got enough saved to buy this boat and choose my own crew.*

"Well the boss isn't here, is he?" She returned to her grisly task.

The knife's handle snagged on the merman's odd braided belt. *Why's he need that? Got no trousers to keep up.* Impatiently, she sliced through it and pulled it clear.

Her vision blurred, and she knuckled her eyes to clear it, wondering at the muffled exclamations and curses. Then she opened her eyes and froze.

"He's got legs now," said Johnny, confusedly running a hand through his mop of brown hair.

And a very respectable set of genitals. Cordie pushed aside her growing feeling of unreality and adjusted her grip on the little knife. The merman's painful gasping had changed to normal breathing, she realized. *Perhaps his gills have turned into lungs too.*

The barb popped free.

"Watch it, Cap!" yelled Harlan.

But Cordie had already twitched her knee out of the way, and the vicious hook was quivering harmlessly in a deck tile.

Blood began pulsing in earnest from the merman's wound. *Got to staunch it, fast.*

After stuffing the discarded belt in the pocket of her yellow overalls, Cordie pulled one of the merman's limp arms—he had passed out when the hook came free—across her shoulders and heaved. "Someone give me a hand."

Geary folded his brawny arms. "Throw him back, Cap."

She gave him a look. "He's got lungs now. He'll drown."

The butcher shrugged. "Not our problem."

"Wrong," said Cordie firmly. "He's our problem until I say he's not."

CORDIE DRUMMED HER fingers on the chart table and considered her options, which in the end boiled down to just one. *But it could bring all kinds of shit down on us.*

The merman was in her stateroom next door, lying in the tiny bunk bed where Bobby had helped her put him. She had packed his wound with sterile ribbon gauze, but he was still bleeding all over her sheets. His skin felt clammy, and his face was much too pale. She had been too leery to give him antibiotics though—who knew how his system might react?

Don't have a choice. He's dying.

She was reaching for the VHF radio when a weathered hand closed round hers. She twisted round to find Bobby regarding her gravely.

"Calling the Coast Guard?"

She nodded.

He scratched his beard. "You thought this thing through, Cap?"

She laughed slightly hysterically. "You bet. I'm all too aware that if anything weird shows up on his X-rays, the scientists and military will be all over him."

"And us. They'll want to know exactly where we caught him." The first mate released her.

"Let's hope it doesn't come to that," said Cordie. "Their presence would certainly screw up the fishing."

"You could always throw him back."

She stared at him. "You're siding with Geary?"

"Just because Geary's an asshole, it doesn't mean he's wrong."

Cordie frowned at her first mate. Without him on her side, she might as well give up now.

"Look, Bobby. I can't act on what *might* happen 'cause of some crazy fisherman's tale. Sure the shit might be about to hit the fan, and it might even be because of a merman's curse. But let's stick to the facts here. Fact: we hauled a man out of the ocean, and he's got my hook in his side. Call me sentimental, but I feel responsible. Fact: he's going to die if we don't get him some help. Do you really think I'm going to just sit on my ass and let Geary throw him overboard?"

Her outburst met with a long silence. "He'll need a name then," said Bobby at last.

She sighed with relief. "Meet my latest crewmember: Mark Harris."

"Why does that sound familiar?"

Cordie feigned a sudden interest in her fingernails. "*The Man from Atlantis*. I loved that show."

"Oh." She could hear the smile in his voice. "He'll need some normal clothes."

She looked up. "Yeah. Can you arrange that? And while you're at it, try to talk the guys round. Tell them . . . I dunno, tell them as far as our good luck goes, putting the merman into a helicopter is as good as throwing him back."

Who knows? Maybe it is.

While Bobby started down the gangway to the galley, she grabbed the microphone from its overhead bracket, pressed the switch, and spoke.

"Whiskey Romeo Alpha nine two nine five to Coast Guard," she said. "This is Cordie Redmond, Captain of the *Eva Larsen*, calling Coast Guard. Come in, please. Over."

The VHF crackled into life. "Coast Guard to the *Eva Larsen*. What can we do for you today, Cordie? Over."

"We have an injured crewmember in need of urgent medical attention. Request immediate evacuation. Over."

A brief interrogation as to the nature of the injury followed.

"Roger," said the Coast Guard eventually. "We'll get a helicopter out to you as fast as we can. What's your current position, Cordie? Over."

She relayed the coordinates from the GPS screen. "And can you hurry it up? He's losing blood fast. Over."

"Roger. Hang in there, Cordie. This is Coast Guard, clear with the *Eva Larsen*."

Cordie spent the next ten minutes cutting the mainline and attaching a beeper buoy to it. The knowledge they were getting rid of the merman had alleviated most of the crew's fears, and they were now more concerned with having to break off the haulback and risk a pay cut. She tried not to roll her eyes and reassured them that they would lose only a few hours' fishing.

After turning the boat onto a new course, one that should intercept the helicopter just beyond the edge of the fishing grounds, she returned to her stateroom to check on her patient.

His dressing was sodden. She wondered briefly whether to change it, then decided it would probably only aggravate the bleeding.

"What the hell were you doing messing with our bait?" she murmured. "Couldn't resist the pretty colours, eh?" She sighed. "Didn't anyone ever tell you about curiosity and cats?"

The merman's eyelids flickered but didn't open. Was he listening? She pursed her lips.

"Look, I don't know whether you can hear me," she continued, "or even understand English, but I'm fresh out of whalesong so . . . Anyway, here's the plan. I'm going to pretend you're one of my crew. Don't know if it'll work. There are too many odd things about you." She fingered the green-tinged blonde hair that lay sleekly against his scalp. "But I think it's your best shot. So play along, will you?"

No reaction.

She rose and walked back through to the wheelhouse. The fog was getting thicker, and that damned blip on the radar was still dogging them. Cordie smiled grimly. Usually, here in mid ocean, she felt she'd left all her troubles behind. This time, they had been lying in wait.

Abruptly, a new blip on the radar claimed her attention. *Thank God for that!*

She crossed to the open door and yelled down the gangway, "Look alive, guys. Coast Guard will be here in a few minutes."

THE HARASSED LOOKING receptionist put down the telephone receiver and turned to Cordie. "I'm sorry about that. Now what name was that again?"

"Harris. Mark Harris. The Coast Guard brought him in ten days ago."

The last Cordie had seen of the merman was his well-muscled legs jutting out of the ascending rescue basket, while the helicopter rotors almost concussed everyone aboard and scared the swordfish for miles. They had been heading back for the beeper buoy when the Coast Guard reported safe delivery of the "crewman" to the local hospital. Since then, nothing.

They'd have told me if he was dead, wouldn't they?

Fingers clattered over the keyboard and the receptionist peered at her screen. "Oh yes. The young fisherman in Room 32. Are you a relative?"

"His skipper."

That got Cordie a raised eyebrow. She suppressed a sigh and wished she were back at *The Lookout* having a drink with the guys.

Cordie had allowed herself a single beer before setting out for the hospital and was looking forward to making up for it later. First night ashore, the crew always went a little nuts, spending their $200 advances like high rollers, buying rounds and lottery tickets for friends and girlfriends. She felt in her pocket for the ticket young Johnny had pressed on her and encountered the coiled belt she hadn't let out of her sight.

The receptionist pointed. "Room 32. Just follow the signs."

"Thanks." Cordie turned on her heel and set off.

Though she knew she had the right room—the blinds were open and she could see the bed and its instantly recognizable occupant through the glass window—an attractive young nurse in starched blue uniform stopped her going in.

"Are you a relative?"

"His skipper." Puzzlement met her and she tried not to roll her eyes. "The one who called the Coast Guard?" she prompted.

"But that was," a cupid's bow mouth pursed in thought, "Captain Cordie Redmond."

"Cordelia Redmond. Yeah. That's me."

"Oh. I was expecting a ma—" The nurse trailed off and flushed. "Sorry." She stood aside. "He's healing well. The only trouble is—" her voice became confiding, "—he seems to have lost his memory."

"He told you that?" Cordie opened the door and walked through. Crisp white sheets rustled as the patient sat up and regarded her warily.

"No, he can't seem to speak either." The young woman had followed her. "In fact, the doctors are slightly concerned about that . . . though it's probably only temporary. They're thinking of calling in a specialist."

People were getting a little too interested in the merman, thought Cordie anxiously, surprised they'd got away with it for even this long. Perhaps she'd better get him out of here before it was too late.

Pale green eyes gazed intently at her. *He recognizes me.* For appearances' sake, she said, "Hello, Mark."

He blinked, once.

"Another thing . . . erm. This is a bit awkward, but we haven't been able to locate his Social Security records. And there's no sign of any medical insurance. So—"

"Bill me," she said shortly.

"Bill *you*?"

Cordie turned to regard the other woman. "He works for me," she said slowly and clearly. "So I'll take care of his medical bills. OK?"

"Oh, OK. I was only asking. I'll get you the paperwork, then." The nurse turned stiffly on her heel and stalked out.

Thank God for that!

Cordie approached the bed carefully and reached out one hand, then stopped as Mark drew back. "I just want to see the wound. Is that OK?"

He blinked at her again, that long slow blink that she was beginning to realize was characteristic.

She raised his pajama top carefully. The wound had been neatly stitched and was healing cleanly. "Nice job."

She became aware that a hand—not hers—was delving in the pocket of her jeans, and recoiled, snatching back the strange belt he had almost managed to grab. "Sneaky!" Her pulse was racing.

He tilted his head slightly to one side and stared at her. She frowned and wished he could speak.

"So you sensed I had this on me, did you?" She held up the belt, which she had repaired with twine. "Well, it *is* yours. And I intend to return it to you." She had been thinking about this a great deal since she had delivered him to the Coast Guard. "But not here."

His expression didn't change. Feeling like an idiot, she mimed putting the belt on, then gasping for breath like a fish out of water. "You put this on here, miles from the sea, and you end up dead. See?"

He blinked again, and she suppressed the urge to shake him. Then she realized that his body language had changed. He no longer looked like he was about to jump her.

"That's right," she told him, relaxing her own stance. "I'll give you your belt back . . . but only when we're back where I found you, not before. Understand?"

The door opened and the little nurse was back, thrusting a clipboard under her nose and glaring at her.

"Fill in these details, please, Miss Redmond. Then sign here . . . and here . . . and here . . ."

Cordie grabbed the clipboard and ballpoint pen. "When I'm done," she said, as she began to write, "I'm taking him home. So you might like to get started on his discharge papers, and get him dressed."

The nurse looked startled. "Oh, but he's not ready. The doctors said . . ."

"I don't care what they said." Cordie let her voice deepen into her fiercest growl, sounding certain but wondering if her bluff was about to be called. "Far as I can see, the wound he came in with is dealt with and healing fine. He can recuperate just as well at home as he can here."

"But his amnesia . . ."

"Is more likely to clear up when he's in familiar surroundings among friends, don't you think?"

The nurse's mouth opened and closed like a goldfish. "Well!" she said eventually, her tone making it clear what she thought about female sea captains who dragged their deckhands back to work before they were fit. "If anything happens, it's your responsibility."

Cordie breathed a sigh of relief. "Yeah, yeah, whatever."

IT WAS EARLY next morning when Cordie joined her crew down at the wharf.

They had just started hoisting the fifteen tons of swordfish out of the *Eva Larsen*'s hold. After that, there was twenty tons of ice to haul, decks to scrub, gear to stow . . .

Damn, I hate unloading. Reluctantly, she pulled on her gloves.

"Where were you last night, Cap?" Bobby grabbed a hundred pound swordfish encrusted with ice and heaved it towards Geary who passed it on. "Not like you to miss free beers."

"Catching up on my naptime," said Cordie, taking her place in the chain.

In fact, she had been installing Mark in the shabby room she rented above The Lookout, figuring that, left to his own devices, he was bound to get into trouble or attract attention. Fortunately, the landlady didn't mind—Kate was used to Cordie's "beaux," as she called them. Cordie herself called the endless stream of men much more colourful names; she had yet to find one who remained faithful when she went fishing.

Mark had spotted the little fish tank at once, and crossed to it, tilting his head to one side. She reached for the carton of fish food, noting that Kate had opened a fresh one—the landlady took care of her goldfish while she was at sea—and joined him.

"Friends of yours?" She sprinkled yellow flakes into the tank and Goldie and Red swam to the surface and gobbled them up eagerly. "Or maybe you're just hungry?"

She wondered absently what they'd fed him in the hospital. Kate made a mean fish chowder. Perhaps she'd try him on some of that later.

He continued to watch the goldfish.

"I've heard plenty of tales about your sort," she told him. "Mortal women up the duff; children with webbed feet. And why not? You're handsome enough. But let's get something clear. Just because you're staying with me, don't get any ideas. No hanky panky. Got it?"

A slow uncomprehending blink.

Might as well be talking to the goldfish. Unnerved by his silence, she switched on the TV. The merman turned to regard the little portable set atop the chest of drawers curiously.

"Wanna watch some TV, huh? Who knows? You might even learn something. Darryl Hannah did in *Splash*."

She flung herself down on the bed, which creaked in protest, and Mark gingerly copied her actions. Far from educating the merman, though, TV seemed to make him sleepy. And after a while, he was curled up beside her, snoring soundly.

Cordie didn't know whether to feel flattered or insulted—she had pictured a night fending off his advances. *He's either simple, ridiculously trusting, or a fatalist.*

But though she wanted to keep an eye on him, there was no way she could get out of the unloading this morning. So after breakfast, she had explained to Kate that Mark was a bit "simple," and asked the reluctant landlady to look in on him. When she left, he was sitting up in bed, sleepily watching a game show.

"Hey, Cap, can you give me a hand here?" Gene was wilting under the weight of a two hundred pounder.

"Sure thing." Ice crunched underfoot as she went to help the little cook.

Can't keep him a secret forever though. Wonder how the guys are going to take it when they hear the merman's back?

CORDIE WAS RELAXING with a few beers—nine hours of strenuous unloading tended to wear a person out—when the door of The Lookout opened and Mark wandered in accompanied by the bar's landlady cum bartender.

"He was wandering around upstairs," said Kate, unaware of any faux pas on her part. "Thought he must be looking for you."

Geary glanced balefully at Cordie. "What's he doing here?"

Cordie sighed. "We gonna get into this again? I picked him up from the hospital last night. He's healing well, so I thought I'd take him home."

"Damned fish men!" Geary signalled the bartender for another beer then gave her a calculating glance. "Maybe I should tell the Marine Biologists about him, Cap. Could be worth a buck or two."

Cordie's stomach lurched. "You do that, Geary, and you can kiss goodbye to your livelihood for the foreseeable future. A fleet of research vessels sending down submersibles and divers is going to mess up the fishing big time, don't you think?"

He blinked.

She pressed her advantage. "And how do you think the boss is gonna like that?"

Geary sneered at her but he didn't raise the subject again.

She was relieved Mark seemed unaffected by the menace emanating from the butcher. *Must use different body language underwater.* Absently, she fingered the belt in her pocket.

"Does he drink beer?" Bobby had come up beside her.

Not everyone's like Geary. Maybe things'll work out. "Buy him one and see."

Her first mate signalled to Kate and a moment later was handing an opened bottle of Bud to the merman who gazed doubtfully at it.

Cordie mimed putting the bottle to her lips and drinking.

"He can't speak English?"

"He can't speak, period."

Bobby stroked his beard. "Oh."

Mark tipped his head back and took a huge gulp of beer. Then he was coughing and spluttering, while the other patrons looked on amused and Geary curled his lip. Cordie and Bobby patted the merman on the back until the fit had subsided.

"Guess that answers that question," said Cordie wryly.

Leaving Bobby to keep an eye on her charge, Cordie wandered over to the table where Harlan and Gene were playing cribbage.

"Room for one more?"

"Aw, Cap!" Harlan gave her a pleading glance. "You always lose. And then you throw the board at us."

"Not always."

The little cook raised an eyebrow. "He wanna play too?"

Cordie followed Gene's gaze to find Mark standing at her shoulder. She glanced towards the bar and saw Bobby gesturing apologetically at her. She sighed. "No," she said. "He can watch."

She pulled up a stool and made Mark sit on it, then grabbed one for herself. "Cutthroat rules?"

Harlan nodded. They cut to see who was dealer, and while Gene reset the pegs in the cribbage board, Cordie dealt the cards . . .

". . . WHICH MAKES 121." Cordie pumped her arm. The last hour had been a lucrative one. "Pay up, guys."

"Three games in a row!" Harlan stared at her in disbelief. "Changed your strategy, Cap?"

She shrugged. "No. Same as always." Harlan and Gene exchanged unhappy glances.

Cordie could take a hint. She scooped up her winnings. "Thanks, guys."

She stood up, kicking back the stool as she did so. Mark trailed after her to the bar, and she was aware of the amused, puzzled, or simply disapproving looks that followed the two of them.

"Got yourself a new beau?" asked Bob Murphy, as she took a stool beside him. She threw the grizzled captain of the *Sea Mist* a glance that would peel paint. He snorted. "Right. Bit too quiet for you."

She thought of her last two boyfriends—Pete, who was now doing a stint as a Coast Guard rescue diver, and Jimmy, who was always brawling . . . *"Quiet" would make a nice change.*

She handed Mark a glass of water and gulped down her Bud, welcoming the coolness sliding down her gullet.

A bell clanged. "Quiet," yelled Kate. "It's time." The bartender turned up the volume on the little TV set above the bar, and the hubbub died to an expectant hush. Cordie scrabbled in her jean pocket for the lottery ticket Johnny had given her yesterday.

The first number flashed up on the TV screen. Mark stared at it, tilting his head to one side.

As she checked off the numbers on the flimsy slip of paper, she was unable to believe what she was seeing. When the last number had been announced and chatter and laughter had replaced the groans and curses, she was still staring at her ticket.

"You OK, Cordie?" Murphy's nudge broke her paralysis.

"Yeah. I won."

"What?"

She showed him her winning ticket. "I won. See?"

Murphy did a double take. "Holy moly!" He twisted round on his bar stool and shouted, "Hey, everyone. Cordie's just won the lottery."

You could have heard a fish blow bubbles in the resulting silence.

"Don't joke 'bout the Cap, Murph," called Harlan. "She doesn't like it." He grinned cheekily at Cordie then his grin became fixed.

Guess I look like a stunned swordfish. "It's true. I won." Her voice came out as a croak and she reached for her beer bottle and found it empty.

Kate, being the good bartender she was, placed another bottle of Bud in front of Cordie. "Guess you'll finally be able to buy that boat of yours."

"Guess so. Depends how many others share the jackpot." *Which reminds me . . .* She looked round for Johnny and found him sitting in the corner with his mates, looking miserable. "Hey, Johnny," she called. "You bought the ticket. So we'll go fifty-fifty. OK?"

His eyes brightened. "Thanks, Cap." A friend tousled his hair and he shook him off.

She became aware that Harlan and Gene were strolling towards her, intent looks on their faces. They halted beside her.

"Hey, Cap. You've been pretty lucky tonight," began the lanky crewman. "First cribbage. Then the lottery."

She shrugged and took a gulp of beer. "So?"

"What are the odds?" persisted Harlan.

"Astronomical, I'd say," added the cook. "Unless something's happened to change your luck. Something like—" His gaze turned towards Mark who returned it with an impassive pale green one of his own.

Cordie finished the sentence for him. "Something like him."

"WHAT WE'RE SAYING, Cap," said Geary, "is you can't take the merman back."

Cordie jutted her jaw. "Says who?"

"Says we." The butcher indicated the rest of the *Eva Larsen*'s crew. The five men had been huddled in a corner of the bar for the past five minutes before sending Bobby to "invite" her and Mark to join them.

"I thought he was bad luck. Now all of a sudden he's good?" Cordie snorted. "Make up your minds, guys." She glanced disappointedly at Bobby who dropped his gaze. Johnny shuffled his feet like a guilty schoolboy.

"Look," continued Geary. "It's only fair." He turned to the others. "It's our turn, right?"

"The lottery win may have been nothing to do with him." She had an uneasy feeling it wasn't just coincidence though.

"We don't want to hurt him, Cap," said Bobby. "Just him being around seems to be enough. We'll take care of him just fine. See he's fed and watered . . ."

Yeah . . . like Goldie and Red. She glanced at the merman and wondered if he knew what kind of future they were planning for him.

"OK." Her apparent capitulation brought grins and sighs of relief. "But if your luck's going to change, it had better do it within the next couple of days." The grins disappeared. "Because like it or not, next trip, I'm taking him home."

"Not without us, you're not." Geary folded his arms.

"I can hire another crew." *Especially if this lottery win pans out.*

Geary laughed. "All this concern over a damned fish."

"He's much more than a fish, and you know it!" She shoved a hand in the pocket of her jeans and encountered the merman's belt. *That might work. Have to act fast though.*

Her rush for the exit took everyone, including Mark, by surprise. She had grabbed his arm and tugged him so roughly he almost lost his footing.

"Hey!" yelled Geary. "Don't let them get away."

Somehow the two of them evaded the hands reaching to grab them, though, and then they were outside.

It was a fine night, but the new moon provided little light. She knew the way towards the wharf like the back of her hand, though. She turned a sharp left and started running, pulling Mark with her.

The Lookout's heavy front door creaked open again, and she glanced back to see Geary and the rest of the crew piling out into the street.

Mark was clearly unused to running, he was already puffing and panting. And behind them, the pounding of feet was getting closer. Fortunately, it wasn't far to the wharf.

She jerked Mark to a halt and gazed down at the black water lapping between the moored boats. Was she doing the right thing? *Over two hundred miles to where we found him. Suppose he gets lost?*

But there was no time for second thoughts. She pulled out the coil of belt and thrust it at him. "Here. Now go."

Strong hands took the belt from her. Then he was stripping off his clothes and wrapping the belt round his naked waist. As he dived into the dock, there was a blurring then Cordie saw a muscular fishtail . . .

A hand on her shoulder yanked her round. "Where is he?" Geary's breath was warm on her face and smelled of beer.

A loud splash from behind answered him, and droplets of water soaked them both. Then the rest of the panting crew came up beside them, and they were staring down at the expanding ring of ripples.

"Shit!" said Geary. "Cap let him get away."

"You once said to throw him back," she reminded him. "Well I did."

Bobby had to restrain Geary from punching her. The big man glared out at the now calm water.

"Over there," yelled Gene, pointing, and they all turned to see.

But it was only a large water rat, swimming rapidly away.

CORDIE HAD BEEN hauling line for two hours, and was looking forward to a hot pizza breakfast, when she saw the leaping grey shapes up ahead. She squinted against the dazzle of the early morning sunshine at the porpoises.

Not again!

"What's up, Cap?" Harlan looked up from his butchering. The *Eva*

Larsen was hers now, and as she'd anticipated, the loss of Geary had proved to be no loss at all.

"I don't kn—"

A loud splash and a squawking of startled storm petrels made Cordie turn. Something was bobbing in the ocean a few yards off the port stern. Something that looked like a man's head and upper torso.

She cut the engine and rushed to the stern rail, then stopped and stared at the familiar face, the pale green eyes, the greenish-blonde hair . . . Bobby and the other deckhands dropped what they were doing and gathered next to her.

"It's Mark," crowed Johnny, pushing hair out his eyes. "He got home OK." He turned to Phil, the newest recruit. "We saved his life you know."

"Yeah. After we nearly got him killed in the first place," said Cordie dryly.

The crew shuffled their feet and gave one another sheepish looks. Relations between them and their new boss had been awkward at first, but things were settling down.

"Hey, Mark," called Johnny. "Got any more good luck you want to send our way?"

"Yeah," grumbled Harlan. "We could sure use it."

Cordie waved but wasn't surprised when the merman didn't wave back. *Don't s'pose he knows how.*

Abruptly, something surfaced beside Mark, something so huge Cordie feared a killer whale was helping itself to a merman snack. The boat rocked alarmingly, and her heart raced.

"Jesus!" breathed Bobby.

Cordie stared at the new arrival. It was three times the merman's size, maybe a little larger. Same colour hair, but much longer. Breasts too. *A mermaid?*

"Must be a fish thing," said Johnny. "Sword females are usually bigger than males." He leaned on the rail and yelled, "She your girl, Mark?"

A vivid memory of a porpoise and its baby came to Cordie, and something clicked into place. *No wonder he never made a move on me.*

"Not his girl," she murmured. "His mother."

Bobby frowned at her. "You're not serious, Cap?"

"Yeah, I am."

She remembered the strange blip on the radar, how it had shadowed the *Eva Larsen* from the time Mark was on the hook to when the Coast Guard airlifted him off. This massive creature could have had them for breakfast. *She still might.*

For now, though, Cordie was relieved to see that the mermaid seemed content to float placidly beside her offspring. *If she'd wanted to capsize us, she'd have done so by now. Perhaps she was just curious.*

"Glad you got back OK, Mark," she called. "Hope you've told your mother we didn't mean to hurt you?"

No reply. Cordie wondered if she should try miming again. Before she had a chance, the two mer-creatures, as if at some unspoken signal, arced high out of the water then curved back down and landed with a loud *smack*.

The boat rocked violently, and by the time Cordie had knuckled salt water from her eyes, all she could see were two muscular fishtails disappearing below the surface.

She darted back up the gangway to the wheelhouse, and was staring at the radar, watching the blip grow fainter and finally disappear, when Bobby put his head round the door.

"The porpoises are gone too, Cap."

She nodded.

He lingered in the doorway. "I'm glad we let him go," he said. "You were right, I was wrong. I'm sorry."

"Me too. Maybe it would have been easier if we'd known he was just a kid. You know: if it's too small, we throw it back."

He scratched his beard thoughtfully. "Doubt if it would have made any difference to Geary."

"True. Sorry son of a bitch." Belatedly she realized her lucky orange T-shirt was sopping wet. Meetings with Mark were always tough on her clothes.

"So. His mother, huh?" said Bobby. "They'll never believe us ashore."

"Then don't tell them."

His brows drew together. "The news'll get out, Cap. It always does."

"Sure it will. But it's just another fisherman's tale, right? The whopper that got away?"

He smiled in sudden understanding. "Right."

AFTERWORD

After reading Linda Greenlaw's autobiographical "The Hungry Ocean," which vividly evokes the sights, sounds, and smells of life on board an Atlantic sword-fishing boat, I couldn't resist using that setting for a story. And what strange creature could a swordfish captain possibly pull out of the sea? A merman, of course.

CAVERNS OF THE HEART

MIRA PUT DOWN her pick-axe and stretched, trying to ease the burning in her back and shoulders. She'd been working flat out—it was time for a break. She glanced at the basket; inside the fraying wickerwork, the raw, misshapen crystals glinted dully in the torchlight. Not a bad haul, she thought with satisfaction. It would soon be full enough to carry to the collection point.

Today she had been assigned the position farthest from the supervisor. To her left, the tunnel stretched emptily into the darkness, while to her right its blackness was lit at intervals by the flickering torches of the other miners. The visibility in these old workings is terrible, she thought. She could only just make out the familiar hunched shape of the nearest man, Old Rog, thirty feet away. He prised something from the dull grey rock and threw it into his wicker basket. Mira's imagination supplied the accompanying faint thunk.

Now she had stopped work, she was all too aware of her smarting eyes and itching nose. She removed her mask—already the creamy muslin was grey with rock dust. Trying not to cough at the dust's acrid stench, she scratched her nose and sighed. It was no use asking for proper protection. The supervisor would only shrug and say, "Company policy." She retied the flimsy mask, looping the strings over her ears and settling it comfortably over her nose and mouth. It was better than nothing, she supposed. Anything was better than catching the black lung . . .

As she rested, she stared dreamily at the tunnel wall, barely aware of the familiar, irregular thud of pick-axes. It was a few moments before she realized what she was looking at—the wall had sheared vertically in two. She reached out. The edges of the man-sized crack were smooth beneath her fingers. Must've been caused by last night's rockquake, she thought. It had almost shaken her out of bed. She had come awake in panic, flinching at the loud rumbling which reverberated round the dormitory. Even when the terrifying grinding noises eventually died away, she was a long time going back to sleep.

Mira squinted at the crevice, afraid to attract the supervisor's attention by holding the rush torch closer. Maybe it was the start of a system of newly formed caves. Impulsively, she squeezed through into the space beyond.

She waited while her eyes adjusted to the gloom, wishing she had brought the torch. When at last she could make out dim outlines, in the light seeping from the tunnel, she felt a stab of surprise. The cave was much larger than she had expected—high enough to stand comfortably erect, and wide. Strange, she thought, glancing round. It looks almost man made. She took a half step forward and stubbed her bare toe.

At first Mira thought the thing was alive—a lizard or a rat perhaps. Cave rats made good eating; she instinctively raised one foot to crush it. Then she realized the movement was caused by the dancing flames of the torch outside. Anyway, it had felt hard . . . probably just a piece of ordinary rock, a fragment torn loose when the fissure was formed. She stooped and grabbed the thing, then squeezed out into the tunnel again.

The other miners were still engrossed in the business of meeting their own quotas, and the supervisor was out of sight—probably round a corner harassing his latest "favourite." Huddling closer to the torch, she peered at her find. Her eyes confirmed what her fingers had already told her. This was no ordinary rock but a piece of red crystal. Not the rough, unworked crystals which filled her basket, however. It was shaped like a tiny rat's heart. Smooth all over too. She had never seen anything like it.

Mira knew she should report her find—there were standing instructions that anything unusual should be handed in at once. But a craving swept over her, stronger than anything she had felt before. It's mine, she thought fiercely, and shoved the crystal deep inside her skirt pocket.

MIRA LAY STILL for a moment, listening. The dormitory was far from silent. From all sides came loud snoring, the muffled coughing of someone in the first stages of the black lung, a child whimpering . . . and beneath everything, like a constant musical drone, the quiet sobbing of a woman who had finally had enough. Such familiar sounds should not have disturbed her. She rolled over, trying to go back to sleep, and something dug sharply into her hip. Belatedly she realized that it was the pain which had woken her.

Carefully she eased the hard crystal from her hip pocket, cupped it in her palm, and stared at it, raising her head slightly to get a better look. It must be man-made. Yet even the best Company craftsmen couldn't cut a crystal as symmetrical and smooth, as perfect as this. The pulse in her temple pounded, as she strained to see in the dim light. Was it her imagination or was there something glowing, deep inside the crystal—a dull, red light? Probably just eye strain, she thought, and knuckled her tired eyes. Then, letting her head flop back onto the pillow and replacing the heart in her pocket, she thought back to its discovery.

Normally the miners excavated new seams, but this time the supervisor had instructed them to rework the tunnels found when the Company first colonized Caltrop. It had become cost-effective, he said. Crystal prices had risen steeply—which meant more offworld food and supplies in exchange. She wondered wryly if any of the extra goods would reach those who actually extracted the crystals.

Mira had never been in one of the original tunnels before, and she noticed at once that its dimensions were subtly different—taller and narrower than usual. No one knew who, or more likely what, had dug them, though rumours abounded—most agreeing that it must have been Caltrop's original inhabitants, who had vanished long before the colonists arrived. Not that the Company would have let a little thing like previous ownership bother them anyway—possession was nine tenths of the law.

Could the heart belong to the mine's creators? An artifact of some kind? And where there was one artifact, she thought with rising excitement, might there be more? But her excitement was tempered by caution. No one must get wind of her discovery until she was ready. She eased back the bedcovers, crawled out of bed, and tiptoed towards the dormitory exit.

AT THIS TIME of night, the tunnels were deserted, and it didn't take Mira long to reach the crevice unobserved. The urge to find more of the artifacts was strong, and without hesitation, she squeezed inside.

This time she'd brought along a rush torch, and the flickering light made the cave look larger than she remembered. Even with the light, she couldn't see the back of the cave. It appeared to stretch far into the rock, sloping gently uphill. Eagerly she stepped forward, scanning the floor for more of the perfect crystals.

Something about the floor tugged at Mira's attention. She stooped and pressed her palm against it. The clammy stone felt as smooth as the walls—as though millions of feet had eroded it, or it had melted and then solidified. Too smooth . . . no sign of any more crystals. She frowned, then shrugged, and straightened. Perhaps they would be further in.

The cave narrowed rapidly, until it was little more than a path between towering walls. She stopped, suddenly indecisive. This could be dangerous. Another rockquake might bring down the ceiling at any time; suppose she became trapped? And what guarantee was there she would find anything? But curiosity kept her pressing forward. What the hell, she thought. It's worth the risk.

The path continued, steeper than before. At this rate it would lead to the very top of the mine. Level One workers, she had heard, were responsible for unloading the offworld supply ships. If she turned in the artifacts—keeping the original heart for herself, of course—the Company might reward her with a Level One job. Imagine having the chance to live a different way of life from that of her mother and grandmother—one in which there was warmth and comfort, and no risk of the black lung.

For the first time in years, she allowed herself to wonder what the planet's surface looked like. According to the history tapes, a thick, poisonous haze obscured everything. The first settlers had seeded Caltrop with the spores of oxygen producing algae; she wondered if it had had any effect yet. Wouldn't it be something, if one day people could actually live in the open?

She laughed, mocking herself for dreaming, and the sound bounced off the surrounding rock. As she listened to the fading echoes of wild laughter, she was suddenly acutely aware of her predicament, squeezed in a narrow crevice, surrounded by tons of rock. She began to tremble. What would happen when the torch was used up? The thought of being left in pitch blackness was terrifying. And all this because she had had some crazy yearning to own a crystal. She really must be mad!

She breathed deeply, trying to regain control. It's just a touch of claustrophobia, she told herself. Just keep putting one foot in front of the other, and the path will emerge soon, you'll see.

MIRA HAD GROWN used to the undeviating nature of the path as it arrowed steadily upwards. Then, all at once, it began to zigzag, the sharp angles ripping skin from her knees and elbows. She wondered what it meant, even considered going back. But she had come this far . . .

Yet there had been no more crystals, or artifacts of any kind. If I didn't know better, she thought, I'd think the heart was bait, used by someone—or something—to lure me here. But that notion was too frightening to pursue.

She plodded on with a sense of growing numbness, from time to time stopping to ease the stitch in her side. Then something tripped her.

It was a moment before she recognized what it was—the first of a series of rock ledges. Steps! Whatever next? She craned her neck trying to see where they led, but they disappeared round an outcrop. Wearily, she raised one foot.

After only a few minutes climbing, Mira's legs trembled with effort—the steps were too deep to negotiate comfortably. Here was further confirmation, if any were required, of the alien nature of the mine's creators. The thought added to her growing feeling of unease. Usually the tunnels were filled with the squeaks of scampering cave rats, but here it was as silent as death. She shivered and hummed a tune to keep up her flagging spirits, then held the torch high to view her surroundings better.

Mira turned the corner and stopped abruptly. The stairs had come to a dead end. A huge slab of rock lay squarely across them, its edges fitting so snugly on all sides that it was impossible to insert even a fingernail. She stared in disbelief. It looked like a door of some kind, but how did one open it? To have come so far . . . Despair welled inside her. So that's it then, she thought dully. I've come all this way for nothing.

She was turning to retrace her steps when she noticed a small indentation in the exact centre of the rock slab. Something about it tugged at her attention—it was heart-shaped. Thoughtfully, she transferred the torch to her other hand and groped in her skirt pocket.

The crystal felt warm against Mira's fingers, sending a faint tingle through them. She pulled it out. It was glowing a dull red, as though proximity to the rock had activated it in some way. She pressed it into the shallow indentation; it fitted snugly. Then she stepped back and waited. For a moment nothing happened, then the crystal flared a brilliant crimson, and a loud click filled the passageway. She heard a dull grinding, as of rock shifting, and took another step back, almost falling down the stairs in her haste. The huge rock slab began to pivot.

Instinctively, she grabbed for the crystal; there was a feeling of slight resistance before it snapped free of its socket. She squeezed through the still widening gap, then stopped, dumbfounded.

The cavern she had entered was massive, stretching in all directions, lit by a ghostly green luminescence which seemed to come from its very walls. Massive stalactites drooped from the ceiling towards Mira, and she gaped up at them. From their size, they must be centuries old, formed even before the Company ship landed. A noise jerked her from her reverie, and she swung round, in time to see the rock door swinging shut.

Her stomach lurched, and she raced towards the door. Too late. It slammed shut with a note of finality that echoed round the cavern. She stared numbly at it. Then she noticed the heart shaped indentation on this side of the slab and relief washed over her. I still have the key, she thought, fingering the crystal which was safely in her pocket. And weary with reaction, she turned back to the cavern.

In the far reaches, Mira could just make out unmoving silhouettes. She wondered what the shapes could be. Only one way to find out. As she walked towards them, bare feet slapping on the cold floor, brilliant emerald light flooded the cavern and she stopped, startled. Its light no longer needed, she dropped the rush torch on the cave floor, where it sputtered briefly then died.

But her attention was not on the torch but on the strange objects the bright light had revealed. There must have been thousands of the things—stone cubes and cylinders of varying heights and widths, each topped with an artifact. She stared round in wonder. There were statues too. It must be a museum of some kind—she had seen such places on the history tapes.

One thing was immediately obvious—everything was dust free. Mira frowned. Did that mean a curator of some kind, someone charged with maintaining the pristine condition of the exhibits? A chill raised goose-pimples on her arm; for a moment she thought it was merely a physical reaction to her fear, then she realized there was a slight through draught. And the cavern smelt fresh. But was that enough to account for the complete absence of dust? She hoped so.

The nearest exhibit was recognizable—a pile of red heart-shaped crystals just like her own. Was she supposed to deposit hers for use by another visitor, then? Not likely. She moved on to the next object, which looked hollow—a receptacle of some kind. Its shape was peculiar, a mixture of spirals and curves; Mira was baffled as to what it might once have held. She examined the plinth, frowning at the alien hieroglyphs. The thing's surface was smooth and shiny, and seemed to invite her touch, but at first contact, rainbow patterns writhed beneath the turquoise glaze, and she withdrew her hand sharply. She stared at it a moment longer, then shrugged and moved on.

As she wandered among the exhibits, her eagerness to turn them over to the Company quickly diminished. These should be seen by everybody, she thought. Even those on other worlds would find them breathtaking.

The unknown sculptors' skills had been so great she was unsure whether the statues were rock or real creatures, somehow petrified. The biologists would have a field day; the cave rats and lizards were familiar, but the others . . . Were these the former denizens of Caltrop, able to survive its poisonous atmosphere? And those things with their fernlike fronds and appendages looking uncannily like toes and toenails! Were they vegetable or animal? Mira's mind brimmed with questions.

One statue towered head and shoulders above the rest. It must be fourteen foot tall, thought Mira, gazing at the strange bipedal creature, which looked as though it had been stretched between the ceiling and floor. The thing was unclothed, yet there was no sign of sexual organs—perhaps they were stowed internally?

She stared up at the massive head. Four eyes clustered above a rat-like snout, and the thumbnail-sized orifices on either side must surely be hearing organs. Four elongated limbs—its arms?—each tipped with four padded digits, sprouted seemingly at random from the long torso. She circled the statue again and again. Was this one of the beings which had created the mine, or merely another of the surface creatures? Eventually, she sighed with frustration and turned away.

A winding path led her into yet more caverns, some containing more artifacts, others strange natural phenomena. When she investigated what sounded like wind chimes, she found green slivers of stone dangling from a coral-like ceiling growth—the delicate wafers were brushing against each other in the air currents. She sat and listened to the restful, almost hypnotic tinkling before continuing her exploration.

In another cavern, the sound of rushing water bouncing off the stone walls led her to a massive waterfall. She had been feeling hungry and thirsty for some time, and she cupped a palm beneath the running water and drank. It tasted fresh and sweet, yet tangy with mineral salts. She drank until her stomach felt near to bursting. As she sat on the waterfall's edge, lulled by the sound of running water, a stronger draught ruffled her hair and made her clasp her arms for warmth. It was coming from the wall up ahead and what she had taken to be the entrance to yet another cavern.

Apprehension washed over her as she crossed towards the gap and peered through. Then she gasped with shock. She was high on a hillside, and down below lay a lush green landscape.

AT FIRST MIRA thought it must be an illusion. She even searched the cavern thoroughly for a projector, like the one which played the old films in the entertainment hall on special occasions. After all, the landscape couldn't be real—everyone knew the planet's surface was murky and hostile. But as she sat, hour after hour, staring out at the view, which she soon concluded wasn't a uniform green after all—there were patches of red and brown, and in the distance a smooth stretch of something which reflected the turquoise sky—she realized it was real. And those things must be clouds, she thought, watching shadows scud over the ground beneath them.

For a while she felt numb. This was too much to absorb. Then a hollow feeling of betrayal crept over her. The Company lied to us, she thought. Buried us deep underground, breathing recycled air and cancerous dust. Condemned us to hunch beneath rock ceilings. Generation after generation living in dampness and darkness, and all the while this . . . Something dripped onto her lap, soaking through her skirt, and she realized she was crying.

IT TOOK A day for Mira to find the courage to venture into the open. At first she thought she might faint—she felt so exposed—but then the pounding in her head eased to manageable proportions. It was gnawing hunger that forced her out in the end.

She ran from one clump of thick vegetation to another, like a cave rat darting between boulders, afraid of discovery by those who had reserved the planet's surface for their own enjoyment. Whenever she found fruits or berries, she crammed them into her mouth. It never even occurred to her that the fruit might be poisonous. She was fortunate that the stomach ache, when it came, was relatively mild, and the attack of vomiting and diarrhoea soon over. After that, she was more circumspect, eating a single berry of each new species, waiting to see if digestion brought no adverse effects, adding it to her mental list of edibles.

Occasionally, creatures scuttled or crawled across her path, or, disturbed by her noisy approach, broke from cover and whirred into the air. All were subtly different from the museum exhibits. Perhaps they've adapted to the change in atmosphere, she thought. There was no sign of anything higher up the food chain—either alien or human.

The first time water fell from the sky and soaked through her thin clothes, she was taken completely by surprise; she had forgotten that clouds could also be a source of wetness. That apart, though, the climate was warm, hospitable.

She was gazing at the huge sun reddening the sky as it rose above the horizon when the supply ship came. It swooped from nowhere with a deafening roar that hurt her ears, and glided towards a strip of flat land to the north. Startled, she watched it go, then broke into a run, arrowing through the shrub and undergrowth towards its landing site.

By the time Mira caught up with it, the ship was standing cooling in the centre of an otherwise deserted strip of gravel, its metal contracting with loud creaks and clicks. She peered from her thicket of scrub and waited for someone to emerge.

A hatch in the craft's belly slid open with a whining sound. Four thin metal struts dropped towards the ground directly beneath, which now she came to think of it looked a different texture from the rest of the gravel. She realized why, when the apparently solid ground suddenly split wide open. Another hatch! The struts slid firmly into four waiting slots, with a clunk. Crunching noises and whirrs sounded for a few minutes, then something like an open cage began to descend between the four rods. The cage contained a large crate.

It's unloading automatically, she realized, astonished. She watched the cage disappear into the ground. Some time later, it reappeared. This time wicker baskets were visible through the superstructure; full of crystals, no doubt. The cage rose slowly into the belly of the ship.

Suddenly Mira understood. The beacon to guide the supply ship's autopilot, the mechanism for unloading and loading cargo . . . all were automated; their design was so basic, necessary repairs could probably be carried out by robots too. When was the last time a human had actually bothered to inspect the surface, and the progress of the terraforming algae? Disbelief replaced her anger against the Company elite. It wasn't their calculated greed which had led to this . . . abomination, but their complacency and stupidity.

Numbly, she watched the loading and unloading, until the last of the baskets had risen into the supply ship's hold. Then the struts retracted and both hatches thudded closed. The engines started with a faint whine which quickly turned into a roar. The craft rose from the gravel landing strip, hovered for a moment, then streaked off towards the horizon, its destination one of the other colony worlds, she supposed. After a while the chirps of the alien birds and the rustle of vegetation in the warm breeze, resumed.

Mira stared at the now empty sky, one hand in her pocket stroking the crystal heart. She was thinking of Old Rog and the other miners who shared her dormitory. They deserved to see this, she thought. To stand tall under an open sky. But she must be careful how she went about getting them here. If the Company got wind of the real conditions on the surface first . . .

She sighed, knowing what her decision meant. It would be hard to go back into the caverns, to experience again the claustrophobia of the path which squeezed between the rocks. But it had to be done. And this time she was prepared. This time she knew where she was going and what she must do when she got there.

She turned and started back towards the caverns.

AFTERWORD

I can't remember where the idea for this story came from, but it's obviously symbolic, the crystal giving my heroine "heart" to reject the consensus and strike out on her own. Whatever its genesis, I set out to evoke the "sensawunda" that got me addicted to Science Fiction and Fantasy in the first place. Whether I succeeded, you be the judge.

BABALAWO'S DRUM

"IS THIS MY new husbandman?"

Rob stared at his dusty shoes and fiddled with his woollen cap.

"Ay, Master Winslade." Justice Philpot's tone was deferential. "His name is Robert Lambert. Fifteen. A vagabond's son."

"He looks strong enough," continued the first voice. "What say you, Rob? Will you serve me?"

Startled to be asked rather than told, Rob looked up warily. Kind grey eyes met his, and the mouth beneath the trim brown beard curved into a smile.

"Speak, lad."

Rob hesitated. Thomas Winslade certainly looked an improvement on his previous master. He was younger, for a start, in his mid thirties, and much more fashionably dressed. A three-inch white ruff fitted over his shirt and round his neck, and he wore a yellow pair of those newfangled Venetian breeches.

"Answer the good gentleman, boy," hissed the Justice.

"If it please you, sir . . . I will serve you to the best of my ability," stammered Rob, at last. It was no choice really. Refuse this master, and Philpot would select another less civilised one, might even send him back to the brutal Finch.

Winslade smiled. "It pleases me, Rob." He turned to a sombrely dressed man who until then had stood by the window at the back of the small, panelled room. "Machyn?"

"Sir?"

"Show him to his quarters. See him fed and instruct him in his duties."

Machyn nodded, and beckoned. Obediently, Rob followed him.

ROB HAD BEEN at Coneyhurst for only a month when the visitors from London arrived. The manor house had been abustle since day-break, rooms being swept, feather mattresses turned, and fresh sheets laid. Rob was ordered to carry a large ham from the smokehouse and a heavy churn of cream from the buttery to the kitchen where Mistress Askew and her helpers were working, red-faced; he didn't mind—it made a welcome change from weeding.

Just before noon, three horses, one of them a pack animal, galloped up, streaked with dust, muzzles frothy. It was the second rider that instantly drew Rob's attention.

"That's Huggarde's servant, Babalawo," said Miles Holinshed cheerfully—the blonde-haired, blue-eyed husbandman did everything cheerfully, Rob had discovered. "Sir John Hawkins, the great voyager, brought him back from Guinea." Miles grinned at Rob's wide eyes.

"His skin!" breathed Rob. "'Tis black as ebony!" He turned to look at the other rider, a foppish-looking, red-haired man currently greeting Winslade like a long-lost brother. "Huggarde?"

Miles nodded. "Charles Huggarde, Antiquary. Captain Hawkins gave him the negro as payment for a rare volume."

Machyn materialised suddenly beside them, and Rob's heart pounded. The sour-faced Steward had a way of moving silently, even over gravel. "Carry our visitors' baggage into the house, if you please," ordered the Steward.

The guest chamber assigned to Huggarde and his man was three times the size of the cramped, windowless bedchamber that Rob shared with Miles. Dominating it was a massive four-poster bed, furnished with linen sheets, tapestry coverlets, and black-and-yellow silk hangings.

Rob moved aside a satin-covered chair and began to stack clothing and parcels on the floor. What he had thought was a container shaped like a skull proved to be a skull. And a drum—a tall, narrow, foreign-looking instrument unlike any he had seen before—fascinated him. Its skin was so taut, the least tap sent sound booming round the bedchamber. He raised an eyebrow at Miles.

"Babalawo is a musician," whispered Miles. "Belike he'll play tonight, for Master Winslade."

"May we attend?" asked Rob eagerly. Sometimes, when Winslade caught sight of Rob weeding, he would halt and enquire after his newest employee's health. Surely such a considerate master wouldn't mind sharing his music?

But Miles shook his head. "Not if Babalawo plays after curfew."

"Curfew?"

"When guests stay at Coneyhurst, no servant must stray abroad between the hour of nine and break of day."

"For what reason?"

Miles shrugged. "By order of our master," he said.

ROB STARED UP at the sloping rafters, at the moonlight shining through a knot hole and onto the small chest beside the bed. For a moment, he wondered what had woken him. Then he heard it: the sound of drumming on the night breeze. He sat up, listening intently.

"What, are you awake?" asked Miles from beside him, his voice sleepy.

The rhythmic drumming seemed to wind itself around Rob's heart and make his pulse keep time. "Do you hear it?" he asked.

Miles yawned, his jaw cracking loudly. "Marry, it must be Babalawo playing for the Master."

Rob remembered the booming notes the drum had made. "Something muffles the sound, or it travels from a distance."

"'Tis after curfew. Go back to sleep." Slow, regular breathing showed Miles had taken his own advice.

Rob lay back, but now he was awake, he couldn't seem to go back to sleep. He had eaten too much, helped himself to too many leftovers. He sucked his knuckles reflectively, remembering the painful rap Mistress Askew had given them when he reached for the fish that she had just removed from the drying rack.

"Touch not that, Rob!" she had scolded him. "'Tis a puffer fish. Poisonous, and besides it belongs to the negro."

He wondered what Babalawo would do with the strange fish with its beaklike snout and tough spiny skin if he couldn't eat it.

A little later the drumming was replaced by a lone voice, a baritone. It wasn't possible to make out the words, and the melody, one Rob had never heard before, was strangely unsettling. He was relieved when the singing finally stopped, or maybe it was just that the breeze had shifted. Later still came a sound of distant rumbling that puzzled him, but soon that too ceased.

Eventually, he slept.

MORNING DAWNED BRIGHT and clear, and since it was Sunday, the whole household, masters and servants, donned their best clothes and hats, and after breakfast walked to the local church.

The Church and its graveyard abutted the land belonging to Coneyhurst, so it wasn't far. The walk was pleasant, through lanes whose hedges had been freshly trimmed. Miles walked beside Rob, whistling cheerily, until Machyn shot him a sour look.

They turned out of the lane and onto the path that led through the sprawling graveyard towards the Church.

"The graveyard is haunted," whispered Miles to Rob, his eyes dancing.

"Haunted?"

Miles nodded. "No one dares come here after dark. Not even the Vicar."

Anxiously, Rob fingered the little cross on the thong round his neck—his only memento of his dead mother—and muttered a quick prayer.

"They appear not in daylight," soothed Miles, noting the gesture.

Rob grunted. Up ahead, Winslade and Huggarde, and slightly behind them Babalawo and Machyn, walked as though there was nothing at all to fear. He took a deep breath and imitated them.

At the Church door, the parish warden greeted Winslade with a smile, licked his pencil stub and wrote down the names of each member of the Coneyhurst party as they made their way to the pews appropriate to their status. Rob squashed in next to Miles at the rear of the church, the heat from his friend's thigh offsetting the coldness of the interior.

The Vicar's voice was monotonous, his sermon tedious, and the pew had turned Rob's buttocks numb before he was allowed out into the autumn sunshine once more. The walk back to Coneyhurst was a relief.

Once back at the Manor, Winslade and his guests retired indoors, Cook and her assistants scuttled back to the kitchen, and Rob and the other husbandmen set off to the butts to practise their archery.

From something Miles had said, Rob suspected that his new master was, at this very moment, celebrating Mass with Huggarde. There was no law against it—unlike her dead sister, Queen Elizabeth contented herself with controlling only her subjects' outward appearance—but even so it carried an element of risk. He began a prayer that nothing terrible would ever happen to his master—

"Wake up, addlepate! 'Tis your turn." Miles' voice jerked him back to awareness.

Rob grabbed the proffered longbow and arrow, and took his place in front of the butts.

ONE TUESDAY MORNING, in the early hours, Rob woke to overwhelming dizziness and nausea. He groaned and clutched his stomach.

"Are you sick?" asked Miles, raising himself to one elbow.

"Ay." Rob lay back, sweating and anxious.

Miles fumbled for the candle, lit it, and held it close to Rob's face. He frowned and began to get up. "I must fetch Master Winslade." In spite of Rob's protests, he hurried from the room.

A little later Rob became aware that someone else was standing by his bed. "Rob, lad," came Master Winslade's voice. "I hear you're not well." A cool hand rested on his burning forehead. "What had you to eat last night?"

"Mutton," croaked Rob. "And bread."

"Nothing more?"

Abruptly, icy cold rushed through him, and he began to shiver. He heard the creak that was the chest beside the bed being opened and felt another blanket being laid over him. It warmed him a little.

"Thank you, sir," he managed, through chattering teeth.

"Nothing more?" repeated his master. "No remnants from my table?"

"A few cold cockles and mussels," admitted Rob reluctantly. "Mistress Askew put them to one side, but I thought them too good to waste."

"Ah," said Master Winslade. "Fetch the box of stibium from my study, Miles."

"At once, sir."

Footsteps clattered down the stairs, growing fainter.

A warm hand grasped his. "Stibby is a deadly poison, lad. But used wisely, it can cure sickness such as this. Do you trust me to use it to make you well?"

Rob squinted up at the blurred face. "Ay, sir. I do."

Then Miles was in the room again. "Your stibium, sir."

While Miles supported Rob into a sitting position, Winslade held something to Rob's lips and urged him to drink. He obliged, then grimaced at the bitter taste.

"Good. It will have effect in half an hour," said Winslade. "Rest now. And keep the chamber pot to hand, Miles!"

"As it please you, sir."

Then Winslade was gone.

For nearly forty minutes, Rob noticed no change. Then came a sudden urge to relieve himself, and no sooner had he finished and with Miles' help climbed back into bed than a wave of sickness overtook him. Soon he was spewing as if his innards would burst. Fortunately, Miles had the chamber pot at the ready.

At last the feverishness that had plagued him began to recede along with the nausea, and he lay back on his pillow, eyelids drooping with relief and tiredness.

"Heaven bless Master Winslade," he told Miles sleepily.

Miles tiptoed away with the foul smelling pot . . .

SEPTEMBER TURNED TO October, and the darkening evenings provided ample leisure time to sit and talk beside the kitchen fire. Rob told Miles something of his early life.

"Father took me with him on the road when I was but two. After my mother had died birthing my sister."

"Your sister?" asked Miles.

"She lived but a day."

Miles nodded. "He travelled out of grief?"

Rob chewed his lip. "Mayhap he was just running away."

"And you with him?"

"What choice had I?" He sighed. "But the constables hate vagabonds worse than the pox. Always we fled, from village to village, town to town. Finally, they caught us. Father died from the whipping they gave him."

Miles pressed his hand in sympathy. "This is your home now."

Rob shook his head sadly. "I am not my own man until my eighteenth year. Until then, I must go wherever the JPs send me."

"Winslade will keep you with him," said Miles confidently. "If you wish to stay."

"Will you be here?"

Miles laughed. "Of a certainty."

But Miles proved unable to keep his word. For the very next week, while they were mucking out the stables together, a horse bridled and kicked him with one massive, iron-shod hoof. By the time Rob reached his friend, it was already too late. His forehead was stove in, his eyes unmoving.

In a daze, he helped the other men carry Miles back into the house. The commotion attracted the attention of the Master, who looked gravely at Rob and told him, "'Tis a black day, Rob. But life must go on."

And Mistress Askew patted Rob on the arm. "Your friend has gone to a better place, Rob. He is with his Maker now."

Rob tried to take comfort from their words. He felt lost and alone, overcome with an irrational anger—Miles had deserted him, as his father had, as his mother had before that. Tears beset him, and he sought a corner where he could weep undisturbed. In the end, a welcome numbness settled over him, and at the funeral, even the anguished sobbing of Miles' parents and two younger sisters couldn't touch him.

For such as Miles and I, decided Rob, life is but drudgery followed by death. At least, he consoled himself, death comes as a release.

THE FOLLOWING SATURDAY, Charles Huggarde and his negro arrived unexpectedly, making the Manor swarm like a disturbed ants' nest. Once more Rob carried belongings from pack horse to guest chamber; once more Mistress Askew was instructed to hang a puffer fish from her drying rack . . .

That night, when the sound of distant drumming woke him, there was no Miles to tell him to go back to sleep or remind him of the curfew. He rose, slipped on his jerkin, hose, and shoes, and tiptoed down the servants' stairs, through the kitchen, and out into the courtyard. A brilliant full moon illuminated his surroundings as he wheeled to face the drumming. It was coming from the Church!

Rob set off the quickest way, across the fields. Unwelcome memories came back as he walked: Miles grinning and saying of the graveyard, "It's haunted!" . . . An owl shrieked, and he flinched involuntarily. At least, it sounded like an owl. Trying not to let his imagination run away with him, he walked on.

He was still some way from the Church when the drum beats stopped and the weird singing started. He paused. Suppose this was a lure, like some will-o'-the-wisp, meant to entice unwary travellers to their death? Then he shrugged and quickened his pace.

At the graveyard he stopped, panting. There was something strange about the moonlit scene. Maybe it was just the unsettling effect of the voice, which had, all this time, floated towards him on the cold, night air. Then he realized what it was. Alongside several of the graves lay mounds of soil. Curious, he padded towards the nearest.

As he peered down into its depths, it became clear that this grave was far from fresh. The coffin at its base had once been occupied; now it lay empty, its lid stacked to one side. He wandered over to another grave, and was met by the same sight—an empty coffin, wood more decayed than the first.

He frowned. There was ample room in the graveyard. Why would a gravedigger reuse old graves and—more to the point—old coffins?

Abruptly the distant baritone stopped.

The seconds of silence lengthened into minutes. There was no way to locate the source of the sound now. He sighed, disappointed, and also, though he was loath to admit it, relieved. Wherever the voice had come from, it clearly wasn't the Church—no candles flickered behind the windowpanes, there was no sign of movement.

He was about to return to the manor house when the rumbling came. He could even feel it through the soles of his thin shoes. And it was coming from nearby, he decided. From the land at the rear of the Church.

LIGHT AND MOVEMENT met Rob's gaze as he peered round the corner of the Church. Lanterns placed on the ground at intervals dimly illuminated a strange tableau. In front of a large barn, its door wide open, stood three carts, from which a dozen labourers were struggling to unload culverins. Cannons, in the Sussex countryside!

As he watched, a culverin thudded to earth, its wheels gouging deep ruts. The labourers began trundling it towards the barn, their movements slow and deliberate. He inhaled sharply as a wheel rolled over a man's foot, then sighed with relief when the lack of reaction showed he must have been mistaken. Surprisingly, although the work looked backbreaking, there were no mutters of complaint—either the labourers were being paid handsomely, he thought, or they were little more than slaves.

Suddenly, those directing the operation came into view—a foppish-looking man with red hair and a man whose skin, even in this dim light, was clearly jet black. Rob recognised the two immediately.

He frowned. What on earth were Huggarde and Babalawo up to? All this activity was clearly the source of the rumbling and of the drumming, perhaps even the explanation for the graveyard's haunted reputation. And judging by the culverins already inside the barn, they had been doing this for some weeks.

A few labourers began to ferry armfuls of hagbuts to the barn as though they were bundles of firewood. Siege weapons and muskets, enough for a small rebelli—

"'Tis pity you saw this," came a familiar voice from behind.

Rob felt his stomach churn. He turned slowly to face Machyn's cold gaze. A sword point rested against his midriff.

"Walk towards the others."

Reluctantly, Rob walked out into the lantern light, conscious of Machyn at his heels and the sword pricking sharply through his jerkin. As he approached the carts and the men unloading them, he slowed. Huggarde turned a face full of dismay towards him. Babalawo's expression remained impassive.

"I came upon him spying," came Machyn's voice.

Huggarde cursed. "'Sblood! We must stop his mouth."

"Babalawo's labourers speak not out of turn," said Machyn pointedly. Rob wondered what the Steward meant by that remark.

Huggarde looked disconcerted. "I thought to bribe the boy not harm him."

Machyn grunted. "The risk is too great."

"I'll speak not of this to anyone," said Rob anxiously. "Upon my honour."

"Honour? What does a vagabond's son know of that?" Machyn's voice was heavy with contempt.

"I trust the boy," said a familiar voice.

"Master Winslade!" As his master stepped out of the shadows, Rob almost fainted with relief. Winslade smiled reassuringly at him.

"Sir," said Machyn urgently. "This is ill advised. If he talks . . ."

"He will not, will you, Rob?"

Just then, one of the labourers, having dumped his load of hagbuts, entered a pool of lantern light. There was something very strange about the man, thought Rob, staring. His eyes were unblinking, black pits that sucked in the light instead of reflecting it. One of his bare arms looked blotchy too, like meat so overcooked it was ready to fall off the bone . . . He shivered.

"Rob?" Winslade's voice jarred him back to his surroundings. "You'll hold your tongue about what you've seen tonight, will you not?"

"Prison him 'til we have taken Nonesuch," said Huggarde helpfully. "Then England will have her lawful Queen, and none need fear reprisals—"

"Be silent, fool!" hissed Machyn.

Rob's eyes widened. Only one faction could refer to a "lawful Queen" and not mean Elizabeth, he thought—supporters of Mary Stuart.

Flushing, Huggarde turned to Winslade. "What say you, Thomas?"

"He will not betray us," said Winslade confidently, "for that would mean betraying me and we are firm friends. Give me your word, lad, and you have mine as a gentleman no harm will come to you."

The labourers had finished the unloading and were now drawn up in two ranks, silently awaiting instructions. Rob glanced at the nearest man and felt the breath rush from his lungs. It couldn't be! Yet the features were as familiar as his own, and the forehead still bore the horseshoe-shaped injury . . .

His vision clouded, and he swayed slightly. He felt someone take his arm, then Winslade was blocking his view, and Rob began to wonder if he had imagined seeing Miles.

"What shall it be, Rob?" Winslade's face was so close Rob could smell the mint on his breath. "May I trust you, Rob? With my life, as you trusted me with yours?"

Rob noticed Machyn staring at him, his eyes glittering. He cleared his throat.

"You may trust me, Master Winslade," he said. "On my honour."

FOR ALL WINSLADE claimed he trusted Rob, he was taking no chances. For the next two days, one of the other husbandmen dogged Rob's every step, even sleeping outside his bedchamber door over-night. When Rob angrily confronted Dirk, he admitted that he was following orders—he had no knowledge, though, of what lay behind them.

At last, however, his chance came. Over breakfast, an undercook upset Mistress Askew by burning the porridge, and it was a simple matter to slip away from Coneyhurst while Dirk's attention was distracted by the loud argument. Mentally, it was far from simple, though, deserting the Master who had saved his life. He tried not to think of it as he ran, retracing the route he had travelled all those months ago, before he had moved to Coneyhurst, before Miles had become like a brother . . .

By the time he reached Philpot's house, his leg muscles were aching fiercely, and his jerkin was soaked with sweat.

The Justice was tucking into a lavish breakfast in his parlour when Rob was shown in. "Pox it! If you've run away, Rob Lambert," he thundered, rising to his feet, "it's the stocks for you."

"Master Winslade and his friends are plotting 'gainst Queen Elizabeth," gasped Rob, pressing his fist into his aching side.

Philpot frowned. "By God, boy, if this is but a malicious rumour about your master I'll—"

"If it please your worship," interrupted Rob, "I have seen cannons and hagbuts. Heard talk of an attack on a place called Nonesuch—"

"The Duke of Arundel's residence?" The Justice looked thoughtful. "I've heard Her Majesty is to progress there."

"I can show evidence. Behind the Church . . ."

Even as Rob stopped once more for breath, Philpot was calling for his cloak and for his horse to be saddled, and for a messenger to fetch the constables.

EVERYTHING LOOKED DIFFERENT in daylight. The graves had been refilled, the barn was padlocked and all traces of anything unusual had been swept away, all ruts refilled.

Rob swung down from his seat on the saddle behind the Justice and pointed at the barn. "In there," he said.

Philpot dismounted, took a crowbar from his saddlebag and unceremoniously levered the lock from the door. It swung open smoothly. And there, to Rob's relief, were the cannons, the shot, and the hagbuts.

The sound of approaching hoof beats announced the coming of the constables.

Philpot fingered the nearest culverin thoughtfully. "Forgive me, boy. I thought you were moonstruck. But this is real enough. Too real." His fingers drummed on the cast iron.

Rob thought suddenly of Babalawo. Exactly how had the negro raised the inhabitants of the graveyard, among them Miles? Something to do with the strange fish, with drumming, and eerie singing in the night . . . ?

Six constables galloped up. Visibly pulling himself together, Philpot turned to their leader, a bullnecked man on an old white nag.

"Arrest Thomas Winslade," he ordered, "and charge him with High Treason 'gainst Her Majesty."

"Ay, your worship," said the man.

Moments later, the constables were galloping across the fields toward Coneyhurst Manor.

WHEN PHILPOT AND Rob reached Coneyhurst, it was just in time to see Winslade being bundled out of the front porch. Huggarde, Machyn, and Babalawo were already taken, their arms bound firmly behind them. Near the huddle of law officers and captives stood four horses saddled and ready—the constables' quarry had been on the point of fleeing, it seemed.

Mistress Askew and the other servants looked on bewildered, and when they saw Rob sitting behind the Justice began to murmur. Dirk glared at him.

Rob noticed that it was taking two men to hold the still struggling Machyn. Huggarde, on the other hand, was almost limp with fright. Babalawo stood like a black statue, his gaze as unresponsive as those he had raised from the dead.

Winslade's air of affronted dignity vanished when he saw Rob. "You!"

Rob nodded.

"By the Mass, but I warned you, sir," hissed Machyn.

"Why, Rob?" Winslade's face was pale. "Did I not treat you kindly?"

Rob clasped his trembling hands together. "For Miles's sake," he said simply.

Winslade looked puzzled. "Miles Holinshed is dead. What has he to do with this?"

"Babalawo conjured Miles from his eternal slumber . . . to do your bidding like some beast of burden." The thought made Rob nauseous.

"It pains me that Babalawo used Miles's corpse," said Winslade evenly, "but 'twas by chance not design, Rob. Besides, it matters not. The negro raises men's bodies not their souls—Miles Holinshed's soul slumbers still!" Winslade sighed. "Is it not better to use mortal clay than living men? To spare them risk of capture and me risk of betrayal?"

Rob scarcely heard his former master's excuses. "Can you not see? What you did was 'gainst God and Nature. To treat Miles in such a way—" He broke off, remembering the travesty that had once been his friend, the empty gaze . . .

"Lad—" began Winslade.

Anger gave Rob the strength to continue. "The dead have no voice, so I must speak for them," he said. "As you betrayed Miles, so I have betrayed you!"

Winslade drew in his breath sharply and for a moment only stared at Rob, his eyes haunted. "I knew you loved him, lad," he murmured at last, "but did not understand how much. If I have erred, I crave your pardon. Can you forgive me?"

Philpot, who until now had hung back, stepped forward. "Enough of this, Master Winslade," said the Justice. "Plotting against the Queen is High Treason, and you and your fellow conspirators must to The Tower, there to furnish the questioners with the names and whereabouts of your accomplices." He turned to the constables. "Take them away."

After Miles's death, Rob had thought nothing could ever touch him again. Watching them drag Winslade away, he realized he had been wrong. Yet for all his kindness and concern, this master had hurt him far worse than Finch, with his beatings and blows, ever had. No, he thought sadly. I can never forgive you.

A hand rested on his shoulder. "Come, Rob," came Philpot's voice, its tone not unsympathetic. "We're finished here. And there is much to be done. For a start, I must find you a new Master."

"Ay, your worship." Rob sighed, tore his gaze from Winslade and turned to face the Justice. "So you must."

AFTERWORD

Sometimes I use a checklist approach to writing. Done vampires and werewolves? Try zombies next. Never used an Elizabethan England setting? Its time has come. But a checklist only gets you so far. Zombies required voodoo and puffer fish venom, and how on earth could I fit those into an Elizabethan setting? As usual a library book about the period came to the rescue. Sir John Hawkins shipped slaves from West Africa to England. Problem solved.

HIGH FLIER

"THERE'S A TABLE in the corner, Jeff. Beer do you?" Before Jeff could disagree, Gavin was easing his way through the crowd of rowdy drinkers towards the bar.

Jeff sighed. He hadn't yet acquired the taste for cheap beer. Back home his parents always drank the fine wines they'd had specially imported from Earth. He felt a pang of homesickness. Idiot! Only two weeks in Copernicus City, and already he wanted to go home.

He peered through the gloom. It was obvious why the table was still empty—the lighting panel above it was flickering annoyingly. As he walked towards it, he hoped no drunken slob would beat him to it. What a place! When he had accepted Gavin's after work drink invitation, he'd imagined they would go somewhere civilized, a winebar maybe, not a dive like The Total Eclipse.

Barring his way was a group of thirteen or fourteen fliers, the cropped hair and wide V-shaped backs unmistakable. They had pushed together several battered tables and now sprawled untidily round them. He'd heard it was best to steer clear of fliers—they were unpredictable, fond of living on the edge—and so he skirted the group carefully. He was almost safely past, when a muscular flier with ash blond hair stood up suddenly, sending his stool flying. It bruised Jeff's shins, almost knocking him over.

Jeff found himself staring up into glazed blue eyes; a badly reset broken nose spoiled what could have been the face of an angel. "What you looking at?" The words were slurred, but the man's tone was aggressive. He grabbed Jeff's arm, digging in his fingers.

"Leave him alone, Raguel," said a dark-haired woman who looked about twenty. "He's only a greenie, and half your size." She grabbed Raguel's hand and bent the fingers back. Jeff winced in sympathy, though the big man hardly seemed to notice.

"Can't a guy have any fun?" Still grumbling, Raguel released his grip, righted the stool, and sat back down.

Jeff quickly made good his escape. He reached the still empty corner table and sat down thankfully, taking deep breaths until his pulse rate returned to normal. A greenie! He supposed he should feel insulted by the term, after all his family could trace its pedigree back to the very first Lunar colonists. But, he conceded grudgingly, compared to the fliers, he probably was rather young and inexperienced . . . He glanced across at the woman who had rescued him. She was deep in conversation, her grey eyes flashing, her hands gesturing extravagantly. She was very attractive, he thought, with her slanting eyebrows and high cheekbones, like a dark elf.

"Cheers," came a voice, and a foaming beer glass was placed on the table in front of him. Gavin took the chair next to Jeff's, gulped down some beer, then sighed theatrically. "I needed that."

Jeff eyed the bitter black liquid and suppressed a grimace. The evening had got off to a terrible start, and already the flickering and buzzing panel above was threatening to trigger a migraine. He felt a longing for real sunlight, but the Terminator was still a day away. He sighed and took a tentative sip of beer.

"How's the flat?" asked Gavin.

"Okay." Jeff's parents had arranged cosy lodgings for him but, in a sudden fit of independence which he now regretted, he had moved. His new place was Spartan and cold, but he wasn't going to tell Gavin that.

"Over here." Gavin signalled to someone.

Jeff craned his neck to see who it was. Margie, Gavin's current girl-friend, was coming towards them, grinning widely. His heart sank. Living at home for eighteen years hadn't exactly taught him how to mix with people, especially girls who seemed to delight in making him feel uncomfortable.

"I knew you wouldn't mind if Margie joined us," said Gavin, kissing his girlfriend.

Jeff caught a glimpse of Margie's pink tongue as it probed Gavin's mouth and looked away embarrassed. Not before he'd seen the mischievous glance she threw at him though. Show off! he thought.

"So, Jeff," she said, after she'd sat down, her plump hand resting on Gavin's thigh, dangerously close to his crotch. "Got yourself a girlfriend yet?"

Jeff didn't think the question deserved an answer.

A burst of laugher sounded; grateful for the distraction he glanced round. The fliers had been joined by several Earthers, their size and oddly uncoordinated way of walking making them immediately identifiable. He watched them for a while, then his gaze sought the woman flier again. To his surprise, she was staring straight at him. He blushed and tried to look away, but somehow he couldn't.

Abruptly, she rose, said something to one of her companions, and pushed her way between the stools. As she walked purposefully towards him, he felt his heart begin to pound. He tore his gaze away and stared fixedly at his beer.

"We skipped the introductions earlier," came a female voice. "I'm Alanna. And you are . . . ?"

Jeff looked up, aware that Gavin and Margie were regarding him with amazement. "Um . . . Jeff," he said, wondering if his ears and cheeks had gone as red as they felt.

"Jeff's pulled. A flier too," murmured Gavin. Margie giggled.

Embarrassed and annoyed with his companions, he glanced quickly at Alanna, but she seemed unperturbed.

"Like to meet a Wave-Rider pilot, Jeff?"

He tried to act as though this was an everyday occurrence. "Sure. Why not?"

"Come on, then." Alanna turned away.

For a moment Jeff hesitated. Then, with a shrug of apology for deserting the others, he stood up and followed the flier.

ALANNA PULLED UP a stool and gestured. Jeff sat down. He was relieved to see the flier with the broken nose was lying face down on the table, snoring harmlessly.

"This is Jeff," said Alanna loudly. The buzz of conversation lessened, and Jeff noticed lots of grins and pointed winks. His cheeks went hot.

A lanky flier with acne scars reached across the table to shake Jeff's hand. "Hi, I'm Mat."

Alanna continued the rest of the introductions. "Raguel's the unconscious one . . . Frans . . . Isobel . . . Vassily . . . Connor . . . Mercedes . . ."

Jeff quickly lost track of the names.

"Slow down, Alanna," laughed a man with a gravelly voice. The sun-darkened skin and network of fine lines round his eyes tagged him as an Earther. "Can't you see he's reaching overload?"

Alanna grinned. "Actually, he's come to meet a real life WaveRider pilot, Stefan, but all I could find was you."

"Bollocks!" Stefan took Jeff's hand in a bone-crushing grip. "So," he said. "What do you do, Jeff?"

"Um . . . I've just started with LunaTrans." Jeff was uneasily aware this would hardly sound glamorous to someone who flew regularly between Earth and Luna.

Stefan arched an eyebrow. "You repair the monorails? You don't look strong enough."

Jeff felt his face flush. "No . . . I work a console, organize the repair crews."

"That explains it . . . You look like you're new to Copernicus City," continued Stefan. "That right?"

Jeff nodded. "My family owns a small dome in the Sea of Rains."

Stefan gave Alanna a sideways glance. "Got yourself a rich boy." She smiled at the Earther and shrugged.

Belatedly, Jeff remembered the hand-to-mouth existence many fliers endured—a job took up valuable flying time. He tried to change the subject. "So, what's it like, wave-riding?" he asked.

Stefan grinned. "It's hard to describe to someone who's never done it." He took a gulp of beer. "The shock-wave's a real kick in the pants. Falling down Earth's gravity well's pretty great too—nothing but you and Sol and the stars, and Earth herself, growing larger and larger . . ." He stared into the distance.

Jeff tried to imagine it but failed. He made a note to try it out in VR.

Stefan glanced at Alanna. "Some say flying is the nearest a Lunie can ever get to it outside of VR. That right?" She shrugged. "Maybe you should try it, Jeff."

"I haven't got the muscles for it," he said.

Alanna gazed assessingly at him, making him go hot inside. "You could soon fix that," she suggested.

"Sure could," agreed Stefan, winking at Jeff. "Girls go for muscular men. Look at how they're flocking round me." Alanna snorted loudly. "So, you ever watched them launch a Wave-Rider?"

Jeff shook his head. "Only on the Net." Most of his education had been via the LunaNet.

"Why don't you come and watch me take off tomorrow morning? Get Alanna to bring you out to Fort Lansberg."

Alanna nodded. "Be glad to."

"I'm working," said Jeff.

"Another time, then," said Stefan.

"Come on!" Alanna looked annoyed. "You can't pass this up. Watching a Wave-Rider launch for real is something you'll never forget." She stared hard at him.

He realized suddenly that if he said no, he'd never see her again. "All right then, I'll come," he said.

JEFF SLEPT THROUGH his sleep alarm. Too much beer, he thought, swallowing a pink mouthful of Fix-U-Up, and waiting for the microbes to settle his stomach and aching head. His throat was sore too—holding a normal conversation in The Total Eclipse had been almost impossible. Still, the rasping voice and bleary eyes had made the lying easier when he finally got up the nerve to call in sick. He'd never played truant before. It made him feel anxious yet at the same time exhilarated. He only hoped Gavin wouldn't mention anything about Alanna to their supervisor.

At last, the microbes began to make headway, and, feeling slightly better, he set off for the local monorail station. He was out of breath and half an hour behind schedule when he arrived. There was no sign of Alanna.

He checked the timetable. Another pod to Fort Lansberg was due in soon. If no one else requested a stop, it should get him there just in time to join Alanna for the launch. He punched the red "call" button. Always supposing she had gone on without him, of course. She could just as easily have returned to the hostel . . . He paced up and down the platform, trying to ease the chafing under his arms caused by the ill-fitting counter pressure suit. He sighed. At home was his own comfortable, state-of-the-art suit, but he had decided to hire one so as not to draw attention to his privileged background again.

Ten minutes later an eight-seater pod pulled smoothly into the platform. He boarded quickly. The pod had seen better days. Its reclining seats were patched and grimy, and traces of graffiti marred the once pristine interior. He located the router panel and punched in the code for the Fort Lansberg Viewing Platform, as Alanna had instructed. Then he strapped himself in.

The door slid closed, and moments later the pod lurched as the magnets raised it off the monorail. It began to move forward, slowly at first, then gathering speed. The pod dived into the southbound tunnel, passed without hitch through the automated airlocks in Copernicus City's crater wall, and hummed out onto the Lunar surface. Jeff could see little except his own helmeted reflection in the pod's canopy. Still, he thought. Seen one moonscape, you've seen 'em all.

He leaned back and thought about Alanna. Why had she chosen him, when she could clearly have had her pick of the fliers and, come to that, Wave-Rider pilots? He was only, as she herself had told Raguel, a greenie and not much to look at. And when she picked him up she hadn't known he was well off. Perhaps she wanted to mother him? But the kiss last night, his first real kiss, hadn't been at all motherly. He remembered her tongue darting into his mouth . . .

They flashed through Fauth and Eratosthenes without stopping, then the seat swivelled suddenly, and he found himself facing the rear of the pod, deceleration pressing him into the seat. The pod flashed into a tunnel, through a single airlock, and came to rest at a platform. Fort Lansberg.

Jeff ran all the way up the steps and was gasping by the time he reached the airlock leading to the Viewing Platform. Moments later, his eyes were adjusting to the blackness and the brilliance of the stars overhead. To his relief, spectators still crowded the platform on the crater rim. None of the helmeted figures who glanced his way was Alanna though.

He stared out into the massive crater with the mountain at its centre, fascinated. There weren't many craters left undomed these days . . . He turned up the helmet's magnification. Pressure-suited figures milled like ants around the floodlit launch complex at the base of the mountain.

A Wave-Rider, its fin and wings like the flights of a dart, its nosecone a shining silver that made the rest of the craft look dirty, was positioned at the start of the track. As Jeff watched, it began to move along the narrow ribbon of monorail. Slowly at first, then more rapidly, it crossed the broad flat plain that was the crater floor then started up the sloping wall, the heavy-duty electromagnets on the sled beneath the Wave-Rider making it look easy. By the time it reached the top of the crater rim, a few kilometres along from the Viewing Platform, the Wave-Rider had attained orbital velocity. The recoverable sled slowed but the Wave-Rider continued, soaring up into the sky, and quickly vanishing over the Lunar horizon. From start to finish, the launch had taken just over sixteen seconds.

The other spectators were talking excitedly to one another and Jeff felt depressed that he had no one to share this moment with. Then someone tapped him on the shoulder and he looked round.

Alanna grinned at him and touched her helmet to his. "Enjoy the show so far?" Her voice was muffled by the two thicknesses of borosilicate lead crystal.

He switched on his comm circuit. "I thought you hadn't come," he said.

"When you didn't turn up, I went to the Launch Complex with Stefan." Her voice was tinny in his helmet. "We've got an hour until the Wave-Rider comes round again. Fancy a coffee?"

He nodded. They followed the other spectators back towards the airlock and the coffee shop.

"Sorry I missed the pod," he said, sipping the strong, bitter brew.

She shrugged. "I guessed you'd probably overslept."

In spite of last night's kiss, he found it hard to talk to her, especially since he was sober, whereas last night . . .

"Why me?" he stammered eventually. "Why not a flier?"

She grinned at him. "I don't go out with fliers." Then she leaned forward and pressed his hand. "Relax, Jeff."

He took her advice. After that, conversation was easier and the time seemed to fly by, and soon they were putting on their helmets and getting ready to venture outside again.

They walked to a spot on the platform that Alanna said would provide a good view. Abruptly she pointed upwards. "Here it comes."

He followed her pointing finger. Something glinted in the star-filled sky, catching the sunlight only hours away from Fort Lansberg. Suddenly, the Wave-Rider was directly above the mountain, and beams of red, orange, yellow, green, blue, and violet light were pulsing up from the launch complex.

"Wow!" breathed Jeff. He had seen the rainbow lasers on the Net, but somehow the colours hadn't seemed so . . . intense. He watched the six beams focus on the Wave-Rider's stern, on the block of ice propellant housed there. As they merged, becoming a dazzling white, ice flashed to steam, and the resulting shockwave punched the Wave-Rider out of orbit on the start of its long flight.

When the lasers snapped off again, Jeff's vision was filled with vivid afterimages.

"FOLLOW THAT!" SAID Jeff, as he accompanied Alanna back down the steps to the monorail station.

"No problem. Come flying with me."

The day stretched emptily ahead of him, but he hesitated. "Our dome wasn't large enough for wings. But I've used a jetpack, and an aircycle once." He glanced at her anxiously.

She shrugged. "Use a jetpack, then."

"You don't mind?"

"It's only temporary, isn't it? Until you get your wings." She smiled at him and reached for his gloved hand.

THE BODYSUITS WORN by the fliers left little to the imagination. As Alanna struggled with the massive wings, the clingy tangerine and turquoise fabric clearly outlined her nipples.

"Give me a hand, Jeff," she ordered.

Embarrassed, he shuffled towards her.

She glanced at him then grinned, leaned closer, and whispered, her breath tickling his ear, "Don't worry. Everyone gets horny up here. Why else do you think we do it?"

Trying not to get too distracted by her nearness, he positioned the heavy harness more snugly on her wide shoulders and back, and tightened the straps.

Earlier, Alanna had let him try on her wings, but as he had feared they made his arms ache after only a few seconds. Disconsolately he fingered the jetpack straps that crisscrossed his own chest. His father had always said wings were for show-offs, but there was something about flying like a bird—especially since the real things were rare, confined to EcoDomes like Daedalus . . .

He glanced at the ground fifteen hundred metres below the balcony, feeling slightly sick. According to Alanna, the Avallon Tower was the highest in Copernicus City, the balconies on its top floor much favoured as launching platforms. He tried to calm his nerves by breathing steadily and concentrating on the details of the crater floor. Unlike Fort Lansberg, it had been landscaped, and groups of Lunies were strolling along the open parkland's many trails or picnicking.

Natural light was filtering through the dome's water shielding again, and sunshine sparkled and flashed off the surface of the lakes in the distance.

"Come on," said Alanna. She brushed past him, climbed the railing, and stepped off the balcony.

She dived for nearly a hundred metres, until Jeff feared she wouldn't pull out of it. Then the tangerine-and-turquoise suited figure spread her wings and turned the dive into a superbly controlled glide. Soon she was climbing, circling back towards the balcony, beating the air with quick, easy strokes.

A flier in a red costume swooped towards her, called out a greeting, and began to perform a series of intricate manoeuvres below her. Raguel, showing off, thought Jeff, recognizing the blond hair and broken nose.

"Come on, Jeff. It's easy." Alanna's voice carried clearly on the air currents, accompanied by Raguel's laughter.

Gritting his teeth, Jeff reached for the control belt at his waist and stepped off into space.

He had been proud of his skill with a jetpack, but beside the acrobatic fliers he felt like a lump of moonrock. Knowing that Raguel was watching and sniggering at his efforts to keep up didn't help. Jeff was glad when Alanna finally signalled she'd had enough and plunged towards the crater floor. They landed on an empty patch of parkland.

"Help me off with my wings," she ordered.

Grumpily, he did so. He cheered up at once, however, when she gazed into his eyes, stroked his cheek with one finger, and asked if they could go back to his flat.

JEFF KICKED THE pile of dirty clothes into a closet and hoped Alanna hadn't noticed the flat's musty smell. She didn't seem to mind her surroundings, however. She made straight for the rumpled bed.

Jeff's mouth was dry. "Um . . . would you like a coffee?"

Alanna shook her head and stretched out full length on the bed. She looked quizzically at him. "You're new at this, aren't you?"

His cheeks were fiery, and he couldn't meet her gaze. "I'd better just check my messages," he said.

He crossed to the ancient comm unit and stabbed buttons. The wallscreen flickered into life, its picture fizzing and popping. Gavin's face mouthed words at him, and Jeff thumped the comm unit. ". . . you're not feeling well, Jeffy boy," came Gavin's voice. "Don't worry, I didn't let on I knew what you're up to . . . or should I say who you're up?"

"Jerk," came Alanna's voice. "Why d'you hang around with him?"

Jeff shrugged. "I work with him." He glanced at her as he spoke and was startled to find she'd taken off her flying suit. He stared at the nipples he'd wondered about earlier, at the dark bush of pubic hair. Heat flooded through his groin, and he turned hastily back to the screen. The blood was pounding so much in his eardrums he barely heard the message his parents had left. Instead his mind was whirling: what if he didn't do it right? what about birth control . . . ?

The screen blanked, and the comm unit switched itself off. But Jeff remained standing in front of it, frozen with uncertainty, trembling with desire.

"Come on. Don't you want to?" Alanna's voice was teasing.

It must be obvious, he thought wryly, that he wanted to a great deal. Feeling as though he were leaping off the balcony at the Avallon Tower without a jetpack, he turned and walked slowly towards the bed . . .

"COMING FOR A drink?" asked Gavin.

"Can't. I'm meeting Alanna." Jeff reached for the sports bag he now kept by his console.

"Look, I know this isn't any of my business," said Gavin, awkwardly, "but don't you think you're getting in too deep?"

"I can look after myself," said Jeff shortly. "And you're right. It isn't any of your business."

"I only meant—"

But Jeff had already left the office and was on his way to the gym.

As he walked, he pondered Gavin's words. Initially, his colleague had made no secret of his envy—Alanna was beautiful, exciting to be with, good in bed . . . Margie couldn't possibly compete. But that view had soon been superseded by one shared by most of Gavin's circle, and Jeff's parents, come to that. As an aunt had once put it to his mother: "Some of my best friends are fliers. But my goodness, you wouldn't want your daughter to marry one!" Or your son, he thought. Which made things difficult, because for the first time in his life, Jeff believed he was in love.

He'd tried to prepare his parents, hinted, in passing, that he was seeing a female flier, omitted to mention that she was three years older than him, had no job, lived in a hostel in conditions they wouldn't expect the maid to endure . . . And even that hint had been too much—he had recognized the panic in his mother's eyes, noticed the involuntary glance offscreen as she looked to his father for guidance . . . Since then, he deliberately hadn't mentioned Alanna.

He walked into the changing room, shucked his work clothes, and put on the navy singlet and white shorts from his bag. Then he went through to the gym. Alanna was on her favourite bench, her turquoise leotard clinging to her in all the right places. She released the pulley bar, letting the attached weight stack thump back into its slot, and nodded briefly at him. Then she methodically wiped the sweat from her upper lip and palms with a towel and reached for the bar again.

The gym was nearly full this evening, the treadmills, exercise bikes, rowing machines, and benches being used by sweating, red-faced men and women in varying stages of physical fitness. As he waited for a bench to become vacant, he watched an Earther lifting weights no Lunie could ever hope to manage. Jeff sighed, wondering briefly what it must be like to live on a planet with six times the gravity, to walk unsuited in the open air, knowing that the nearest he could ever get to it would be in VR.

A flier vacated a bench, and Jeff quickly staked a claim to it, adjusting the weights to his liking. He slid on to the black foam upholstery, made himself comfortable, and reached for the barbell. He gripped the bar firmly, and began to lift, concentrating on establishing a rhythm and trying to ignore the strain in his arms.

He was pleased with his progress of the last month. At this rate, it wouldn't be long before he was strong enough to try out a set of wings. His strength and stamina was increasing daily, and not just in the gym. He smiled wryly. It was hardly surprising, considering the athletics he and Alanna practised in the bedroom . . . With difficulty, he wrenched his thoughts back to the weights.

A shadow across his face made him rest the barbell on its stand and look up. Alanna was standing by the bench, gazing down at him, her expression serious. She used one end of the white towel draped round her neck to wipe her face, then gave him a slow grin that made his pulse race.

"I think you're ready for your wings, Jeff," she said.

THEY SET OFF for the Avallon Tower, each carrying a set of wings—Alanna had borrowed a pair for Jeff from another flier. She had also hired him a cheap purple-and-yellow bodysuit, which unlike hers clung in all the wrong places and itched abominably.

When the moment to jump off the balcony came, he was almost paralyzed with fear, even though as a concession to him they were only six storeys up. Alanna had judged his condition just right, though, and he was able to flap the wings strongly for several minutes before his shoulders and arms tired and he was forced to land—minutes during which he swooped and soared like a bird and Alanna joined him in the air, flying so near that he feared she would knock him out of the sky. She spiralled around him, laughing wildly, before arrowing away for another run. One thing was for sure, thought Jeff. It was nothing like using a jetpack.

Afterwards, he and Alanna returned to his flat and made love on his bed. Since his arms were still trembling badly, Alanna took the lead, pushing him onto his back and straddling him. The exertion used up the last of Jeff's meagre resources, and immediately afterwards he sank into oblivion. As he did so, Alanna's lips, soft and warm against his skin, brushed his left cheek.

When he awoke, she was gone. The note on the pillow said simply, "Goodbye."

HE TRACED HER to the Adams Hostel and doggedly refused to leave until she had agreed to see him face to face. He hadn't banked on it being in the shabby lobby surrounded by a crowd of interested onlookers though. He ran a finger round the inside of a collar that seemed suddenly too tight.

"So?" she said. "What do you want, Jeff?" Her expression was impatient.

"Surely that's obvious? I want you to come back." His voice wobbled. "Did I do something? Maybe it was something I didn't do?" He stared at her, thinking she had never looked so beautiful . . . or so heartless.

She laughed.

"What's so funny?" His cheeks began to burn.

"It was nice while it lasted. You were quite sweet, in fact." She shrugged. "But it was only a crush, Jeff. You must have known that. And now it's over."

"Look, if it's because I didn't introduce you to my family . . . I'll fix that. I'll take you to see them. Next weekend. How about it?" He willed her to accept, but instead she frowned.

"You're not a greenie any more, Jeff, so don't act like one. You're a flier."

A lump in his throat made it difficult to speak. "I don't understand."

"I don't go out with fliers." Her voice was flat, uncompromising.

The crowd of onlookers began to shake their heads and murmur. "Give it up, son," advised one.

"But—" began Jeff.

"For God's sake!" said Alanna. "What more do you want? It was fun while it lasted. Now it's over. Go find yourself another girl, Jeff, and quit bringing me down."

"Bringing me down"—the worst thing that could happen to a flier, he thought numbly, feeling the last vestige of hope drain away.

And with that, she turned and walked away.

TWO DAYS LATER Alanna found herself a new greenie. Jeff was drinking cheap red wine with Stefan in The Total Eclipse when it happened. Through a bleary haze, he watched her target the bemused young man, whose name he later learned was Jose, saw him go with her as naively as any fly into a spider's web. Jealousy settled in his stomach like a lead weight.

"Don't take it to heart, son," rumbled the Wave-Rider pilot in his ear. "She's always been that way. Experienced older woman educates grateful young man . . . Trouble is, once he's educated, she loses interest. Guess it's some kind of power trip—y'know. It's nothing personal."

"I wish I'd known that," said Jeff bitterly. "I wish you'd warned me."

"And if I had, you'd have acted differently?" Stefan's smile was disbelieving.

"Well, no," admitted Jeff. He reached for the bottle, poured red wine into his glass, and stared glumly at it for a long time. "Does it always hurt this much?" he asked eventually.

"The first time's the hardest," said Stefan. "You make mistakes, you get burned. But that's how you learn."

Jeff sighed and raised his glass. "To becoming older and wiser," he said.

"I'll drink to that," said Stefan.

AFTERWORD

One of the most exhilarating books about Space that I have ever read is Marshall T. Savage's, The Millennial Project: Colonizing the Galaxy in Eight Easy Steps. *His vision may have turned out to be wildly over-optimistic, but it was a pleasure to share his dream for a while. And I couldn't resist using a setting based on his ideas for a moon colony.*

JOURNEY TO NISKOR

VIRO HAULED UP the frosted entrance flap and peered inside. Immediately he was reeling back, eyes streaming at the sudden warmth and the overpowering stink of body odour and smoke. The tent's four inhabitants gazed out at him, startled.

"Yes?" said the man, scrambling to his feet and following Viro out into the cold, fresh air. "Can I help you?" He was shorter than Viro by at least a foot, with the coarse, black hair and flat, high cheekbones of the region. His gaze lighted on Viro's woven armband, on the intertwined threads of red and green. "Healer?"

At least the peasant could recognize a healer's armband when he saw one, thought Viro. Perhaps he would do. "I need a dog-sled and driver," he said, "to take me to Niskor. There's an outbreak of the coughing sickness."

So far he had dealt only with minor ailments and fractures, and his teachers had always been available for consultation. Niskor, deep in the northern ice-fields, would be his first encounter with the coughing sickness; his first time unaided too. The mere thought of it scared him, but if he was to become a fully fledged Healer . . .

Black eyes assessed him, then looked at the sky. A pink tongue tasted the air. "There's bad weather coming."

Viro frowned. There had been only a few wisps of cloud during the first part of his journey north. It must be a ploy to raise the fare. He reached inside his tunic and pulled out a bulging cloth bag. The coins inside it clinked faintly. "I'll pay you the standard fare, no more," he said shortly.

The man's dark brows drew together. "Nevertheless, bad weather is coming."

Viro wished he wasn't wearing clothes more suited to the city. The spare tunic and extra pair of leggings in his bag were just as thin. The cold had penetrated his boots and his toes were turning numb. He stamped his feet noisily and slapped his upper arms for warmth.

"You are cold," exclaimed the man. "Forgive my poor manners."

He stepped back and held the tent flap wide. "My name is Erlik. Please share my family's hospitality."

"My name is Viro." Reluctantly, but willing to put up with the stench for the sake of warmth, Viro stooped and eased himself inside.

"Sit." Erlik pointed to an unoccupied rug on one side of the small fire that burned in the middle of the floor.

Viro sank onto the fur, which had once belonged to something large and white. He crossed his legs awkwardly, imitating the posture of the other inhabitants—a middle-aged woman, busy sewing, and two small children, a boy and a girl. Their faces were ruddy from the fire's heat. The girl held one hand over her mouth and giggled nervously. The boy seemed interested in the bag Viro carried. Viro placed it in the protective triangle of his legs.

"Ajysyt, my wife," said Erlik.

Viro nodded politely, his gaze assessing the woman quickly and dismissing her. Strong boned and wide hipped, good for child bearing, he thought. Very plain; the ragged fringe of hair didn't improve her looks much either. He turned back to her husband.

"And these are our children, Mamaldi and—"

"Will you take me to Niskor?" interrupted Viro. "And if not, is there another who will?"

Erlik exchanged a glance with his wife. "No one will take you until the coming storm is past," he said.

Viro fought down his annoyance. "It is my understanding," he said, keeping his tone reasonable, "that a contract exists between your village and the College of Healers . . . to provide dogs, sleds, and drivers when required."

"That is true," said Erlik, just as reasonably. "But what good will a dead Healer be to the citizens of Niskor?"

Why were people always so lacking in respect? wondered Viro tiredly. Perhaps if he weren't so young, if his beard were grizzled like the Master Healer's instead of this fine blond fuzz . . . He became aware that Ajysyt had stopped sewing and that the children were looking curiously at him.

"You are welcome to stay with us until the storm has blown itself out," suggested Erlik.

"No, husband. I will take him," said a low female voice.

Viro frowned. Why didn't Erlik rebuke Ajysyt? But Erlik was looking thoughtfully at his wife.

"Surely," said Viro quickly, "you are the sled driver!"

Erlik grinned, revealing strong discoloured teeth. "In this weather, you will be safer with Ajysyt." He turned to her again. "Is it wise?"

She shrugged. "Probably not. But if we lived in Niskor and one of our children had the coughing sickness . . ."

Her husband nodded. "True."

There was silence while Viro digested Ajysyt's offer and assessed the chances of receiving a better one. At last, reluctantly, he reached inside his tunic and pulled out the bag of coins once more.

Ajysyt took the bag and nodded her head formally. "I will drive you to Niskor, Healer," she said.

VIRO HUDDLED INTO the skins which covered the body of the sled and pulled the warm fur hat Erlik had given him further over his ears. The cold slashed his exposed skin like a knife. Up ahead, the team of twelve huskies pulling the sled seemed blithely unaware of any discomfort; the air above their muzzles was steamy with breath.

Movement from the rear, a slight creaking pressure on the foot plate or the brake to correct the sled's course, was the only sign of Ajysyt's presence. So far she hadn't spoken. Viro wondered idly how, without reins or a whip to guide them, the dogs knew when to pull harder on the rope harnesses, when to turn right or left.

There was no sign of the storm Erlik had predicted. The air was still and clear, full of the tiny sharp sounds of ice and twigs cracking. Viro found the panting and soft thudding of paws, the hiss of the runners over the snow, hypnotic and in spite of the cold he started to doze.

Something hard dug into his hip and woke him—an axe handle by the feel of it. He shifted and investigated with one hand, easing the implement to one side. A sled was not the most comfortable way to travel, especially when one was bundled next to tentskins and poles, sticks of tallow, a cookpot and vast quantities of frozen fish—"For the dogs," Erlik had said, seeing his guest's eyes widen. It was a bumpy ride too, over icy ruts and ridges, and already he ached all over.

They had left the plains behind and were now passing through dense woodland smelling strongly of pine. The trail was barely visible beneath a thick layer of snow and ice. As it rounded a bend, the sled creaked, reminding Viro uneasily that all that lay between him and a freezing death was a flimsy contraption of wood and rope, drawn by a pack of barely tamed wolf-dogs. He shivered, not only from the cold. Then the sled began to slow.

He turned. The driver, her eyebrows white with frost, was almost unrecognizable beneath her thick layers of clothing. "Why are we stopping?" he yelled. "We're still in the middle of nowhere!"

"The dogs," came Ajysyt's muffled reply. The sled stopped.

The dogs looked fine to Viro, sitting on their haunches, panting happily, tongues lolling. Drops of steaming saliva pocked the snow below their muzzles. Blue-white eyes looked expectantly at Ajysyt.

She got down from the sled and crouched and stretched oddly a few times, concentrating on each limb in turn. Then she walked over to Viro, pulled back the skins, and began to rummage among the supplies.

"What are you looking for?"

With a satisfied grunt, she found the axe then crossed to a nearby tree. She gathered a few fallen branches and chopped them into smaller pieces. Soon a small fire was burning, the pine sap making it crackle and spit. She filled the cookpot to the brim with snow and placed it on the flames. Then she walked over to the dogs.

Thinking it best to stretch his legs while he had the chance, Viro scrambled off the sled. He imitated Ajysyt's strange exercises and found, to his surprise, that they were extremely effective; his stiffness eased and the blood began to circulate through his limbs.

Ajysyt had removed her gloves and was doing something to one of the dogs' paws. She finished, put her hands deep inside her clothing, then moved on to the next. Curious, Viro went to join her.

"What are you doing?"

She finished her examination of the paw before answering. "Ice balls can get between the pads, make the dogs lame." She shoved her hands, red with cold, deep inside her clothing. "Next to the belly is good for cold fingers," she explained, following his glance.

He flushed and looked away.

By the time Ajysyt had finished examining all forty-eight paws, the cookpot contents were steaming. Viro settled himself back under the skins and watched her take the pot off the fire, licking his lips in anticipation. She poured the water into bowls for the dogs. They lapped it up thirstily.

"What about me?" he asked, annoyed.

"Dogs first, then humans."

He had heard that tone of voice, as though stating the obvious, often from his teachers, but it stung to hear a woman use it. But before he could protest, she was reaching into her furs, feeling between her breasts. She held out a small waterskin; he took it. It felt warm against his ungloved fingers, and he tried not to think about where it had been kept. He unstoppered it and took a gulp. Warm liquid filled his mouth and trickled down his throat, followed by a burning sensation that brought tears to his eyes.

"Gods!"

A warm glow spread through him, and his fingers and toes began to tingle. He knuckled his blurred eyes and realized that Ajysyt was watching him with amusement.

"Fire cordial," she said. "Good for warmth."

He nodded, finding himself temporarily unable to speak. She reached for the waterskin and took a small mouthful—it seemed to have no noticeable effect on her—then re-stoppered it and pushed it back inside her furs.

Viro snuggled back down among the supplies, while Ajysyt collected the now empty dog bowls and stowed them in the sled.

"Are you ready, Healer?" she asked, securing the skins back in position.

He grunted.

Feet crunched round to the rear of the sled, and it rocked slightly as Ajysyt climbed on board. The huskies looked back, giving little yelps of eagerness. Viro waited for a word of command, but none came. Instead, the dogs suddenly leaned into their harnesses, and the sled slid forward with a jerk.

IT WAS NIGHTFALL, frosty and clear, when they finally set up camp. Ajysyt tethered the huskies loosely, and fed them hot water and fish. Then she expertly and quickly erected a tent beside the fire.

While she prepared fish stew for them both, Viro warmed himself. He hadn't offered to help; healers' hands must be protected at all times—besides, it was women's work. Not that Ajysyt was like any woman he had met before. And she was less stupid than she looked.

He had realized there was method to Ajysyt's seemingly random trail stops. Every four leagues, she checked the dogs' paws—

removing any ice balls and coating the sore pads with a salve she carried in one pocket. When the paw checking was complete, she gave the dogs a drink. Every twelve leagues, she added some of the frozen fish to the dogs' boiling water.

The thawed but uncooked fish was unsuitable for humans, but in spite of Viro's entreaties, Ajysyt refused to stop anywhere long enough to cook a proper meal.

"Time is short," she had said, looking at the sky, which to Viro's eyes still appeared perfectly normal. She offered him a piece of dried meat to chew, but it was as tough as old boot leather. The mouthful of fire cordial that went with it was much more welcome.

Consequently, he was now ravenous. He also had a severe headache—probably from drinking cordial on an empty stomach. Automatically, he pressed his fingers against his temples and willed the headache to disappear. The pain faded and a glow of well-being flooded through him, followed by a slight lassitude—healing always depleted his strength.

Ajysyt gazed at him as she stirred the stew. "You have a gift?" she asked.

He nodded stiffly. The subject was far too personal to discuss with a complete stranger, and a woman at that!

The flickering firelight had softened the hard lines of her face. Or perhaps it was just that she had brushed the ragged fringe out of her eyes, leaving a streak of ash on her forehead in the process. She returned his look frankly, and he dropped his gaze, frowning. Ajysyt reminded him of someone. But all his friends were fair-haired, blue eyed, and certainly not slant-eyed . . .

She ladled out fish stew and handed him a wooden bowl. Eagerly he gulped its steaming contents straight down. Still hungry, he held out his bowl for more. Ajysyt smiled and refilled it.

Of course, thought Viro. It's her expression, like a mother looking fondly at her son. He glanced at her again, but the driver had finished eating and was now gazing up at the stars.

"I don't know why you were so fearful of the weather," grumbled Viro, to take his mind off thoughts of mothers—he hadn't seen his own since she had sent him away to the College of Healers. "It looks fine to me."

"It is coming," she said, absently.

He frowned. "Will we make it to Niskor in time?"

She turned and looked at him, her face half hidden by shifting shadows from the fire. "Perhaps."

VIRO WOKE EARLY from a fitful sleep—the pile of rugs had done little to soften the frozen ground. He rose stiffly, feeling more like an old man than a nineteen-year-old, and watched, yawning, as Ajysyt packed up the tent and fed the dogs. To Viro's distaste, breakfast was cold fish stew left over from the night before. They ate to the accompaniment of impatient yelps, then resumed their journey.

By midday, the sky had turned a pale yellow and the wind had risen sharply. It had also started to snow. Viro huddled deep into the body of the sled, pulling his earflaps down against the slashing wind and its burden of snowflakes.

He peered back at the driver, now a mere silhouette coated in white. "Shouldn't we stop?" he yelled. But the wind whipped his words away and he doubted that Ajysyt had heard him. Besides, he thought ruefully, I'm the one who wanted to get to Niskor in spite of the storm.

Visibility had dropped considerably. Viro wondered how Ajysyt could possibly see where they were going and keep the dogs under control, but somehow she managed, and their speed barely slackened. He burrowed deeper into the skins, trying to stop the shivering that had become his constant companion.

They had travelled for what seemed like hours, the wind a constant deafening roar that made Viro want to scream with irritation. Then the runners suddenly hit something buried beneath the snow. A shudder ran through the sled and a sickening splintering sound was audible even above the wind.

For a moment, Viro thought the rearing sled would simply settle itself back on its runners, but it continued to tilt. He reached desperately for something to hold on to, but found himself falling amid a shower of supplies. Then something rolled on top of him, and everything went black.

"MOUSER'S VERY ILL, Viro." Mother gazed sadly at him, at the limp black body he clutched tightly to his chest.

Viro's eyes felt puffy, and there was a painful lump in his throat. "Make him better, Mother. Please."

The cat's head flopped to one side, and Viro felt something grate beneath the smooth black fur. Mouser mewed piteously, a thin weak sound that scraped at his nerve endings.

"There's nothing I can do, child." Mother patted his shoulder. "Sometimes, things get broken and can't be fixed." She looked meaningfully at the cat and reached for it.

"No!" Viro pulled away from her. It was his fault Mouser had fallen. They had been playing on the balcony, and the cat had followed him along the railing as it always did, but then a bird had distracted it and the next minute . . .

"I won't let Mouser die. I won't!" he shouted. And closing his eyelids so tight his vision was flecked with white, he willed his pet's broken body to heal.

Mother's protestations faded, and time stretched. Then Viro's head seemed to grow hot and the limp weight in his arms suddenly squirmed and miaowed loudly, protesting at his tight grip. Mother made a strange sound in the back of her throat.

Viro opened his eyes. He felt tired. Mouser was wailing to be set down, so he stooped and placed the cat on the kitchen floor. He grinned up at his mother. She was gazing at him, her blue eyes filled with a mixture of pride and dread.

"Viro! What did you do?"

"I made him better," he said. "Can I go and play now?"

"Of course, child." Then she was turning away, moving slowly like one struck blind, muttering something about the Law and how she must inform the authorities of his gift immediately . . .

VIRO AWOKE, DISORIENTATED. His bedroom was freezing, so cold his feet and legs had gone numb. He also had a splitting headache and a burning sensation in his side.

"Mother," he called, his voice echoing oddly in the darkness.

While he waited for her to come and draw the curtains, he strained to make sense of the muffled noises drifting up from the yard below his window. Wind whistling, dogs whining . . . Abruptly he remembered the sled crash.

He tried to sit up and almost fainted as pain lanced through him. Gods, but it hurt! He pressed one hand to his side; something hard and cold met his fingers. Puzzled, he explored the thing's shape. It felt like . . . an axe. Gods! How deeply was it embedded? Desperately Viro tugged at the axe handle. For a moment it held firm, then, with a wet, tearing plop, the axe head came free. Something hot and sticky pulsed over his fingers and a wave of dizziness overtook him. He hung on to consciousness grimly, aware he must staunch the wound quickly before he bled to death.

Trying to ignore the fear and pain, he centred himself, breathing deeply, invoking the healer's trance as he had been taught. It took slightly longer than usual, but after a few moments he was ready.

Carefully, he visualized his side, remembering the diagrams he had studied for long hours, the layers of fat and muscle cushioning the bone, the veins and arteries . . . He was wringing wet with effort by the time his head grew hot and, deep in his side, something began to tingle. The pain eased slightly, becoming a dull ache. He pictured the two edges of the gash meeting and knitting together. The ache vanished, and he sighed with relief.

Viro lay still for a while, recovering, but gradually it dawned on him that his legs weren't just numb, they wouldn't move. He reached out and explored his surroundings, squinting in the gloom. With a sinking feeling, he realized he was pinned beneath what must be the edge of the upturned sled. His feet were protruding into the still raging blizzard.

"Ajysyt," he shouted, remembering the driver suddenly and wondering where she was. "I'm trapped. Can you get me out?" There was no reply.

He struggled again to pull his legs free, then flopped back breathless onto the snow. Perhaps there was something he could use for a lever? He looked round. Near the far end of the sled, something moved slightly and let out a faint human groan. He realized immediately who it must be.

"Ajysyt," he called. "Are you all right? Can you hear me?"

After a long pause, he heard a faint sigh, then a mumbled word: "Healer?" He didn't like the sound of the wet gurgle at the back of her throat.

"I'm trapped," he said helplessly. "It's my legs."

Ajysyt said something else, but her words were indistinct against the background noise of the wind and the whining dogs.

"What? I didn't catch . . ."

". . . the dogs," she repeated.

Was she still more concerned for her precious dogs? he wondered angrily.

Silence fell so suddenly, for a moment Viro feared he had gone deaf. The storm must have blown itself out at last, he realized. And then he noticed something else. The dogs had stopped whining.

Without warning, something touched his boot. He flinched, but couldn't pull his leg away. Something nosed at his boot again, then began to scrabble at the underside of his calves. He began to panic. His unprotected legs must look very tempting to huskies that hadn't been fed for hours.

"Get away," he shouted. "Leave me alone."

From outside the upturned sled came scraping sounds and snuffling noises. From inside came Ajysyt's irregular breathing. "Harmless," she gasped. He frowned. Was she referring to the dogs?

Suddenly, the packed snow and ice beneath his trapped calves gave way. He tucked his legs in and rolled clear, then he looked back. Light was flooding into the cramped space beneath the sled. Then wet noses poked through the gap where his legs had been, and blue-white eyes stared at him. The huskies. And thankfully, their gazes were friendly.

He turned to Ajysyt. "They dug me out!" But the light showed her chest was barely moving, her breathing had almost stopped.

Viro couldn't work in such a confined space. So he eased himself through the opening made by the dogs, getting his face thoroughly licked in the process. Once out, he braced a shoulder against the sled and pushed. It wouldn't budge.

At first he tried to chase the huskies off, then he realized that far from hindering him they were actually trying to help. Startled, he watched as some leaned their heavy bodies against the side of the sled, while others squeezed into the gap under its rim, and lifted. He joined his weight to theirs and pushed. The sled lurched upwards, rolled over, and settled onto its mangled runners with a loud crunch.

Ajysyt lay unmoving in a tangle of supplies, the dogs forming a silent circle around her. Viro pushed his way between them, knelt, and felt for a pulse. Nothing. He leaned close to the slightly open mouth, trying to feel her breath, but either his cheek was too numb or she had stopped breathing. His mind raced. Where was she wounded? Other than a trickle of red down her chin, there were no signs of blood, no torn clothes. He was going to have to go in blind.

He placed a hand on Ajysyt's forehead and invoked his trance. Awareness of his surroundings and of the dogs' trusting gazes, dropped away. Heart first, he thought, willing it to resume beating. Then lungs—breathe, damn you. Next, the spine—he visualized the vertebrae one by one.

Viro was working on her major arteries when a tired voice said, "Healer?"

He rocked back on his heels, limp with relief and exhaustion, and found himself staring into black peasant eyes. "How do you feel?" he asked.

"Better," said Ajysyt, smiling weakly up at him. "Much better."

THERE WAS NO question of mending the sled until they were both stronger. Together, Viro and Ajysyt managed to erect the tent, throwing the tentskins haphazardly over the poles. Then they crawled wearily inside and collapsed on the floor.

"What about the dogs?" he asked, hanging onto the remnants of consciousness with difficulty.

"They'll sleep too," said Ajysyt, pulling a skin over him, then crawling onto her own pile of sleeping furs.

"That's good," he said, wondering how she knew but too tired to pursue it further, "that's very—" He tumbled into the dark well of sleep.

"YOU HAVE A gift too, don't you, Ajysyt?" Viro glanced sideways at her. They were mending the broken runner, roping a replacement branch into place. It was far from perfect but would serve to get them to Niskor, she'd said.

"Mind your fingers."

He nodded and stood clear. "It's the dogs, isn't it?" He had been worrying at the thought since he woke up. "You can talk to them, tell them what to do . . . With your mind, I mean." He had heard rumours others had gifts different from those of a healer. But a peasant woman, of all people!

Ajysyt looped another coil of rope round the branch and tied a knot. She leaned her whole weight on the makeshift runner, grunting with satisfaction when it held firm.

Viro watched her. "If you hadn't told them to dig me out . . ." he began.

She shrugged matter-of-factly and threw the coil of unused rope into the sled. "A fair exchange. You healed me." She glanced at him. "To help others, it is the way of things. Erlik knew my gift would be needed if you were to reach Niskor safely."

He looked down at his boots. "I just assumed . . ."

"It is a common assumption among the young men from the College." Her tone held no resentment. "But already you are learning, Healer. That is a good sign." She brushed her hair off her sweating face.

Sheepishly, he met her gaze, wondering what else he had misunderstood. His mother's rejection, for example? In the still vivid dream, she had seemed less eager to send him away than he recalled. Suddenly everything seemed very complicated. He sighed.

Ajysyt turned and shaded her eyes, seeking the dogs which she had freed to exercise—an unacceptable risk, Viro would have thought previously. Muffled yelps became louder, and the twelve huskies suddenly emerged from the edge of the dense woodland. They lolloped over the snow towards the driver, tongues hanging out, breath steaming.

Boisterous but obedient, the dogs allowed Ajysyt to harness them. She patted each gently on the head before moving to the next.

Viro climbed on board the sled and made himself comfortable, thinking of what lay ahead. The injuries he and Ajysyt had suffered had been much more serious, surely, than the coughing sickness could ever be, yet he had successfully dealt with them. A new confidence in his own abilities surged through him, and he liked the feeling.

Ajysyt finished with the dogs and walked past him to the rear of the sled. He felt the shift in balance as she boarded. He turned round and looked at her.

"Ready to go to Niskor, Healer?" she called.

He nodded. Ready as he would ever be, he thought.

The lead husky strained at its harness, and the others followed its example. Slowly, the sled began to move.

AFTERWORD

One weekend, my newspaper's colour supplement contained a vivid travel article about the annual Iditarod dog sled race. Reading it left me wanting to write a story about Siberian huskies and their mushers. So I did.

TIME AND THE MAID

"SO, IT WORKS with a rat simulacrum. Have you tried sending or retrieving anything sentient with it yet?" A series of loud beeps cut short Marcus's question.

Anna reached for the phone, her sleeve catching on a circuit board and sending it clattering along the workbench. "Scoop Lab. Dr Grant here. I'm in the middle of a demo. Can't it wait?"

Anna's young research students started talking about football. Marcus preferred to watch Anna twirl a strand of her long, dark hair round one finger as she talked into the vidphone. He could just see the tiny viewscreen; on it a bull-necked man in a navy, peaked cap was gesturing—Tyler, Chief of Security.

Anna turned and held out the receiver. "It's for you, Marcus. Something about a break-in."

"Sorry," he said, taking it. "Professor Williams here. What is it?"

"We've caught some intruders in your Viewing Lab, Professor. Three kids. A student here," Sgt Tyler consulted an ID card, "name of Lee Anderson—"

"For heaven's sake! Anderson's doing research for a history project; he has my full permission to use the lab." Marcus rolled his eyes at Anna, who smiled and began to tidy the bench.

The Sergeant gave Marcus a wounded look. "He was with two girls, Professor. And what they were doing wasn't on any syllabus I've ever seen!"

Marcus frowned. "You must be mistaken. Lee Anderson is hardworking, reliable . . . I wish all my students were like him—"

"That's as may be, but he and his playmates were caught red-handed mucking about with the machinery."

A cold lump began to form in Marcus's guts. "What do you mean 'mucking about'? Anderson would never—"

"If it's proof you're after, get over to the Security Block pronto. Anderson's quite happy to boast all about it; he'll probably feel different when the whisky wears off, though."

"Whisky?" But the Sergeant had already hung up.

Slowly, Marcus replaced the vidphone receiver and turned to the others. "I'm afraid I'll have to catch up with your demo another time, Anna. Something urgent's just come up."

"I DON'T KNOW what all the fuss is about, Prof."

Anderson's fair hair was rumpled, his face slightly flushed. Probably alcohol rather than embarrassment, thought Marcus; from the evidence on Sgt Tyler's desk, the culprits had finished two bottles of whisky.

"The girls wanted to see how the Viewer worked, so I showed them." Anderson smiled reasonably at Marcus then turned to the dark-haired girl noisily chewing gum beside him. "We were just having a bit of fun, weren't we, Steff?"

"'S right," she drawled. "You got a problem with that?" She resumed her aggressive chewing and folded her arms.

"And it's not as if we changed history or anything, is it, Claire?" Anderson turned this time to the long-legged, skinny blond, but she was slumped in her chair, snoring loudly. He shrugged, then returned his gaze to Marcus.

Marcus looked into his student's apparently open and guileless blue eyes, his thoughts roiling. Betrayal and anger warred with dismay; he had trusted this young man, and now this . . . "What did you do, Lee?"

Anderson shrugged. "Like I already told Judge Dredd over there—" he glared at Sgt Tyler, who glared back, "—we didn't mean any harm. The girls wanted to see Joan, that's all. So what?"

"Joan of Arc? The subject of your history project?"

"All I did was dial up Domremy . . . that day in 1425 when she had the visions, y'know?"

Marcus remembered reading about that: noon, a fine summer's day, thirteen-year-old Joan in the garden of her parents' house. The lump in his stomach hardened as he asked, "What did you do next?"

"I spoke to her."

It turned out that Lee Anderson had done more than speak to the Maid of Orleans. He had convinced her that he was the Archangel Michael and his two companions were the Saints Catherine and Margaret.

"Never thought I'd be a saint," murmured Steff, grinning crookedly at Marcus.

"Why all the fuss, Prof?" asked Anderson. "I kept to the rules. Nothing anachronistic. Joan thought we were her voices." He seemed genuinely puzzled.

By now, Marcus was almost speechless. Why the hell hadn't he disabled the Communication Circuit? He should have done it months ago, when the Ethics Committee first ruled it too dangerous. If Anderson had accidentally changed the past . . .

The pulse in Marcus's temple began to throb. Time paradoxes were as insoluble as the riddle of the chicken and the egg; just thinking about them gave him a migraine. He patted his jacket pocket and cursed inwardly—the tube of pills must be in his office desk.

"Listen very carefully, Lee," he said, trying to hang on to his temper. "I want you to tell me everything you and your friends did in the Viewing Lab this afternoon. Every single thing. Do you understand?"

"Sure." Anderson clasped his hands comfortably behind his head and crossed his bony ankles. "Well," he began. "You know Joan's first sword? There was quite a mystery about how she knew it was buried behind the altar at Fierbois. For starters, I told her where to find it . . ."

MARCUS LAY ON the shabby couch in the office adjoining his Viewing Lab, waiting for the migraine pills to work. The desk phone rang, and he reached for the receiver blindly.

"Professor Williams." A tiny version of the Vice Chancellor's round face, even more florid than usual, glared out at him. "About this incident in your lab this afternoon . . ." The bloodshot eyes became puzzled as they registered the fact that Marcus was sitting in the dark.

He took advantage of the pause. "It won't happen again, Vice Chancellor. I've changed the combination on the Viewing Lab door." He tried to ignore the son-et-lumiere show going on in his head. "As a matter of fact, I was just about to ring you. I've sent Lee Anderson down—he obviously can't be trusted to continue his studies here. Now, about pressing criminal charges—"

"I think it would be best not to pursue the matter," interrupted the

Vice Chancellor. "There's the risk of adverse publicity. And we don't want to upset the Institute's sponsors, do we?"

Marcus frowned. "But surely—"

"I trust you'll keep me informed of any further developments, Professor Williams?" He rang off before Marcus could answer.

Slowly Marcus replaced the receiver. As he did so his headache faded and his distorted vision cleared. Muttering thanks to the inventor of the pills, he rose and opened the blinds. Then he checked his watch—still a few hours left before it was time to call it a day. He strolled through to the Viewing Lab and switched on the Viewer . . .

HE WAS IN a cramped market square. Around its edges, ranks of men-at-arms, their plate armour newly burnished, were keeping thousands of spectators at bay. The atmosphere was taut and sweaty with expectation focussed on four large platforms in the centre.

Elaborate tapestries hung from the largest of the four—its wooden benches held important dignitaries, if their ornate robes were anything to go by. Two other platforms were more humbly occupied, and the remaining one was empty, apart from a stake almost obscured by faggots of wood.

Two armed guards were dragging a young woman away from Marcus across the square. A shapeless, long, brown robe hid the details of her figure, but he could tell she was short and rather thickset. A white bonnet covered her hair. She turned her head, and he saw the sunburned face and wide-set eyes of someone of peasant stock.

The woman seemed to be asking for something. Marcus watched a soldier tie together two tiny pieces of wood and shyly present them to her. She kissed the makeshift cross and pressed it to her chest. Then the guards impatiently tugged her up the steps onto the fourth platform. It was obvious what was about to happen.

I must stop this, thought Marcus, watching the guards bind the woman securely to the stake. But for some reason he couldn't move or speak. Numbly, he watched them replace her bonnet with a paper mitre, realizing, with a shock, that she had no hair—merely a fine black stubble. Then all at once, the faggots were aflame.

Marcus had a grandstand view. The young woman's brown eyes seemed to be staring straight into his, and he felt his breath catch.

Then, to his horror, he realized that she was speaking to him. "I trusted you, Marcus," she said. "This is all your fault."

The flames were now a vicious curtain of orange and yellow, reaching as high as her neck. Her eyes were rolling in agony. Oh God, he thought. Somebody stop this. Then the young woman began to moan, low at first, but gradually rising in pitch. "Jesus," she cried, "Jesus, Jesus . . ." Her last shriek was indecipherable . . .

Time seemed to skim past, then Marcus found himself watching the guards mount the platform and rake aside the embers. What the hell were they doing? She was dead, wasn't she? Couldn't they leave her alone even now?

With a flourish, the guards revealed the charred and naked body to the waiting crowd. Marcus suppressed a wave of nausea; it was hard to believe that misshapen thing had once been living, breathing flesh and blood. The crowd let out a huge roar, but he couldn't tell if it was approval or outrage. It didn't seem to matter to the guards; they were busy stoking up the fire again.

They're trying to reduce the corpse to ash, he realized. Perhaps they're afraid if anything remains it might become the focus of rebellion. And they were certainly doing a thorough job of it. But no matter how long they left it in the flames, the woman's heart stubbornly refused to burn. Even the addition of sulphur and oil made no difference. In the end, the frustrated guards doused the fire and gathered the mass of cinders and other remains into a blanket.

He watched them carry the blanket towards the River Seine . . .

MARCUS CAME AWAKE, drenched in sweat, his heart pounding as though it would burst. He threw back the duvet and padded into the bathroom for a glass of water, his trembling hands spilling half of it in the process.

I should never have used the Viewer to watch the execution this evening, he thought, as he drank. For it was clear who the woman in his dream must have been. He took a final gulp of water and straightened up.

The man in the shaving mirror rubbed his bleary eyes and ran a hand through his thinning hair, but Marcus was scarcely aware of his reflection. Instead he saw again the sunburned face and wide-set brown eyes of the young woman who had burned to death. And a nagging thought remained. She had said it was all his fault. What if the Maid of Orleans was right?

"YOU LOOK AWFUL." Anna frowned at Marcus. "And you're not eating enough to keep a gnat alive." She poked a fork at Marcus's barely touched ham salad.

He pushed his tray away. "Maybe I'm cracking up," he said. "I feel it's my fault that Joan of Arc got burned at the stake."

"Come again?" Anna looked up from her lasagne, startled.

"Night after night she's there in my dreams, Anna. Blaming me."

"If anyone's to blame, it's that student you sent down. What was his name? Lee Anderson?"

"Anderson!" The name was an expletive. "He had me completely fooled!"

"Well, he must have done some research. You said his notes on the False Joan of Arc were very comprehensive."

Marcus grimaced. "They were. He did good work to start with. It was later on, when he got bored with pure research . . ." He sighed. "He used the Viewer like some kind of personal, hi-tech video game. How could I have been so blind?"

Anna patted his hand. "You treated him as a responsible adult. It was a brave thing to do."

He stared at her fingers, absently noticing the calluses caused by her nonstop work on the Scoop prototype.

"Brave, or foolish? The Viewer is my invention, my responsibility," he said. "I should never have let Anderson loose in there without disabling the Communication Circuit. Who's to say, if he hadn't meddled, Joan might never have heard any voices, never have set out on the road to martyrdom?" He regarded her miserably.

"When it comes to observing or changing history, we're all in the same boat," she said. "My Scoop may be able to transfer people through time and space. Think of the possibilities!" Her eyes, which had brightened, dulled again. "But I expect the Ethics Committee will restrict me to retrieving urns from ancient tombs, or something equally harmless." She shrugged. "It's so frustrating!"

He envied her the fact that her problems were still theoretical, whereas his—

Anna's wristwatch beeped and she crammed the last piece of lasagne into her mouth. "Sorry. Tutorial. I've got to go."

She kicked back the refectory chair and stood up, then frowned down at him for a moment. "Look, Marcus. I know you feel really bad about all this, but you've got to keep it in perspective. I've got the name of a shrink somewhere. Why don't you see him, before this gets completely out of hand?"

But Marcus had the uneasy feeling that it was already too late for that.

THE VIEWING LAB door hissed open, and Marcus hesitated. For five consecutive nights now, he had been unable to sleep. Each time he closed his eyes he had the same dream, heard Joan of Arc blame him for her agonizing death, watched her die. He could barely function, he was so tired. He'd toyed with Anna's suggestion of seeing a shrink—she'd given him a name and telephone number—but somehow he couldn't bring himself to act on it. He, and he alone, was responsible for this mess; and he was damned well going to clean it up. One idea had begun to preoccupy him: if he could just get Joan of Arc's death sentence commuted to imprisonment . . .

He strode towards the silent bank of machinery that was the Viewer and flipped the power switch. Red and green lights danced across the board, and a low hum filled the lab. The sudden tang of ozone made his nostrils twitch. Digits whirred, and meter needles flickered, while on the VDU screen rapidly scrolling text showed the auto-startup sequence was in progress. Marcus pulled up a chair and sat down. At last the words "ready for instructions" blinked at him.

He pulled out the notebook he had confiscated from Lee Anderson and turned the pages. Joan's life riffled beneath his fingers. Ah, here it was. 25th May 1431, the day after she had repudiated her voices. A few days later she acknowledged her voices once more, and from that moment on her fate was sealed. If he could just convince her to stand firm in her repudiation . . .

He keyed in the coordinates for the cell in Philippe Auguste's chateau at Rouen, trying not to think about the ethics of what he was about to do.

The large vidscreen flared into life. A young woman in a shabby red dress was sitting on a pile of straw in the corner of a room. Her legs were chained. She seemed half asleep, and the sound of her slow breathing echoed round the lab. Marcus grunted with satisfaction and keyed the Communication Circuit on.

"Joan," he said. "Can you hear me?"

Suddenly, her large, liquid eyes were staring straight at him. Even though Marcus knew she couldn't see him across the centuries, the effect was unnerving. Her lips began to mouth words in medieval French, while the Translator broadcast English. The result was like a badly dubbed film; in other circumstances it might have been comic.

"Is that you, Michael?"

He took a deep breath. "Listen carefully—" But before he could continue, a man's broad, leather-clad back had blocked the screen.

"What are you doing, witch?" The gruff voice was trying hard to conceal its owner's fear. "Speaking to one of your demons? It's not enough that you are in league with them, but that I must hear them too?"

Marcus hastily keyed off the Communication Circuit. There was a guard in the Maid's cell. What the hell had he done?

But already he could hear the guard calling for help, and then the cell was full of men, and Joan was being dragged roughly to her feet.

"You are caught, witch. Your abjuration was patently false," said a sour-faced man wearing the robes of a bishop. "You have relapsed and must bear the consequences. What have you to say?"

Joan was clearly waiting for the Archangel Michael to speak to her again. She twisted in her captors' grip but said nothing. When no voice came, she sighed and bowed her head. "So be it," said the Maid.

With a cry of anguish, Marcus switched off the Viewer.

"YOU MUST BE crazy, Marcus!" Anna looked shocked. "We've never tried it on anything sentient."

"I don't know what else to do. Everything seems to twist itself so that history remains unaffected . . . Just show me how to operate the Scoop, Anna, and I'll do the rest myself."

She stared at him. "You're serious!"

Marcus nodded tiredly and ran a hand over his chin. Bristles rasped, and he realized that he had forgotten to shave again. "I'll take full responsibility. I know what I'm doing."

"I wish I could be sure of that." She gnawed her lower lip.

The silence stretched, and Marcus held his breath. If Anna turned him down, he didn't know what he was going to do. Go completely out of his mind, probably.

"Okay," she murmured, at last. "But it'll have to be this weekend. I'm in Tokyo for a conference, and my research students are coming with me. The Scoop Lab will be empty." She smiled wryly. "I must be as crazy as you are, Marcus . . . If the Ethics Committee get to hear of it . . ." She pursed her lips in a silent whistle.

Relief flooded through him. "You won't regret it, Anna."

"I hope not." She regarded him steadily for a moment. "I'll get the door combination and instructions for working the Scoop to you later today, then you're on your own."

CARRYING THE ROLL of carpet from the van to the Scoop Lab in between security patrols was the worst bit—Marcus didn't fancy having to explain to Sgt Tyler what he was doing with the Axminster, let alone the body inside it.

Not that it was a real body, but a "sim" speed-grown in a local Bio-lab's vats. Marcus had had to call in a huge favour to get the sim. It had also taken him some time to locate the heart which had been sitting in a jar of preservative for nearly three years. But details, such as the heart that wouldn't burn, were important if history were not to be affected more than strictly necessary. He hoped he hadn't over-looked anything else that mattered.

Marcus was sure the lab assistant thought him some kind of pervert. He'd had to saw open the chest cavity himself—she flatly refused to help—remove the sim's own heart, and stuff the preserved organ in its place; God alone knew what the acrid fumes had done to his lungs. He'd sewn the incision closed with a bodkin that had once belonged to his grandmother—luckily no one should be near enough to notice the uneven stitches. The Scoop Lab door hissed shut behind him. He dumped the carpet on the floor, unrolled it, then started to drag the contents to the far side of the lab. It was much harder to manoeuvre the heavy sim than he had imagined; its limbs kept flopping all over the place, getting tangled in wiring or trapped between banks of hi-tech machinery. And it felt unnervingly like the real thing, he thought, finding his hand grasping an ample breast. He pushed aside the image of the sim as a sex toy—he seemed to have perverts on the brain tonight—and struggled on. By alternately pushing and pulling, he managed to steer the sim into the massive egg-cup shaped container. He was sweating and gasping for breath by the time it was stowed to his satisfaction, and he could at last pull down the hatch.

He switched on the Scoop console and keyed in the complex series of instructions he had decided on—this particular combination of sends and retrievals was a first, as far as he knew. Then he typed "Initiate," followed by "Confirm."

There was a blue flash, and the sim disappeared.

BACK IN HIS own lab, Marcus set the Viewer for Rouen Marketplace, 30th May 1431. His hands were shaking. This was the moment of truth.

Once again, he watched the young woman receive the makeshift cross, saw the guards place the paper mitre on her head and set light to the faggots . . .

As he reviewed the familiar details of the horrific execution one by one, he began to feel uneasy. The palms of his hands were sticky as he tried to spot something, anything, that would reassure him that his plan was working. The only discrepancy he could detect was one of sound not vision. Joan hadn't cried out when the flames leaped higher. A small seed of hope began to sprout . . .

On the vidscreen, the procession was finally carrying the blanket and its gruesome contents towards the River Seine. Marcus rummaged through Anderson's notebook; there was one last thing for him to check.

"Orleans, 28th July 1439," read the scribble. "At that time there came a pretended Pucelle, who was very honourably received at Orleans." It was obviously a quote from some manuscript Anderson had used when researching the False Joan of Arc. With beating heart, Marcus keyed in the coordinates.

On the vidscreen now appeared a crowd of men and women, dressed in brightly-coloured costume—their best clothes by the look of them. Cheers and shouts filled the lab.

"It's Madame des Armoises," said someone. "Let her through!"

The crowd parted. A handsome, dark haired lady was smiling and waving, leaning affectionately on the arm of a man obviously her husband. There were crow's-feet round her eyes now, but it was unmistakably the woman Marcus had just seen burned at the stake.

The breath left his lungs in a whoosh of relief—the Scoop had worked, and so had his plan. It felt as though a huge weight had been lifted from his shoulders. He would have to congratulate Anna when she returned from Tokyo. Hell, he would have to do much more than that . . .

He would love to have seen Joan's face when she found herself alive and in the back street of a strange town. He hoped she wasn't too traumatized; no doubt she would ascribe her deliverance to the good offices of the Archangel Michael. He had picked Metz deliberately; it was well-documented that the false Joan's future husband, Robert des Armoises, lived there. It had been a calculated risk that the real Joan would meet him . . . Marcus smiled and watched the radiant Madame des Armoises for a moment longer, then switched off the Viewer.

He stretched. There was still a niggling doubt that he had actually changed anything, of course. Suppose "the pretended Pucelle" had been the real one all along? Perhaps Marcus had merely done what he was always meant to do. Perhaps—But there was time enough to think about chickens and eggs later. In the meantime—he yawned widely—it was time to catch up on some well-deserved sleep.

AFTERWORD

Whenever the topic of Joan of Arc comes up I get furious on her behalf. It's routine to blame the English for her fate, but the French and the Burgundians were just as culpable. In fact treacherous men of all nationalities treated her abominably. This was my way of giving her a happy ending.

THROWBACK

MILOS HAD JUST turned fourteen when he found out he would never become a proper vampire.

"It's one of those unfortunate things that happen from time to time," said Dr Ionesti. "Those genetic things."

Milos fiddled with a hangnail and dared not look at his parents.

"It's my fault, isn't it?" said his mother. She sounded close to tears.

"In a way, Mrs Severin," said the doctor. "Your Great Great Great Grandfather married a non-vampire, I believe?"

"There weren't many eligible females in the Kingdom at that time—"

"Quite so. Quite so." The doctor held up a hand. "Anyway, that would account for it. Normally vampire genes are the dominant ones, but just occasionally you get a throwback—a recessive, we call it."

Better not mention such terms to the boys in his class, thought a glum Milos. He had enough nicknames as it was!

His father cleared his throat. "You're certain, Doctor? After all, he looks more like one of us than any of his friends."

Milos imagined his father's stern black eyes gazing at him in disappointment.

"His fangs are very fine," agreed Dr Ionesti. "Though superfluous, of course, since we all drink Cordial these days." He turned to Milos. "Talking of which—"

"I've never liked it," admitted Milos. He threw his parents a resentful glance. "But everyone kept telling me it was an acquired taste."

The doctor nodded. "And finally, there's this." He pointed to the X-ray he had clipped to an illuminated panel at the start of the interview. "Most vampires are fully fledged by fourteen. But this shows quite clearly that Milos has no wing stubs at all. He will never be able to fly."

During the silence that followed, Milos's father reached for his mother's hand and squeezed it.

Milos sighed. He had always suspected he was different. And the feeling had intensified recently, as one by one his friends' wings appeared. His mother had said he must be a late developer, but he had known it was worse than that. Hearing it put into words such as "throwback," though . . .

Behind his lenses, the doctor's eyes were sombre. "No, I'm afraid there's no mistake, Mr and Mrs Severin." Then his eyes brightened and he smiled. "Fortunately, we have a fine counsellor attached to this practice. I'll make you all an appointment, shall I?"

"COME ON, MILOS," shouted Pavel. "Tibor and Stasio are threatening to go without us."

"I'm coming." Not having proper night vision was a bugger, sometimes, thought Milos, as once again he narrowly avoided twisting his ankle on a tree root.

From overhead, came the muffled sounds of conversation. "You two go on then," shouted Pavel at its finish. "We'll catch you up. I'll give Milos a lift."

"I don't want a li—" But the downdraft from Pavel's wings was already ruffling Milos's hair, and then his school-friend was standing next to him, folding his wings and resettling his cape over them—in the moonlight, its satin lining looked black rather than crimson.

"Get a move on, Milos. Grab hold."

Milos sighed. It was all so humiliating. He switched off and pocketed his torch, then grasped Pavel round the waist, twisting his fists into the broad leather belt Pavel had donned for this purpose.

"Ready." He braced himself.

Pavel's muscles bunched under his grip, and the ground dropped away beneath them. Milos tried to ignore the thought of the trees rushing by below—a fall from this height would be fatal.

"You should have let me walk!"

"Fledged vampires never walk." Pavel sounded as though he was stating one of the Laws.

"That's just it," said Milos. "I'm not even a proper vampire, let alone a fledged one. And I never will be."

He tried to keep the bitterness from his voice. What was it his counsellor had told him? For others to accept you as you are, you first have to accept yourself. Easier said than done, he thought. It didn't help that some of the boys at school had found out the truth and took great delight in pointing out his deficiencies nightly. He was lucky Pavel hadn't shunned him. As it was, their friendship was cooler than it had been.

The sound of rushing water was suddenly deafening, and he looked down at the river that marked the Kingdom's boundary. Moonlight glinted off the roiling surface. It was ironic, he thought, that humans believed vampires couldn't cross running water. In fact, the turbulent river had prevented all but the most determined of *humans* from venturing into the Kingdom. Then they were over dry land again, the sound of the river receding rapidly behind them.

The night air was chill on his neck, and he hunched further into his cape-collar. Already, his hands and arms were burning from the effort of holding on. He tried to think of something else, concentrated on the rhythmic sound of wings flapping. But his thoughts soon turned to what would happen if the Elders found out what he and his school-friends were up to. He hoped the fair would be worth it.

"Not far now," came Pavel's encouraging voice. "I can see the lights."

"Really?"

Milos twisted round awkwardly and squinted. In the distance, he could make out smudges of scarlet and apricot, emerald and ultramarine, gold and silver . . . As the lights grew closer, he could hear, above the wind, what must be music of some kind.

"Hang on. We're going down," yelled Pavel.

For a moment, Milos felt the familiar sickening sensation of falling. Then there was leaf-mould beneath his feet, and the sound of organ music loud in his ears.

Thank the Ancestors that's over, he thought. Releasing Pavel's belt and massaging the blood back into his numb fingers, he turned to see what his friend was staring at.

They had arrived at what was unmistakably the fair.

MILOS WAS SUSPENDED upside down, hair tickling his face and straying in his eyes, a strong metal rod locking him into his seat.

"Scream," came a man's voice from thirty feet below, barely audible above the din of music and machinery. "I won't let you down until you scream."

"Does he really think he's scaring us?" asked Pavel, from the seat next to Milos.

Though the Top Spin's attendant was glaring up at his customers, he sounded merely bored, thought Milos. All around them, though, humans were screaming—it was clearly expected. He opened his mouth and screamed too.

Pavel's startled look turned to amusement and understanding. His lips drew back, revealing his own fangs. "Aaargh!"

Milos screamed louder still. He was beginning to enjoy himself.

Soon after their arrival at the fair, they had found Tibor and Stasio sampling the dubious contents of one of the numerous food stalls.

"It's ghastly," said Tibor, after only one bite of something called a toffee apple. He would have thrown the rest of it in a litterbin had Milos not prevented him—he found he quite liked the crunchy texture, the contrast of the apple's tartness with the toffee's sweetness. Even he, however, had disliked the sickly sweet confection called candyfloss.

Tibor and Stasio had already tried the Dodgems and the Hoopla (they were now the proud owners of a shocking pink teddy bear) and were thinking of trying the Ghost Train next. Milos and Pavel joined them.

It was disappointing though. The so-called vampire that swooped out of the darkness at them was laughable rather than terrifying, and if spiders and webs were supposed to be scary . . .

"Its fangs were all wrong!" said Tibor, afterwards. "And why the lipstick and eye-shadow?" He rolled his eyes.

"Not to mention those gross fingernails," complained Stasio, admiring his own manicured fingers. "Non-vampires!" He shook his head, then glanced guiltily at Milos. "Sorry. I forgot."

Milos shrugged. "'S alright," he muttered.

By the time they'd worked their way round to the Galloping Horses, almost all their money was gone.

"Roundabouts are kid's stuff anyway," said Stasio. "That's much more like it." He had been gazing up at the strange contraption that was the Top Spin.

Which was why Milos, against his better judgment, was now suspended upside down thirty feet above the ground. A sudden wave of nausea overtook him and he swallowed. Maybe he shouldn't have eaten the toffee apple after all.

When he glanced back at the ground again, the attendant had

stopped glaring and was now pushing a huge lever into gear. For a moment nothing happened, then, with a deafening groan, the ride juddered into motion. Milos gave a sigh of relief as his seat swivelled the right way up again.

As he watched the ground drawing nearer, movement attracted his attention. Beside the Top Spin's kiosk stood a knot of four teenagers, all boys, all in jeans, T-shirts, and baseball caps. One of them, a tall blond lad, was pointing straight at him. Abruptly, the youth withdrew his arm and turned away, but his movements were stiff, as though he knew he had been spotted. Milos frowned. He had last seen the boys queuing for the Ghost Train. Was it a coincidence? Or were they following him?

His shoes touched what had once been grass but was now pitted dirt and the Top Spin ground to a halt. Then the attendant was standing next to him, reaching for the lock that held the metal rod in place. With a screech of metal, he was free. Milos stood up and stretched the cramp from grateful limbs. Beside him, Pavel did the same.

"Someone's taking an interest in us," said Milos, under his breath.

Pavel stopped stretching and glanced at him. "Who?"

But the attendant was indicating they should step clear of the ride and allow the other passengers to disembark. Milos hastened to obey.

When Pavel joined him, he continued. "There were four boys in baseball caps . . . standing next to the kiosk." But by now, the youths in question were moving away, intent, so it seemed, on trying their luck at a nearby coconut shy.

Pavel looked doubtful. "Perhaps it's just our clothes. We're a bit overdressed, aren't we? We'll know better next time."

Milos bit his lip. "I could've sworn . . ."

Then Tibor and Stasio were with them. "Perhaps they fancy you," said Tibor. Milos turned away exasperated.

"Anyone got any more money?" Stasio had been searching his pockets but had come up empty-handed. "I'm broke."

"It's time we were getting back, anyway." Pavel was glancing at his wristwatch. "We've got Double History in an hour. If we're not to run foul of Voislava . . ."

Milos sighed. Mr Voislava believed in strict discipline. He would take keen exception to members of his History class being absent without permission.

They left the fair and trudged back to the woodland that bounded it.

THEY WERE JUST entering the trees when bright torches shone out of the darkness and a male voice said, "That's far enough."

Milos shaded his eyes against the light and squinted. If it was dazzling to him, it must be blinding to his friends. Beside him, Pavel sucked in his breath. "Damn! Left my sunglasses at home."

There were three—no four, it was difficult to see—people barring their way, and they were all wearing baseball caps. Milos's heart sank.

"We know what you are," continued the voice. "And we don't like it." It came from the tallest of four boys, obviously the leader. He was slapping something rhythmically into his palm, something long and thin and . . . a baseball bat?

Milos sighed. "Leave us alone," he said. "We haven't done you any harm."

"Hear that?" jeered the boy. "The bloodsucking vampire says he hasn't done us any harm. Not yet, anyway. Not at all, if I have anything to do with it."

"Let's fly," murmured Pavel.

"I can't," said Milos under his breath.

"When I take off, grab for my belt—"

"It's not just that. We'd be breaking the Law." Louder, Milos said to the blond boy, "Don't talk rubbish."

"Rubbish, is it?" The boy stepped towards Milos. "I don't think so. Just look at you! Pale white skin, widow's peak, fangs . . . Oh, you're definitely vampires."

"Milos is right," hissed Tibor. "'Never provide proof that the People exist.' We break that Law, we're for it."

"So what are we going to do?" asked Stasio. "Stay here and get beaten to a pulp?"

Milos chewed his lower lip. "There may be another way," he said.

"Oh, right!" Pavel's tone was sarcastic.

"Trust me." Taking a deep breath, Milos placed himself nose to nose with the blond boy, or rather nose to chin—the boy was taller than him. "Prove it," he challenged. "I'll pass any test you like— short of a stake through the heart—that would kill anyone! And if I pass, you stop bothering us. Deal?"

The boy seemed disconcerted, and his friends muttered. "Don't believe him, Danny," urged one. "It's a trick," said another. "Let's just beat the crap out of them," said the third.

"Wait." Danny stared calculatingly at Milos. "Nothing to say we can't have ourselves a little fun." He glanced up at the moon then shrugged. "Pity it's not daylight. Still, I've got enough other stuff to use." He looked at Milos again and smiled; it wasn't a pleasant smile. "Deal," he said. "Bring me the bag, Steve."

One of the boys disappeared into the darkness then reappeared with a holdall. The leader took it, unzipped it, and began to rummage inside.

Pavel stepped up behind Milos and whispered in his ear, "Are you sure you know what you're doing? We could make a break for it. Once in the trees, they wouldn't see us take off, wouldn't know what had happened to us for sure . . ."

"It's not enough just to escape," muttered Milos. "We have to prove we're not vampires. And I'm the only one who stands a chance."

Pavel squeezed his arm. "OK. But look out for yourself. After all, you're *part* vampire. And that Danny's a nasty piece of work."

Milos nodded.

"Ready, vampire?" asked Danny.

Pavel rejoined Tibor and Stasio in the shadows, and Milos nodded. "Ready," he said.

THE FIRST TEST was easy. Danny thrust a bulb of garlic at Milos's face, clearly expecting him to flinch. Milos, though, had always liked French and Italian food. He sniffed the bulb and smiled.

A crucifix came next. When that had as little effect as the garlic, Danny reached into the holdall for a silver flask, unstoppered it and threw its contents—holy water, he claimed—at Milos's face.

Milos touched a tongue to the water still dripping from his upper lip. "Not bad," he said, thanking the Ancestors that, as he had suspected, these humans subscribed to the usual erroneous myths.

"Come on, Danny," urged a boy with bad skin. "It's a trick," said the one called Steve. "Must be."

Danny frowned at him, clearly baffled, then stooped once more to the holdall. After a few moments, he gave a grunt of satisfaction and held up a small silvered circle of glass.

Milos took the mirror and stared at his reflection. There was a smudge of dirt on his nose, and he removed it with one finger. He returned the mirror to its owner.

"Shit!" said Danny. One of his henchmen whispered something in his ear and his frown cleared. "Of course," he said. "Shadows. Everyone knows they don't have 'em."

As one, everyone turned to stare at the ground. Milos's shadow stood out black and clear on the woodland floor in the moonlight.

"Anything else you want to try?" he asked. He had a feeling the holdall was now empty.

For a moment it was silent in the clearing, then Danny shoved his hand into his pocket. "Iron," he said. "They don't like iron."

Milos felt his belly clench. A sudden scuffling noise on the other side of the clearing made him look across—Tibor and Stasio were restraining Pavel, who had decided enough was enough.

"It's OK," called Milos, trying to look calm and confident, even if he didn't feel that way. "No problem." Pavel looked unconvinced but ceased his struggling.

Milos watched Danny pull a penknife from his trouser pocket and open it—the blue-sheened blade had been lovingly honed and oiled. Milos licked his lips. Suppose Dr Ionesti was wrong. Iron could blister and burn vampires, even kill.

Aware that Danny was watching him avidly, Milos held out his left hand. Danny grinned, leaned forward, and cut him on the forefinger.

Blood began to well from the cut. Milos watched it drip onto the leaf-mould, looking black rather than red in the moonlight. His finger stung like crazy . . . but that was all. Almost sagging with relief, he pulled a cleanish handkerchief from one of his many cape pockets and wrapped it tightly round his finger.

Danny's silence spoke volumes. He had lost the wager, and he knew it.

"We could keep him here until daylight," said someone. "See if he shrivels up and dies."

Milos shrugged. Sunlight would merely give his friends migraines. Much worse would be the reaction of Mr Voislava if they didn't get back to school right now.

"Why waste your time and mine, Danny?" he said. "Come on. We had a deal. I passed your stupid test, so let us go."

Danny stood back. The three boys behind him didn't budge however. "Let them through," ordered Danny. "Want them to call me a liar?"

Grumbling, they gave ground.

Milos eased through the cordon of boys, trying not to hunch his shoulders—he wouldn't put it past them to throw a punch or two as a parting gift. Then he turned and waited. After a pause, Pavel started after him, followed by Tibor and Stasio. No one tried to prevent them.

When they were all safely through the cordon, they walked away from the human boys, into the trees.

MILOS AND THE others didn't quite make it back to school in time. And when they were forced to explain why they'd missed History, Mr Voislava reported them to the Head who gave them detentions and then called in their parents, who grounded them for a month.

Milos got eyestrain from all the worthy books he was forced to read that month and writer's cramp from the lines and essays he wrote.

"I still don't think it was fair," said Pavel, when the four of them were free to seek out each other again. "Weren't they ever young themselves?"

Milos grinned. "Yes, but that was nearly two centuries ago."

"I suppose you're right." Pavel sighed. "At least we can say we've been to a fair."

"Even if it *was* rather disappointing," added Stasio.

"Yeah, what happened afterwards was much more exciting than the actual fair!" said Tibor.

"It was a brave thing you did, Milos," said Pavel. "After all, that knife could have killed one of us."

Milos shrugged, then surprised himself by adding, "One of the few advantages of being a non-vampire." Perhaps he was getting used to the idea of being different after all.

Pavel smiled. "I tell people one of my best friends is a non-vampire."

Stasio rolled his eyes. "Cliché city."

"'Best' friend?" asked Milos, feeling suddenly shy.

"Sure."

He realized that this was as much of an apology for the coolness of the past few months as he was going to get.

Then a look of pure mischief came into Pavel's eyes and his voice dropped to a conspiratorial whisper. "And that being so, I feel sure you'll want to join me on a little expedition I'm planning for next

Tuesday night. It seems, guys, that the circus is coming to a spot not far from here . . ."

With a sigh, Milos leaned forward and began to listen.

AFTERWORD

It's hard to come up with an original take on vampires, so I decided to subvert reader expectation and make vampires the norm rather than the exception. Teenagers are notoriously vulnerable to peer pressure, so it seemed obvious to make Milos that age. Oddly, considering this story features a whole kingdom of vampires, it's probably the least "fantastic" in this collection.

A QUESTION OF GENDER

A RHYTHMIC CRUNCH came from the packed snow path outside.

"Sounds like Greg's back," said Dorothea. Navila looked up from her computer and nodded.

The door banged open, and Greg stumbled in, accompanied by a cold flurry of snowflakes. His six-foot frame was hidden beneath layers of thick clothing, and a white fur cap with earflaps protected his head. He stamped snow from his boots and closed the door behind him. "Brrr. I wish I had an Otarri's skin. It's freezing out there."

It was just as well the three of them were scheduled to leave in the next fortnight, thought Dorothea. The weather here on the Northern continent was turning arctic. It had dropped ten degrees in the last week alone, and their batteries were already overstretched powering the few heaters they had brought down with them on the shuttle.

"Have I missed the Mercury's transmission?" asked Greg.

Dorothea nodded. The orbiting starship had signed off only five minutes ago, and wouldn't be back within range for the next hour at least.

"What did they say?" He removed his gloves and awkwardly began to unbutton and unzip the top layer of clothing; his fingers were blue with cold.

"Have to wait for the Committee to decide." She watched him struggle with his heavy boots, but, as his superior officer, didn't offer to help. Eventually he glanced exasperatedly at Navila, who rose and went to assist him.

"How did you get on with Harkri?" continued Dorothea, trying to hide her envy. Greg wasn't stuck back at base for fear of offending the natives—unlike the two female members of the Team.

"I think I made some kind of breakthrough this morning." He grinned with relief as the last boot came free with a jerk. "Thanks . . . Here's the recording I took, Navila."

The Survey Team Linguist took the tiny silver disc from Greg, flicked the shiny, blue-black hair out of her eyes, and gazed anxiously at him. "Any trouble with the translator?"

"Nothing I couldn't handle," he said. "Though there were one or two moments when I wasn't sure we were talking about the same thing."

She grunted, crossed to her computer, and inserted the disc. At the touch of a symbol, the huge figure of Harkri ap Krishar, Warlord of Nashkiri Fort blossomed onto the screen.

Large as life and twice as ugly, thought Dorothea, gazing over Navila's shoulder at the pendulous snout and two large, thickly lashed, yellow eyes. Yet Harkri was probably considered a fine figure of a male by his own kind. She had seen recordings of the wild Otarris that inhabited the equatorial regions—none reached even three-quarters of the Warlord's twelve-foot height.

He was slumped on his cushioned throne, barking something unintelligible. Navila touched another symbol, and subtitles appeared.

"<Welcome> <concern for welfare> is offered to the <stranger> <guest>," said the Warlord. "What <tribute> <bribe> have you brought me this sunrise?"

"Grateful thanks are returned, mighty Harkri." Greg's distorted voice came from somewhere off screen.

Considering Greg's speciality was engineering—it was he who had constructed the two-room Base Camp—he had mastered the guttural consonants and glottal stops of the Otarri language surprisingly well, thought Dorothea. She gave Navila a sympathetic glance. Had circumstances been otherwise, the linguist would herself have been interviewing Harkri. Still, at least she could analyse the recordings Greg brought back.

"Much <honour> <face> to you," continued Greg's voice. "I bring more of the <metal> <source of female status>. May I approach your <throne> <symbol of power>?"

"Assent is given," barked Harkri.

The picture swayed, and a human hand appeared and placed a large chunk of rock at the Warlord's feet. As Greg backed away from the throne again, a wave of vivid pink flowed swiftly across Harkri's creamy skin, then vanished.

"He's pleased," said Navila.

"What did you give him? More copper ore?" asked Dorothea.

Greg nodded. "He can't seem to get enough of the stuff. All those females, I suppose."

Early in the mission, the Mercury's scanners had detected a massive copper deposit not far away. It had proved invaluable in negotiations—as a source of adornment for the females. The Survey Team had envisaged the copper providing weaponry not jewellery, but with hindsight it should have been obvious. Otarri males were formidable creatures, in little need of weapons. At first sight, they resembled large Terran elephant seals, with clawed limbs instead of flippers. But appearances were deceptive. Underneath that smooth skin was a layer of thick armoured platelets. And on all sixes, their speed was breathtaking. The smaller females stood little chance when a male decided to add them to his harem.

"So where's this breakthrough you mentioned?"

"It's about half an hour in."

Navila obligingly altered the time parameter. When it came, the moment was unmistakable. Harkri's skin turned an intense red, and remained so for at least a minute.

"Wow." Navila touched "hold." "He's really turned on. What's that all about, Greg?" Without waiting for his reply, she backtracked thirty seconds.

"I have been a <male> <superior being> since birth," came Greg's voice. Navila froze the recording, and Dorothea looked questioningly at the engineer.

"We were talking about females," he said. "First he wanted to know how large my harem was, then he asked when I became a male . . . 'was honoured with maleness' as he put it!"

Dorothea grunted. Gender again. It kept cropping up. Her own work had been curtailed to an unforgivable degree simply because she was a woman. For a female to question a male was apparently a severe breach of etiquette, and access to the females was controlled by their male owners. It didn't help, either, that she was black. Had they known in advance how the Otarris would react, the Mission Committee would undoubtedly have chosen an all white, all male team of athletes like Greg. But restricted shuttle flights meant there was nothing they could do about it now.

"How large is your harem, then?" asked Navila.

Greg gave her a sidelong glance. "I told him I own five females."

Navila spluttered with laughter and put a hand over her mouth. "Good job Harkri doesn't know you're gay."

He grinned.

"Why five?" asked Dorothea.

"I figured status must relate to harem size. At the last count, Harkri had thirty wives. Five seemed about right—just enough to earn his respect, yet not enough to be threatening."

She nodded approval. "And then he asked when you became a male?"

"I think so. One or two words were new to me," he confessed, "so I may have got it wrong."

The Warlord's interest was feasible. Towards the beginning of the mission, Dorothea had found the decomposing body of a baby Otarri. There had been something odd about its sexual organs, which led Dorothea to think the natives only attained a specific gender at puberty. If so, it was no wonder Harkri had been impressed with Greg. She sighed. The theory was mere speculation. If only she could do a first hand examination of a living Otarri—but that depended on the Committee's decision.

"I'll analyse this latest recording," said Navila, "and add the new words and phrases to the translator's data banks ready for next time."

Dorothea nodded. With luck, before Greg's next meeting with the Warlord of Nashkiri Fort, the Mission Committee would have considered her request. And Greg could ask Harkri if a member of his own harem could examine one of the Warlord's wives.

THE HAREM GATES looked strong enough to withstand a force ten gale . . . or an angry male Otarri, thought Dorothea. Greg had described Nashkiri Fort, and she had viewed all the available recordings, but nothing had been able to convey its solidity and barbaric splendour, or the overpowering reek of musk. Stakes of Lersha formed the bulk of the stockade. The gigantic red reeds, with stems the same texture and density as Terran wood, grew abundantly by the lowland rivers now thick with ice, and Greg had used them to construct the base camp too.

According to Greg, Harkri's male followers were not only fierce warriors, assigned their own female as a reward for services rendered, but also skilled at smithing and carpentry; everywhere she saw signs of their work. They had hewn the Lersha to fit so snugly only hairline cracks remained. Dove grey animal pelts covered the inner walls. The skins looked like Brekah, the small four legged ruminants that were the Otarri's main food source. The result was surprisingly cosy—not that the Otarri appeared to feel the cold.

The Committee had been split about allowing Dorothea to ask permission to visit the harem. Some thought it might antagonise Harkri, and a full-grown male Otarri on the warpath was something to be avoided at all costs. But in the end the chairperson, who was a biologist too, gave the OK. The Planetary Survey was almost complete, she said; the risk was worth taking.

And Greg had overcome Harkri's initial reluctance with a massive gift of copper ore and an undertaking: Dorothea would enter and leave the Fort at predetermined times while the males remained in the main hall to avoid contamination or loss of face.

So here she was at last, outside the harem. Dorothea placed her folded jumper with her other outdoor clothes—the Fort was warm enough without them—and straightened her uniform shirt and trousers. She checked the micro-camera pinned to her collar and the little recorder threaded on her belt. Everything appeared to be working smoothly. She took a deep breath, clutched the tiny translator tightly in the palm of her left hand, and swung open the massive door.

The room was huge, its walls and floors covered with yet more Brekah pelts. Several recessed doorways led presumably to the sleeping quarters. Some wives must still be dozing because only fifteen adult Otarris, their small body size and short snouts proclaiming them female, reclined on the skins. Two had newborns clamped to their swollen teats, sucking vigorously. In the corner six youngsters were mock fighting, making excited yowls and barks. At Dorothea's entrance, the hubbub faded to a profound silence. Yellow eyes stared warily at her.

She opened her hands wide in the Otarri gesture meaning "no harm intended." For a moment, the females remained tense, ready to defend their young from this strange, two-legged apparition. Then they relaxed, and a low background murmur of barking resumed. Dorothea let out her breath in relief. The first hurdle was over.

As her gaze travelled slowly round the room, Dorothea didn't know quite what it was she had expected, but it wasn't this. She was used to pictures of sleek well-fed males. Outside the Fort, there was an abundance of food, yet these females looked emaciated, their skin riddled with sores which must be due to malnutrition. They moved slowly and lazily, walking on all sixes rather than erect—trying to conserve what little energy they had?

The largest Otarri female, covered from head to foot in copper chains of varying widths and lengths, approached Dorothea and stopped directly in front of her. She was obviously waiting for an explanation.

Dorothea placed her tongue and lips in the position Navila had taught her. "Your <husband> <owner> has generously given permission for me to speak to you," she began.

The female barked softly in reply. Dorothea glanced down at the translator and read, "<Welcome> <concern for welfare> is offered to the <stranger> <guest>. I am Nikvah, the senior <wife> <possession>. My <husband> <owner> has ordered me to help you."

It looked like this was going to be easier than she had thought. "I wish to examine a <baby> <future rival>," she said, feeling the guttural consonants scour her throat.

Nikvah reared up, her seven-foot height dwarfing Dorothea's five-and-a-half and making her step back quickly. But it appeared to be no more than an acknowledgement of her request, because the senior wife then dropped back to all sixes and led the biologist to one of the two nursing mothers. If Nikvah was just a small female, thought Dorothea, awed . . . No wonder Greg treated the Warlord with care.

Nikvah barked something, and the mother pulled her newborn, despite its limpet like grip, from her teat. While the mother held the squirming baby firmly with her fore- and mid-arms, Dorothea ran her fingers through its downy covering, feeling the ridges of the tiny platelets beneath the skin. It wriggled even more, and gave a tiny, high-pitched bark—perhaps she was tickling it. She glanced up anxiously, but the mother seemed unconcerned.

Dorothea tried to concentrate on the information her fingertips were sending to her brain. The baby's platelets felt thin and pliable. Presumably the down was for temporary warmth and protection until the platelets thickened. But she had waited two months for this opportunity and mustn't waste it. She homed in on the bulge between the baby's hind legs, parted the fur gently, lifted the little flap of skin, and saw what had so intrigued her before: two sets of tiny, undeveloped sexual organs—one male and one female. She sighed with satisfaction, released the baby, and stepped back. So the dead Otarri had not been deformed; this baby was a hermaphrodite too.

"You have finished with the <baby> <future rival>?" asked the senior wife.

"Assent is given."

The mother plonked her baby back onto a teat with a force that would have crushed a human infant, but it merely mewed slightly before resuming its eager sucking.

"I must talk with you and some of the other <wives> <possessions>," said Dorothea.

Nikvah led her to an unoccupied pelt, then barked. Two more females joined them, lolling in a circle around Dorothea. I hope they don't turn nasty, she thought.

"Is it correct that each <baby> <future rival> is born neither <male> <superior being> nor <female> <inferior being>?"

"Assent is given," barked the shortest of the females, with a gesture unfamiliar to Dorothea, but which she was sure would translate as "Who is this idiot?" She would have to ask Navila when the linguist had had a chance to look at this recording.

"When did you become a <female> <inferior being>?"

Again that gesture, but Nikvah barked something which made the female cower and answer meekly enough. "Shortly before I first felt the urge to mate," she said.

"And when was that?"

"The seasons had turned full circle eight times."

Dorothea nodded. "Show me what makes you a <female> <inferior being>."

The Otarri obediently rolled onto her belly, spread her hind legs and twitched the muscles which raised the flap of skin between them—as though presenting herself to a male, Dorothea realised. In this position the sex organs were visible. The tiny male protrusion had remained at its birth size, but the female orifice had enlarged several times over.

Nikvah barked at Dorothea. "Is this sufficient?"

"Assent is given," she said, rather shamefaced. She was finding it hard to reconcile her scientific curiosity with the possible humiliation she was inflicting. But the worst was over now. She had confirmed that the Otarri shared hermaphroditism with the rest of the planet's flora and fauna. The Committee would be pleased.

Dorothea glanced at her watch. Perhaps one last question? It seemed natural to ask the gaunt females about food.

"We are always hungry," confirmed Nikvah. "Our <husband> <owner> feeds us once every two days."

Another female who had been eavesdropping joined in. "We have all the food we need to be <attractive> <copper clad>, <feminine> <sexually arousing>. Any more and our <husband> <owner> will not protect us and breed with us."

Dorothea was amazed. These females had been captured shortly after puberty, then held for the Warlord's pleasure; they were starving, yet seemed to approve of their lot. Some cultures and customs had a lot to answer for. But her time was up, and she rose from the pelt.

"The visit is ended?" asked Nikvah, also rising.

"Assent is given. Grateful thanks for your help."

"Good journey."

As she retraced her steps, Dorothea could feel eyes staring after her. I wonder what they made of all that, she thought, hurriedly donning her outdoor clothing. I hope I haven't offended them too much. She pulled up her hood and knotted the drawstrings tight. The wind was whistling outside the stockade; it sounded like the blizzard had intensified. Dorothea sighed. She wasn't looking forward to the trudge back to Base Camp.

THE OTHERS WATCHED Dorothea's harem recording, and Navila transmitted its contents via fast beam to the Mercury.

The sight of the ill-treated wives shocked the Committee members, but they were strictly bound by the Non-Intervention Policy: on no account must they meddle with alien beliefs and activities. Besides— they salved their consciences—the females must benefit from the arrangement somehow. Left to fend for themselves, they would run the risk of being killed in battles between competitive males.

For a moment, Dorothea's emotions got the better of her. "Harkri shouldn't treat them so cruelly," she protested. "And there shouldn't be such a high ratio of females to males."

But the Committee members pulled rank. "And what's more—" they added huffily, "—according to our scanners, the same sort of gender imbalance occurs in the wild, so it's perfectly natural."

Dorothea wasn't so sure. The balance should have been fifty-fifty. Was there some other factor at work? But she gave in ungracefully, determined to solve the question of gender in the little time remaining to her. In the meantime, Greg continued his visits to the Fort, and Navila used his reports to expand the Otarri/Universal dictionary she was compiling.

"I DON'T KNOW quite how to put this," said Greg.

Dorothea looked up from the latest report she was preparing for the Mercury. "Spill it. I haven't got all day."

"Harkri's given me a present."

"Copper chain? Brekah skins? What?" Her mind was still half on her report.

"One of his wives—to add to my harem."

"What?"

"It's an honour, a gift from one male to another. I couldn't refuse without insulting him."

"But, Greg," said Navila, "what will you do with her?"

He shrugged. "We can't take her with us when we leave. There's no provision for aliens on board the Mercury, never mind the Non-Intervention Policy. Have to set her free, I suppose."

"Will you tell the Committee, or shall I?" Dorothea was trying not to laugh.

"It's not funny. These are sentient beings!"

That sobered her up fast. Greg was right. "Where is she at the moment?"

"Outside."

She shot out of her chair. "You left her out in this weather?"

"It's too small and hot for her in here, so I thought . . ."

"You're right. Sorry." Dorothea rubbed her eyes. "I'm not thinking straight. You'll have to build her an enclosure of some kind."

He nodded. "That's what I thought."

Curiosity made her pull on her outdoor clothes. "I'll just take a look. See if it's one of the wives I met." She opened the door and stepped out into the cold.

Dorothea didn't recognise the Otarri female sitting placidly in the snow. She was even skinnier than the other wives and wore a single copper chain around one forelimb. Obviously one of the Warlord's lesser wives. She was appalled to see a clear impression of platelets beneath the raddled skin.

"Just look at her, Greg."

The engineer had followed her out. "I chose the worst looking one," he said. "Thought the least we could do before we leave is give her a good feed."

Dorothea squeezed his arm.

THE HUT GREG built his new wife wasn't quite up to Otarri standards—the planks didn't fit with the precision of Harkri's fort, and draughts whistled through when the wind blew from the north—but Jornek seemed happy enough.

If the Survey Team had thought Otarris were fussy eaters, Jornek soon proved them wrong. She ate everything and anything they put in front of her, mostly a mixture of Brekah meat and vitamin concentrates. She had been with them only three days, but already her body had filled out, the platelets hidden beneath a thick layer of fat. Her skin developed a healthy sheen, the sores healing fast. She was growing taller too.

Dorothea's knowledge of Otarri physiology had increased vastly thanks to Jornek, but there were still many unanswered questions. And she only had one week left.

She was astonished at the efficient way the native's system converted food into body mass. "How often are you feeding her now, Greg?"

"Six times a day," he said. "And she'd eat even more if I let her."

"Hmmmm. Yet she barely excretes anything."

"Making up for all those years of starvation?" suggested Navila.

"Perhaps," said Dorothea.

"She's been getting a bit stroppy lately, too," said Greg. "I thought female Otarris were supposed to be placid." He grinned wryly. "The honeymoon is obviously over!" Then he checked his watch. "I'm due at the Fort. Can you give Jornek her next meal, Navila?"

"She's your wife not mine, Greg," objected the linguist.

He frowned. "But I won't be here—"

"Enough, you two," said Dorothea. It was just as well the mission was drawing to a close. They had been cramped together for nearly three months solid and she could feel the tension level rising by the day. "Go on, Greg. We'll take care of Jornek."

He pulled on his snow gear and went out.

"DID YOU HEAR that noise?"

Dorothea groaned and sat up sleepily. "What?"

"A few seconds ago . . . that noise," said Navila. She sounded scared.

It was pitch black, so Dorothea switched on the torch she kept beside her sleeping bag. The wind had dropped at last, and there was complete and utter silence. What was Navila talking about? Then she heard a muffled roar, followed by the sound of wood splintering.

The sleeping bag on the far side of the room stirred and sat up. "What's going on?" asked Greg, peering out the top. Then all of them felt the vibration which ran through the floor of their sleeping quarters. Thump!

"What the hell?" Dorothea scrambled to her feet. "Something's attacking Jornek's hut. It must be a male, trying to get at her. Is she in season or something, Greg?"

"How would I know? I'm not the biologist!" He disentangled himself from his sleeping bag and pulled his outdoor clothing over his night attire.

Dorothea did the same. "You stay here, Navila. We may need you to radio the Mercury for help . . ."

The linguist nodded.

". . . and we need the laser pistols," she continued. "I don't like the sound of that thing."

Greg snorted agreement.

Moments later, Greg and Dorothea were outside, pulling their hoods up over their heads and peering through infrared goggles. Dorothea clutched her pistol tightly. "Can you see anything?"

"Jornek's hut!" He pointed.

They ran through the gently falling snow towards the place where the hut had been and gaped at the smashed remnants. The padlock was the only thing still intact. Matchwood covered the trampled snow, red splinters showing up clearly against the white background.

Dorothea peered at the wreckage.

"Is she in there?" asked Greg.

"No."

He turned. "Jornek," he shouted, his smoking breath causing the snowflakes to dance. "Where are you?"

"I can't believe Harkri would do this," said Dorothea. "After all, he's still got twenty-nine wives. And I'm sure he can easily get more."

"It's not Harkri."

"One of his warriors with delusions of grandeur?"

Greg shook his head. "They wouldn't risk setting up in Harkri's territory."

Dorothea scanned their surroundings uneasily. "Well who the hell is it then?"

"Jornek," yelled Greg again.

She saw movement on the edge of her vision. It couldn't be Jornek—females didn't move that fast and it was at least eight feet high. When she had last seen Jornek two days ago . . .

There was a deafening roar, and something huge dropped to all sixes and charged at them out of the darkness.

"Greg, look out," yelled Dorothea.

It came with the speed and force of a rampaging rhino; there was no time to run. They fired their pistols point blank, but the weapons had no effect. The platelets, thought Dorothea, amazed at the way her mind was coolly analysing the situation even as adrenalin flooded through her and her pulse rocketed. The lasers can't get through. We're done for. The Otarri reared to its full height, screamed its defiance . . . and crashed to the ground like a tree trunk felled by the axe.

Dorothea stared stupidly at the dead alien, and became aware of the numbness in her fingers and toes, and the prickle of sweat running between her breasts and shoulder blades. Gradually her pulse slowed and the pounding in her temples eased.

She scanned their surroundings through the infrared goggles. There was no sign of Jornek. "We'd better leave it 'til morning, Greg. We'll never find her in this." There was no reply, and she turned sharply.

Greg stood like a statue, his head bowed, the laser pistol dangling loosely in one fist. Then he looked up and shook his head.

Dorothea patted him on the back. "It couldn't be helped, Greg. It was him or us."

There was silence except for the persistent hissing of the snow.

DAYLIGHT REVEALED THE full extent of the destruction. Even under the new coating of snow, it looked like a hurricane had hit Jornek's hut. Greg was trying to find and follow his wife's tracks; the deep footprints wouldn't remain visible for long.

"That's funny," he said. "I can only see the tracks of one Otarri. And it must be the intruder."

Dorothea stared at him. "Are you sure?" There was something nagging away at her, something important, but she couldn't quite get hold of it.

"Maybe the snow wiped the other set away."

"Maybe." But she didn't think so. She wandered over to where the intruder's body lay, crouched, reached out one gloved hand, and began to brush the snow off the frozen skin.

"What are you doing?"

"It's just a hunch." Greg watched her for a baffled moment, then shrugged and bent to help her.

"Did Jornek have any distinguishing marks?" asked Dorothea conversationally. She thought she could remember something, but she needed confirmation.

He considered for a moment. "Her right forelimb," he said. "One of the three digits was missing. She said it was damaged when Harkri captured her."

"Like that?" Dorothea pointed to the missing digit on the dead Otarri's forelimb.

Greg froze with astonishment. "Just like that," he said.

The body was now completely uncovered, and Dorothea reached between its hind legs. The flap of skin was difficult to lift—it was stiff with cold, and rigor mortis had set in—but eventually, it moved. She studied the now exposed sexual organs, aware of Greg's gaze. The female orifice showed signs of once having been functional—it was shrinking, but had not yet reached dormancy; the male member had grown to almost adult size.

Dorothea rose stiffly to her feet. "I'm sorry, Greg. This is Jornek."

THEY BURIED JORNEK as best they could—the frozen earth and the cumbersome corpse made the going difficult. Then they signalled the Mercury that it might be best to terminate the survey a few days early. If Harkri discovered what they had done to his former wife . . .

"I should have seen it earlier," said Dorothea, packing the remaining equipment into boxes, careful to leave nothing which might affect native development. "Remember how Jornek changed after we fed her all that food? She used to be small and placid, didn't she? Then she grew much larger, became more aggressive. Last night, she completed the transition from female to male. The humiliation of being locked up in the hut must've proved too much for him."

Greg grunted and unplugged a heater.

Dorothea continued to talk, rehearsing what she would tell the Committee. "The surplus of females in the equatorial regions makes perfect sense given the shortage of food there. At puberty, all Otarris become female. Then the strongest takes most of whatever food there is, changes into a male, and breeds with the others . . . I should have seen it, but it never struck me that their gender wasn't permanently fixed. Besides . . . that business of the food . . . it goes against the grain. Everyone knows malnourished mothers have malnourished offspring—yet here it seems to be the way of things. This godforsaken planet has got everything backwards!"

"So Harkri has artificially recreated desert conditions for himself?" asked Greg.

"He had no choice," said Dorothea. "He had to restrict the food or all his wives would have become males. It wouldn't do, would it? The species would die out."

"No, I suppose not." Then he grinned. "Might be fun while it lasted though!"

Navila popped her head round the door. "Shuttle's on its way. Ten minutes, they say. All packed?"

"Just about," said Dorothea. "Right, let's get going then."

They carried the boxes outside, then watched the base camp burn, warming themselves by the blazing Lersha wood.

Navila was worried. "You can see the smoke for miles."

"We'll be gone before they get here," said Greg. "Harkri will assume we died in the fire. Maybe he'll give me a warlord's funeral."

"You hope!" said Navila. "I don't know about you, Dorothea, but I'll be glad to get back to civilisation for a while."

Dorothea grinned and held out her hands to the flames. "I'd settle for somewhere nice and warm."

Sunlight glinted off something high above, and they looked up eagerly. Moments later they heard the roar of the shuttle's drive as it came in for the final descent.

AFTERWORD

In parts of the animal kingdom, gender depends on calories, temperature, population density etc. A friend, Gareth Davies, decided to use this fact in a story, and we spent many enjoyable hours discussing plot possibilities. Unfortunately, he died soon after, without ever publishing his story. It seemed a terrible shame to let the ideas we'd concocted go to waste, so I wrote my own story.

THE HOUSE ON THE VIA AURELIA

[Author's Note: Taking into account supernatural beings, the households of Ancient Rome must have been densely populated. While the *Lar Familiaris* protected the house and the *Penates* guarded the store cupboard, each Roman also had a guardian spirit (males had a *genius*; females, a *juno*). Unfortunately the *Lemures*, mischievous ghosts of the dead, were less benign.]

QUINTUS WOULD HAVE liked to go to the funeral. He had never met Decimus Flavius Calvus, but over the years, the ugly old man's exploits had piqued his curiosity.

When Marcus and Julia arrived back at the house on the Via Aurelia, Quintus waited impatiently for them to don their sandals and join their four children in the dining room so he could eavesdrop. Several of the other guardian spirits and ghosts had had the same idea, and as the family members settled on stools placed round the table, Quintus floated over to join them.

"The urn was chipped," said Marcus, while his two house slaves served supper. "But what can you expect?" He popped an olive into his mouth. "I warned Decimus not to choose the cheapest funeral society, but he wouldn't listen. He never did."

Mouths full of *chicken fronto* didn't stop the children from asking questions about the ceremony. Marcus answered circumspectly, but Quintus was able to get the gist.

Not for old Decimus the pomp and circumstance of Quintus's own funeral. There was no traffic-stopping procession to the Forum, no wearing of death masks, no mimes and dancers, and only one flute player who could barely hold a tune. But then, times had changed since the Republic, and even if they could afford it, only the most prominent of Rome's citizens had lavish processions these days.

"At least my eulogy went well," finished Marcus, before explaining what a eulogy was to four-year-old Secundia.

Marcus's *genius* snorted.

"What?" Quintus asked the guardian spirit, who resembled his charge in his prime, as did all *genii* and *junos*.

"Marcus made Decimus's life sound so respectable, the mourners must have thought they were at the wrong funeral!"

Quintus smiled and switched his attention back to the conversation.

"Did Great Uncle Decimus leave us any money?" asked Marcus's oldest boy.

"Yes, Papa," said his brother. "There's this hobby horse I'd really—"

"Show a little respect, boys!" said their mother. "You should be mourning Great Uncle Decimus, not making plans to spend his money."

"Did he have any children, Mama?" asked Secundia, sucking sauce off her fingers before scooping up more chicken.

"No, dear. He wasn't married."

"Then why didn't he live with us?"

Julia sighed. "Because your grandfather barred him from this house."

"Why?"

She glanced at her husband, who scratched his shiny pate before answering. "Decimus inherited half the family property, as did your grandfather," explained Marcus, "but he frittered most of his away."

"On drink, chariot racing, and whores," announced his eldest daughter.

"Primia!" said Julia. "Where did you hear such a thing?"

The ten-year-old blinked. "Flavipor was telling Caenis about it this morning."

The house slave winced and hunched his skinny shoulders in an attempt to disappear as Julia frowned at him.

"Um. What *are* whores, Papa?" continued Primia. The three *Lemures* hooted and even Quintus found his lips twitching.

"*Not* a fit subject for the dinner table." Marcus's cheeks and the tips of his ears had gone bright red. "And we won't know if Decimus has left us something until the will is read," he said, steering the conversation back on course. "But I'm not expecting much. That run-down place of his on the Via Flaminia is probably in hock to his creditors." His older children looked disappointed.

"Are you sad that Great Uncle Decimus is dead, Mama?" asked Secundia.

Julia pushed back a stray gold ringlet before answering. "Of course, dear." She turned to the waiting house slave. "Call Caenis, will you, Flavipor. It's past Secundia's bedtime."

THE FAMILY HAD finished their meal, placed offerings of food, wine, and incense on the various shrines, and gone to bed. The house slaves, having finished sweeping up the food scraps from the dining room floor, were now tidying the atrium. Quintus floated back a step to let them pass. Occupying the same space as a household god didn't hurt a mortal, unless the god concentrated really hard, but it always made Quintus feel nauseous.

"Did we miss anything juicy?" came a voice from behind him.

He turned and gave the two *Penates* a welcoming smile. "No. Decimus's funeral seems to have been uneventful." Claudia and Gallio's faces fell.

The fattest member of the *Lemures* shared their disappointment. "Given the old man's reputation for being a randy old goat," grumbled Titus, "I expected a cat fight at the very least." He scratched his beard. "Some scratching, hair pulling, tearing of stolas and scarves . . . What a missed opportunity!"

The guffaws that met his remark disturbed the caged finches in the atrium. Their frantic twittering made the two slaves exchange a glance, shrug, and resume their sweeping.

The spirits' conversation turned down other avenues, and soon the *Lemures* were goading Primia's *juno* by placing bets as to when and how the girl would next embarrass her father at dinner.

The house slaves put away their brooms, extinguished the last of the lamps, and retired to their room for the night. Quintus stretched and looked at the *Lemures*.

"So. Whose turn is it?"

"Julia's," answered Drusilla, whose curves were much more generous than her nature. Titus and Vibius nodded. "We thought . . . a mild fever." She glanced at Julia's guardian spirit. "Only enough to keep her in bed for a day."

The *juno* pursed her lips then nodded. "Seems fair. She'll think she caught a chill at the funeral."

It was hard for Quintus not to feel smug at the minor nature of the proposed torment and the amicable negotiation. Before he had introduced his rota system, it had been constant battle between the *Lemures* and the guardian spirits, with the household gods caught in the crossfire. Nowadays, punishments were fairer, the house more ordered and peaceful—in fact visitors frequently commented how charmed a life Marcus and his family led. Some also warned that such good fortune couldn't possibly last, but what did they know?

"Good. That's settled." He gestured. "Now . . . Everyone to their posts."

The guardian spirits departed to join their charges, and the *Penates* retired to the kitchen once more, while the *Lemures*, bickering as always, floated towards the master bedroom to inflict fever on the mistress of the house.

Quintus drifted over to his own shrine, with its statue of a dancing boy, clad in an indecently short tunic, clutching a drinking horn in one hand and a cup in the other. There, he settled down to watch for burglars and those with malign intentions towards the house on the Via Aurelia. As he had watched for centuries since he first became a *Lar*.

IT WAS NINE days since Decimus's funeral. Marcus had arranged to have his uncle's house hung with branches of yew and cypress, and today it would be ritually swept—the last thing anyone needed was Decimus's ghost returning to haunt the place. Tonight there was to be a feast, to which a few of Decimus's old friends had been invited, followed by the reading of the will.

Quintus would be glad when life returned to normal. As, no doubt, would the family. It would have been hypocritical to not comb their hair, wash, or cut their nails, but they still had to wear drab woollen clothes that made them itch. And the Nine Days of Sorrow had kept Julia and the children cooped up indoors.

He floated into the kitchen to check on the bustle that had been underway since the early hours. A neighbour had lent Marcus two of his house slaves for the day and they were banging elbows and tripping over each other's feet as they washed, sliced, and diced. On every surface lay food in different stages of preparation. *Leeks, sliced eggs, snails, and sea urchins* . . . Quintus hoped Marcus would remember to put some of the choicest morsels in the Lararium.

The *Penates* looked up from their post by the crackling hearth fire and gave him a wave. He drifted towards them.

"How's it going?"

"A few minor setbacks," said Claudia. "They were going to have sow's udders but the butcher let them down at the last minute."

"They're having pheasant instead," added Gallio. "And cutlets, and lamprey."

"Sounds good." Quintus had always been partial to lamprey.

Flavipor staggered into the kitchen under a heavy basket full of apples, pears, grapes, nuts, and figs.

Caenis paused in the middle of plucking a pheasant and pointed. "Over there."

The skinny slave nodded and placed the basket in a corner. He straightened his rucked tunic, then stretched the ache from his back with a groan. "What next?"

"Well, that Falernian wine wants bringing in . . ."

"LET'S HOPE THIS is the final draft," said the bony-nosed lawyer.

At his feet lay earlier versions of Decimus's will, which Marcus had found at the bottom of a chest in the old man's study. They had left Decimus's fortune, such as it was, to, variously: the first girl he had sex with; a local wine merchant; Marcus; a courtesan; a winning team of charioteers; Marcus; and, in a fit of uncharacteristic piety, the Vestal Virgins.

From their expressions, the guests sprawling on the couches that had been moved into the atrium shared the lawyer's hope.

"Get on with it," called a paunchy dealer in scent, whose bulbous nose betrayed his love of the grape.

"I, Decimus Flavius Calvus," read the lawyer with a sniff, "do bequeath all my worldly goods and chattels to my nephew Marcus Flavius Calvus, currently residing on the Via Aurelia. And much joy may they bring him, the stiff-necked young prig." Marcus's lips thinned at this unflattering description, but he said nothing.

Glad the old goat saw sense in the end, thought Quintus. *The family could do with the money.*

The lawyer rolled up the scroll.

"But he promised!" protested a butcher with a greying comb-over, whose toga was fraying at the edges.

Discontented mutterings from the other guests showed that he wasn't the only person whose expectations Decimus had falsely raised. Marcus sighed and gestured to Flavipor to top up the wine cups.

"Thank you, Aulus." The lawyer relinquished the scroll into Marcus's hands and resumed his place on the second couch. "Music," called Marcus. The hired cithara players struck up a tune.

THE LAST OF Marcus's guests had called for his shoes and set off on his litter along the deserted streets of Rome, and the relieved host was tucked up in bed with his wife. The slaves had cleared up the mess and shifted the furniture back to its rightful place. Now muffled chatter and laughter coming from the kitchen indicated they were enjoying themselves with the leftovers.

Quintus didn't begrudge them their treat. On Marcus's instructions, they had distributed choice portions of food and drink to each of the shrines, including the Lararium. He had been delighted to find some lamprey waiting for him.

The *Lar* was about to start his nightly inspection when a ghost he had never seen before materialised in front of him. He halted, frowning at the ugly young man with a slight paunch. He was wearing the short-sleeved white tunic that seemed to be standard issue for ghosts.

"Who are you?"

The ghost stuck his thumbs under his belt. "Are you the ferryman?" He surveyed his surroundings and frowned. "Where's your boat?"

The *genii* and *junos* floated over to join Quintus, the *Penates* on their heels.

"Trouble?" asked Marcus's guardian spirit.

"Maybe." Quintus turned back to the stranger. "It should be obvious that this isn't the Underworld."

"Then what am I doing here?"

"I have no idea. All I know is that you can't stay." Quintus took a dim view of uninvited guests, human or ghostly. He ushered the intruder towards the street door that led between two shops out onto the Via Aurelia. At the exit the ghost stopped.

"Please leave."

"I'm trying to." The ghost surged forward again, and this time Quintus saw that some kind of invisible barrier was preventing him from going through the doorway. Just like the barrier Quintus himself faced if he ever tried to leave the house.

He blinked. *But that must mean* . . . A feeling of unease stole over him. "What is your name?"

"What does *that* have to do with anything?" The ugly ghost's voice was querulous. He was still trying to float through the doorway, with as little success.

"Only ghosts and household spirits related to the Flavius Calvus family have a right to be here. *What is your name?*"

Movement from the corner of his eye made Quintus turn. His raised voice had brought Flavipor into the hall to investigate. The house slave looked round, saw nothing amiss, shrugged, and returned to the kitchen. Quintus turned back to find the other ghosts and spirits staring at him as if he had lost his wits. He hoped he had. The alternative was too horrible to consider.

"Well?" He folded his arms and glared at the ghost.

"My name, since you asked so nicely," said the new arrival, his tone sarcastic, "is Decimus Flavius Calvus."

"SO YOU'RE SAYING I won't be going to the Underworld?"

The new arrival was still having trouble grasping his situation. Quintus could sympathise. It had taken him weeks to come to terms with the unexpected change to his own fate. Worst of all had been the dawning realisation that he wouldn't be joining Helena and their three children for decades, possible centuries. Decimus had no family of his own, of course, but even he must have been looking forward to meeting the loved ones who had gone on ahead.

Decimus glanced at the faces surrounding him and frowned. "What am I supposed to do here anyway? All the jobs seem to be taken."

Quintus had opened his mouth to reply, when raised voices interrupted him. He turned and saw Vibius and Drusilla rushing towards him.

"Where's Titus?" demanded Vibius, a wild look on his gaunt face.

The *Lar* blinked at the two *Lemures*. "Isn't he with you?"

"If he was, do you think we'd be asking?" hissed Drusilla.

A terrible suspicion crept over Quintus, and he glanced from Decimus to the two ghosts then back again.

Vibius followed his gaze. "Who's this?"

"His name's Decimus Flavius Calvus."

The *Lemures* exchanged a startled glance. "Marcus's Uncle?" Vibius's brows creased and he tugged on an earlobe. "You don't think . . ."

Quintus nodded.

"What?" asked Secundia's *juno*.

"Shift change," said Vibius. "Titus must have gone on to the Underworld. This," he pointed at Decimus, "is his replacement."

"That doesn't make any sense," objected Gallio. "If Decimus's ghost is to haunt anywhere, shouldn't it be his own house?"

Quintus thought for a moment. "Marcus said the place was in hock to creditors. Maybe that's why he came here instead." He turned to address the two *Lemures*. "Sorry about Titus."

Vibius tried to look as if he didn't care. "Plenty more where he came from."

"Never did like that beard of his," said Drusilla, scowling.

"We'll just have to make the best of things." The *Lar* ran a hand over his bald pate. "Can you bring Decimus up to date on his duties and the existing agreements?"

"Oh, all right," said Drusilla. "Seems like we don't have much choice."

THE HOUSE ON the Via Aurelia was no longer a happy one and it was all Decimus's fault.

The ugly ghost refused to abide by the agreements the *Lar* had brokered and which had served the Flavius Calvus household well for many years. And with Decimus's encouragement, the other *Lemures* were falling back into their bad old ways.

The first shot in Decimus's campaign to bring chaos and discontent was to smash all the containers in the larder and empty their contents on the floor. The *Penates* were almost beside themselves at this disrespect for their domain, but the gentle guardians of the store cupboard were no match for the *Lemures*. And no sooner did the harassed slaves clean up the mess, buy new containers from the market, and restock the shelves, than the ghosts repeated the exercise.

Marcus sensed at once that something in the house had changed for the worse and sacrificed a portion of black beans, the usual appeasement for angry *Lemures*. Drusilla and Vibius would have accepted the offering, but Decimus growled, "I hate black beans," and refused.

When the situation didn't improve, Marcus pursed his lips then placed extra food, wine, and incense in all the shrines and decorated them with fresh garlands of flowers. It was a waste of time. Did the master of the house but know it, the household gods were already on his side. His gesture also backfired.

"I don't know why you're complaining," Decimus told an increasingly frustrated Quintus. "They've increased their sacrifices to you too. This is how things are *meant* to work. We torment them, and they sacrifice to us to make us stop."

"But you aren't stopping."

"Of course not." The ugly ghost picked his teeth and grinned. "A ghost has to get his fun where he can."

Decimus's next idea of "fun" was to douse the brand kept burning in the hearth all night, by pouring wine over it—something he could only achieve by getting Vibius and Drusilla to distract the *Penates* from their duties at the vital moment. For the first time since Quintus could remember, the house's eternal flame was extinguished.

For Flavipor, relighting the fire was a simple though time-consuming procedure, but the trembling slave was visibly appalled at what this omen might portend. As was his master. The anticipated run of bad luck began the next day.

As though making up for all those years of good health, illness (or rather the *Lemures*) began to stalk the family—nothing lethal, even Decimus wouldn't go *that* far, but still debilitating. The boys were now rarely well enough to attend school let alone play with their friends, and the girls spent every other day in bed, alternately shivering and sweating. Their parents weren't exempt. Diarrhoea melted the flesh from Marcus and Julia's bones, and they gained dark shadows under their eyes.

The slaves remained healthy, but they didn't escape the *Lemures'* attentions. Flavipor and Caenis's buttocks were black and blue and they took to tiptoeing around the house with wary looks. And after concerned friends and neighbours had experienced the invisible nipping fingers, they stopped calling.

Quintus tried to restore the status quo. But for the first time in years, his oratory went nowhere, and he was forced to take physical steps. In his youth, he had been a considerable wrestler, but Decimus proved to be just as skilled. The *Lar* was forced to call the contest a draw. It was humiliating.

And so the days progressed, until in desperation Marcus consulted a soothsayer about the problems of the house on the Via Aurelia. He came back that same afternoon, jaw jutting with determination, and ordered his family to pack. They were going to one of his country estates for a few weeks, he announced. Their *genii* and *junos* would be able to accompany them, but the ghosts and household gods wouldn't. The respite should allow the family and slaves to regain their former health and equanimity.

That his descendants had been forced to leave at all Quintus took as a personal affront. He could remember as if it were yesterday discussing the plans for the house on the Via Aurelia with the architect, supervising the laying of the first foundation stone, then the first layer of bricks. Choosing the decor and furnishing. Helena's admiration when he brought her to see the home where they would be spending their married life . . .

"You idiots!" he shouted at the *Lemures*. "Can't you see? If you push Marcus too far, he'll sell this house and then we'll all be in the midden."

"Not all of us." Marcus's *genius* shot Quintus an apologetic glance. "Guardian spirits can go where their charges go."

"And I wouldn't say the rest of us are 'in the midden' either," said Decimus, "since we'll simply be allowed to continue our journey to the Underworld." He gave the *Lar* a mocking smile. "Really, Quintus. What's all the fuss about? You're always going on about your wife and children." Drusilla nodded and Vibius mimed a yawn. "Can't you see? This way you'll get to see them earlier." Decimus chuckled. "You of all people should be pleased."

IT WAS THE very early hours of the morning. The *Penates* were sulking in the kitchen, where the hearth was cold and the larder half empty. In the atrium, the *Lemures* were finishing off the remnants of the last sacrifice.

Quintus gave a wintry smile. *No Marcus, no more sacrifices.* Decimus hadn't taken that into his calculations. Not that lack of food would make much difference—eating wasn't vital to ghosts, it merely alleviated their boredom.

An owl's hoot, wafting in through the atrium's open roof, suited his melancholy. As he drifted from room to room, noting that little

Secundia had forgotten her hairbrush and that one of the boys had left a dirty toga crumpled on the floor, he wondered if things would ever return to the way they'd been. He hadn't realised quite how much he depended on his ordered existence until Decimus came along and upturned everything.

Far from the altruism the ghost claimed, a wish to free others so they could complete their journey to the afterlife, it was clear that what really drove him were hurt, anger, and revenge. Why should Decimus care about Marcus and his family when they had never cared about him? But knowing what drove the newest of the *Lemures* didn't bring Quintus any closer to stopping him. Which brought him face to face with a bitter truth. A *Lar*'s responsibility was to protect the house and family. And so far he had done a lousy job.

A splintering sound made him turn. It was coming from the exit that gave access onto the Via Aurelia. As he floated over to investigate, the door burst open, and two cloaked figures surged through. One carried a crowbar, which he had evidently used on the door, his companion was holding a couple of large sacks. Behind them floated their respective *genii*.

The intruders shucked their cloaks, revealing shabby tunics—less restrictive than togas if you were intending to do a spot of housebreaking. The taller man had pocked cheeks and a shock of bright red hair. His shorter companion was balding, and his belly strained the seams of his grubby tunic.

"Sorry about this," called one of the *genii*, looking sheepish. "I tried to put him off the idea, but . . ." He shrugged.

Vibius had come up beside Quintus. His shout of "Uninvited guests!" brought the other *Lemures*, and the *Penates* also appeared from the kitchen.

The two burglars took a sack each, then fanned out and began stalking around the house without a care in the world.

"This is all your fault," Quintus told Decimus between gritted teeth. "Word must have got out that Marcus was taking his family to the country."

Decimus shrugged. "He should have asked someone to keep an eye on the place."

"And get pinched black and blue for his pains?"

The ugly ghost ignored Quintus's sarcasm. He was watching the burglars opening iron-bound chests, jewel cases, and cabinets. They curled their lips at Marcus's books and the wax masks of his ancestors but tipped the jewellery into their sacks.

Quintus had to do something. He rushed at the red-headed burglar, concentrated hard, then pushed the man's chest. The man let out a surprised "Oof" and sat down.

A plucking at his tunic made Quintus turn. The burglar's *genius* was trying to draw him away from his charge. "Leave Manius alone."

"Ooh, I love a good fight," called Decimus. Vibius and Drusilla backhanded one another in the ribs and grinned.

"Get off me." Quintus pushed the guardian spirit away.

"Watch out!" called Claudia, just as the red-headed burglar's arm accidentally swiped through the space occupied by Quintus's midriff. He gasped and doubled over, trying not to retch.

"What is it, Manius?" The balding burglar in the grubby tunic looked up from examining one of Julia's heavy twisted gold snake bangles.

"I think the damned *Lar* just knocked me over."

"Ignore him," advised his companion, popping the bangle in his sack with a satisfied grunt. "We'll be out of here soon."

But a belligerent Manius scanned the atrium for the Lararium and strode towards it. "Even a household god doesn't push me over and get away with it, Servius."

He swept the sacrifices from the little shrine dedicated to Quintus, then picked up the statue of the dancing boy, popped it in his sack, and headed for the dining room.

"Sorry," called Manius's *genius*.

The nausea had faded and Quintus straightened in relief then headed for the dining room, where the red-headed man had turned his nose up at the spoons but taken the silver salt-shaker Marcus and Julia had received from her parents as a wedding gift.

Next stop for the burglar was the kitchen. The *Penates* were hovering anxiously by the unlit hearth when Quintus joined them. Manius was peering into the larder, eyeing the shelves. It was well known that some householders hid valuables in flour sacks.

Quintus surged towards the burglar. But once again the burglar's guardian spirit tried to protect his charge.

"Don't touch him!"

"A *Lar* is entitled to defend his house."

"And if he messes with the store cupboard," chimed in Gallio, "we're entitled to defend it too."

"All right." The reluctant *genius* stood aside. "But don't hurt him badly."

Quintus lunged, focussing his energy and hitting Manius in the kidneys with his fists. With a shout of surprise, the red-headed man fell forward, reaching hands pulling down a shelf, and the sacks upon it. Some were open, and clouds of white flour billowed everywhere.

It was too much for the *Penates*, they dodged past Quintus and began slapping the burglar around the face. "Stop wrecking our larder."

Manius raised a hand to protect himself and yelled, "It was an accident." He struggled to his feet and ran, almost knocking over his companion, who had come to investigate the yelling.

Servius gaped at Manius's flour-spattered hair and tunic. "What happened?"

"*Penates.*"

The plump man sighed. "What is it with you and household gods?"

The *Lemures* floated up. "Having fun?" asked Decimus with a wide grin.

Quintus turned on him. "No wonder you never got married, or had any children. You may look young now, but inside you're still just a dried up old cripple with no family feelings."

Decimus's eyes flashed. "Mind your own business."

"It's odd, don't you think," continued the *Lar*, unable to stop his tongue now it had decided to run away with him, "that you should end up here. Maybe the gods decided you still had something to learn, hmm?"

Vibius and Drusilla looked at one another.

"And what might that be?" asked Decimus. "*Do* tell."

"By Jupiter, don't you get it?" asked Quintus. "Without adversity, how can anyone learn resourcefulness and endurance? How can they appreciate the good if they don't experience the bad? You're here to *help* Marcus and his family, not make their lives so bad they flee."

For the first time since his arrival, the ugly ghost seemed at a loss for words.

A loud crash followed by the sound of stamping feet made everyone turn and head back to the atrium.

"Hey!" Vibius tugged his earlobe in agitation. "Look what he's done."

Manius had swept the statues and offerings out of the *Penates'* alcove—the plaque on which figures danced lay in fragments on the tiled floor. And whether accidentally or on purpose, he had wrecked the shrine to the *Lemures* too.

Servius gave his companion an appalled glance. "Idiot!"

Decimus's expression was thunderous as he took in the carnage. With a shout, he lunged towards the burglars. Vibius and Drusilla exchanged a gleeful glance and followed him.

For the next ten minutes the three ghosts threw everything they had at Manius and Servius. Fevers and chills racked the burglars, pinches turned them black and blue, and objects lurched into the air then came crashing down on their heads. The sacks upended themselves, dumping their booty onto the atrium's mosaic floor.

The intruders' *genii* tried to save their charges from the worst, but when the *Lemures* are on the warpath, there is little anyone can do. In the end, the guardian spirits decided that their best course was to flee. They tugged at Manius and Servius's tunics, eventually managing to pull the now terrified and battered burglars through the splintered doorway out into the street.

The sound of running footsteps had faded into the distance, when Quintus turned to regard the smiling, panting *Lemures*.

"On behalf of Marcus and the family, thank you."

Claudia clapped. Gallio joined in. "Yes, thank you," they chorused.

"I didn't do it for you or the stupid family," protested Decimus. "They wrecked our shrine." But there was a light in his eyes that hadn't been there before.

Could this be a turning point? Quintus tried not to get his hopes up.

Decimus patted his paunch. "That was fun." He gave his fellow *Lemures* a thoughtful glance. "Maybe we could hang around here for a bit longer."

"What about the Underworld?" objected Drusilla.

The ugly ghost shrugged. "It's not going anywhere, is it?" He turned and looked Quintus in the eye. "You know, when you were lecturing me earlier, something occurred to me. Maybe the gods sent me here to teach you a lesson too."

Quintus opened his mouth to ridicule Decimus's suggestion, then closed it again. Suppose he was right?

"The way I see it," continued Decimus, "I may have been too hard on the family, but you've been far too soft."

Quintus swallowed and considered that idea for a long bitter moment. Had he become a little smug, a little complacent in recent years? Had his orderly regime been more about his own comfort than the good of the family? *What kind of a Lar am I?*

He cleared his throat twice before the words would come out. "Let's suppose for a moment that you're right. What do you suggest we do about it?"

"Simple. We need a new regime."

Quintus blinked. But if it meant some of the house's former harmony was restored . . . He sighed. "Very well."

"Splendid!" Decimus beamed at him. "I suggest we get the details of our new agreement ironed out before the *genii* and *junos* come back and want to stick their oars in."

Heads bobbed in agreement. Quintus gestured Decimus to continue.

"First," Decimus ticked the point off on a ghostly finger, "I propose that we three," he nodded at Vibius and Drusilla, "go back to inflicting milder torments on the family . . . But we must occasionally be allowed to inflict stronger ones."

To see little Secundia suffering even slightly was something Quintus always hated. But they couldn't go back to the way things had been. "Agreed." He thought for a moment and saw a glimmer of light in the darkness. "I suggest once a year."

Decimus frowned.

"No, no, once a month," said Vibius.

The *Penates* had been listening to both sides, and now Gallio stepped in. "How about once every six months?"

If Quintus was any judge, these negotiations were going to be torturous, not to mention protracted. But if a *Lar* had one thing it was plenty of time.

"Once every six months sounds fair," he agreed. "Next?"

AFTERWORD

Fantasy stories set in Ancient Rome inevitably focus on the major gods in the pantheon (Jupiter, Mars, Mercury etc.) rather than minor deities. For a change I wanted to shift the focus to the personal gods that Roman citizens sacrificed to daily in their own homes.

DOG AND KAT

DOG

Mistress is staring at the wall again. It's not as if it's even activated. All she does is stare at nothing and rock, and light an endless chain of those foul white sticks. She's been like this for weeks.

The room reeks of smoke; it drowns out all the other scents. Well, almost. There are still traces of cleaning chemicals in the carpet, and no matter how hard the maid scrubs, she can't eradicate my own smell from my basket and blanket. I sniff, searching for my favourite scent, that unique combination of salt, sweet, and sour that is Mistress.

I don't remember what my real mother smelt like. It's years since I was taken from her and my siblings, since the people in white coats altered me. Mistress is my mother and pack leader now.

Tired of being ignored, I leave my basket and trot across the room towards her. I nose the hand lying limply in her lap and lick first her palm and then her long fingers—they taste of salt.

She puts aside the keyboard and reaches for me. Her fingers trail through my fur, causing tingles of pleasure. I whine softly and wag my tail to show my happiness. If only it could always be like this . . .

The door opens, and Master walks in accompanied by the cloud of acrid fumes he calls aftershave. Mistress stops stroking me and turns towards him. I go back to my basket, curl up, and rest my muzzle on my paws.

He frowns at her. "You can't go on like this, Heather."

Her eyes are dull. "What am I supposed to do, Robert? How can I paint when I know the critics are waiting for me to fuck up?" Tiredness radiates from her. I growl softly at him, warning him, but he ignores me.

"You mean 'critic,' don't you?" He sighs. "Would it have hurt to pretend to be flattered by Roarke's attentions, to let him down lightly?"

"The little turd disgusts me. How could I hide that?"

He stares at her for a long moment. "Anyway," he continues, "you've been blocked before. You got through it in the end."

Abruptly, she stands up, knocking over her chair. "You couldn't give a fuck about me, could you?" I shrink down in my basket. "All you care about is what my work will fetch. God forbid the goose that lays the golden eggs should stop laying!"

Master's face remains expressionless. "You know that isn't true, Heather." He shrugs. "But if we're talking about caring . . . all you really care about is being able to paint. I have no illusions."

She glares at him, her fists bunching.

"Shout at me, by all means," he continues calmly. "Or take it out on Boy. But that won't get past your block. You ought to know that by now."

Mistress rights her chair and sits down again. She looks thoughtful. I relax, thankful her rage has dissipated as quickly as it came.

Master rests a hand gently on her shoulder. "You need someone to inspire you. It worked last time."

She looks up at him. "Any suggestions?"

He shrugs. "Check your e-mail messages. They've been building up . . ."

While Mistress reaches for her keyboard, he crosses to my basket and crouches. I let him scratch the spot behind my ears.

"Don't," mutters Mistress, and immediately he withdraws his hand and stands up.

The wall's activation makes my skin prickle and my fur try to rise, as always. It has pictures and writing on it now. Some of the words are strange or too complicated for me, but "Artist" I recognize. Mistress is an artist.

"This one's from the ArtNet." There is a note of interest in Mistress's voice. "They want an interview. Hmmm. The programme director's an unknown: Kathryn Morrison."

Her fingers tap the keyboard. A picture of a young woman appears on the wall; short dark fur covers her head, and she's dressed in blue. "Recently moved here . . . lots of gay topics in her CV . . . I wonder . . ."

Mistress turns her head toward Master. "What do you think, Robert? She'd probably be flattered by the attention of a celebrity, wouldn't she?" She smiles.

"I told you something would turn up," he says, smiling too.

KAT

"Up the stairs to the top. First on your left," says a husky female voice from a speaker in the hall wall beside me.

I heft the bulky case and start up the stairs, looking round for anything that might prove useful in the coming interview—such as the fact that this house screams money . . . On the first landing I pause to peer at a painting in an ornate gilt frame. An original! What will the Brookfields do with it when they get bored?

On the next landing is the usual vid-wall, currently displaying "Timescape for the New Century," the work that made Heather Brookfield's name when it was shown at the Exhibition of the Millennium, ten years ago. As I stare, it fades, and is replaced by another piece of com-art, a more modern Brookfield.

"Are you lost, Ms Morrison?"

I look up the stairwell to see a woman's upside-down face peering down at me. I feel myself redden. Caught gawping like a fan! "Sorry." I hurry up the remaining steps.

At the top I come face to face with my subject. She's older than the woman in the library footage. The immaculate make-up can't quite hide the tracery of fine lines around her eyes, and there are strands of silver in her long blond hair.

At her side stands a large black Labrador. It sniffs at me suspiciously, then, embarrassingly, thrusts its wet nose into my crotch. She clicks a finger and thumb at it. "Leave her alone, Boy."

Obediently, the dog turns, trots along the landing, and disappears through a doorway.

Then her eyes, which are a very pale blue, are assessing me.

So this is what it's like to be an artist's model, I think, feeling her gaze travel over every inch of me. I am suddenly acutely aware of my scuffed boots and the fact that my old jeans could do with a wash. I'm strapped for cash, so anything not visible on camera is low priority. At least my new blouse is presentable.

The blue eyes release me, and I find I can breathe again.

"Hello, I'm Heather Brookfield," she says, her smile revealing even white teeth. She gives me a firm handshake then turns and walks towards the doorway the dog went through. "My studio's this way."

I follow close behind her, watching the movement of her well-muscled calves below the hem of her crimson kimono, recalling the various stories I've heard about her.

According to my ArtNet colleagues, Heather Brookfield has had no shortage of lovers of either sex. And I can quite believe it—physical attraction is tugging at me like a magnet. There are other more disturbing stories, though. Like the time her wealthy husband beat her dog to death in a fit of jealous rage . . .

She stops inside the studio door and waits while I look round. The room smells of cigarettes—something only those who can afford protective gene therapy indulge in these days. It is large and airy, the wide open blinds allowing sunlight to pour through the large windows. On the wall is a huge vid-screen, inactive at the moment, and in front of it, on a table, the keyboard, electronic palettes, and brushes which she must use to "paint" her com-art.

"I thought this room would suit your cameras best," she says. She directs me to one of the two easy chairs and sits on the other, her kimono sliding slightly open with a murmur of silk. I try not to look at the expanse of thigh it reveals.

"Is that what you'll be wearing?" I ask carefully.

Heather looks surprised, then glances down at herself. She throws back her head and laughs throatily. "My God . . . You must think . . ." She gets up and strides from the room.

This interview isn't turning out at all like I'd imagined.

I start to unpack my case. I've brought along three microcams—for long shots, close-ups, and question- and reaction-shots. Carefully, I place them on the carpet and activate each in turn, tapping the commands into the master keypad. The microcams lurch into the air and hover, humming faintly, looking like giant metallic insects. Something in a large basket in the far corner moves in response. Startled, I glance at it. The Labrador is on its feet, its brown eyes fixed on the nearest microcam, its hackles raised. It starts to growl, deep in its throat.

"Easy, boy," I say quickly. "It won't hurt you." I can't afford to injure my subject's pet or lose an expensive camera.

Much to my relief, the growl stops, and the dog sinks back onto its haunches. Eying one another warily, we wait for Heather to return.

This time, she's wearing an expensively cut, emerald green dress which flatters her. "Will this do?" she asks, twirling around, the dress flaring out over her long legs.

"It's fine." I wonder briefly if she is flirting with me. "Um, maybe we should get rid of the dog . . . these seem to upset him." I nod at the microcams hovering beside me.

She glances at the Labrador, then back at me. "Did you tell him not to worry?"

I nod.

"Then he'll be fine. We had Boy genetically enhanced, Ms Morrison. He understands simple things." The Labrador whines softly at her words then rests its muzzle on its paws.

Genetically enhanced? One of the benefits of having an outrageously rich husband! Not that Heather has done too badly herself—these days her work commands impressive prices.

"Right," I say. "Shall we get started?"

Heather sits down and smoothes her dress over her knees. I instruct the microcams to move into standard configuration and try to ignore the lens trained on my own face. Heather's gaze seems to make it more difficult than usual to concentrate.

I ease her in gently, flattering her a little, recapping her history for the viewers. Then I get straight to the point. "Ms Brookfield, when can our viewers expect a new work from you? It's been over a year since the highly acclaimed 'Fractals in Indigo and Tangerine.'"

Heather smiles. "I'm about to start a new piece, untitled as yet. But I'd rather not say any more at the moment." Her eyes are suddenly opaque.

"I'm sure we'd be interested in anything you can tell us . . ." I begin.

"It's really much too early to talk about it," she insists, smiling, yet managing to convey steely resistance.

"That's fine, I understand." Smoothly, I switch to a more congenial topic. "Is it true that the President was so taken with an earlier piece of yours, she programmed every vid-wall in the White House to display it for well over a year?"

Heather relaxes and begins to tell an amusing anecdote . . .

At last I decide to call it a wrap. The microcams settle gently to the floor, their activity lights winking out.

"Is that it?"

I nod. "Thank you, Ms Brookfield."

She gets up and stretches. The dog gets to its feet too, but, when Heather continues to ignore it, lies down again.

As I start to pack my equipment away, she gazes quizzically at me.

"When is the interview likely to be transmitted, Kathryn? . . . I may call you Kathryn?"

I try not to show surprise at her request. "Of course." I press the last microcam safely into its moulded slot and click the case latches firmly shut. "Probably tomorrow night. There's the editing to do, but that won't take me long."

Her gaze is unsettling. "I really would love to see your latest work," I find myself saying impulsively, and then, remembering her reaction during the interview, wish I hadn't.

Her reply disconcerts me. "And I'd love to show it to you." The ghost of a smile curves her lips. "But not until it's finished."

We gaze at each other, an assessing, speculative gaze which sets my pulse racing, then her eyes flicker towards the doorway behind me. I turn. A distinguished-looking man in a dark business suit is standing there. He must have been handsome once, I think, but too much good living has softened his jaw and thickened his waistline, and his grey hair is receding fast. How long has he been watching us?

He smiles easily and steps forward, hand outstretched. "I'm Robert Brookfield, Heather's husband. You must be from ArtNet. Got everything you need?"

I nod. "Kathryn Morrison." We shake hands; his grip is limp.

He places a kiss on his wife's forehead. "Everything going as planned, darling?"

"Fine," she says, glancing at me.

I stand up. "Well, I'm sure you're very busy, Ms Brookfield—"

"Call me Heather," she says.

"Um, Heather. So I'll let you get on." I reach for my case.

She murmurs something I can't catch to her husband and comes towards me. "Let me show you to the front door, Kathryn."

As we descend the stairs, she walks closer to me than is strictly necessary. I'm acutely aware of her, of the mixed scent of freesias and stale cigarettes she exudes.

At the front door she touches my arm. "I hope you and I can become close friends, Kathryn." Her gaze is frank. I find I am holding my breath again. "You have my private number. Will you call me? We can meet somewhere that suits you. Not here, of course . . . A time that suits you . . ."

Her gaze holds mine until I look away. This is happening too fast. "Of course," I murmur awkwardly. "I'd like us to be friends too."

DOG

Mistress is pacing up and down, looking at the phone every few minutes. She smells edgy. I'm edgy too; I haven't been out for my walk today, and my muscles are itching. She's totally unaware of me, focussed on the phone. I rest my head on my paws and stare at her.

The phone rings and she snatches up the receiver. "Hello?" Her shoulders relax. "I'm really glad it's you . . . Yes, I meant what I said. Now? . . . How about the park? I was just going to take Boy for his walk."

My ears prick up at the mention of my name.

"Okay, I'll meet you there in five minutes." She puts down the receiver. "That's good," she mutters. "I was beginning to wonder . . ."

She turns to me and clicks her fingers. I bound towards her and she stoops and runs her fingers through my neck fur. I pant at her and wag my tail. She attaches my lead.

Mistress is in a hurry; she won't let me stop at my usual lampposts and trees, or snarl at the two mangy cats from number 10. But she is happy and excited, so my disappointment soon passes. I bounce along beside her, feeling full of energy.

We turn in through the park gate, and I immediately spot the woman from yesterday. She is wearing blue jeans and a thick black jacket with the collar turned up, and is frowning at her boots as she walks up and down. She looks up and sees us, and a smile lights up her face. She hurries towards us, then stops awkwardly, her hands twisting, nervousness exuding from her pores.

Mistress grins, leans forward, and kisses her on the cheek. The woman blushes. "You're shaking, Kathryn," says Mistress. "Is it the cold?" Her voice is teasing.

"I wasn't sure you'd . . ." The woman clears her throat and tries again. "I'd begun to think I imagined . . ." Her voice peters out.

Mistress slips an arm through hers. "Let's walk."

She releases me from the leash, and I dash from one end of the park to the other, revelling in my freedom. I look for other dogs to impress, but there's only one, an ancient and incontinent cocker spaniel, and he's more interested in sniffing territorial markers and making his own replacements than in anything more intellectual. I leave him to his dull pursuits and search for Mistress.

She is walking slowly across the park, her arm round the other woman's waist. They are deep in conversation, their faces so close they are almost touching.

I run huge circles round the two of them until Mistress laughs and says I'm making her dizzy. She picks up a stick and throws it for me. I take it back to her as quickly as I can and drop it at her feet, but by then she has lost interest in me. She is kissing the other woman on the mouth.

Panting, I sit and watch them, waiting for their attention. At last they pull apart, gasping a little.

"Your place?" murmurs Mistress.

The other woman nods.

KAT

From the start Heather questions me closely about my life, my thoughts, my feelings . . . It is flattering to be the focus of her attention. Being involved with an interviewee like this probably breaks all the rules, but somehow I don't give a damn. I'm intoxicated by her, in a state of constant euphoria.

It takes a conscious effort not to let my work suffer. During one interview in the ArtNet studio, a voice in my earpiece jolts me back to attention after a pause has gone on longer than it should have. I was daydreaming about Heather, of course.

I rearrange my schedule so that my afternoons are free—it's the only time she can get away without her husband becoming suspicious, she says. On afternoons when she isn't with me I itch for the phone to ring, for her to say she's coming over and will be here soon. And when she arrives she always has with her the black Labrador she calls Boy—her alibi, she explains, in case Robert should ask where she went.

I've never felt like this about anyone before, and I want to tell the world about us. But she won't let me.

Boy is in the dining room, chewing on a marrow bone I bought especially for him. We are in my bedroom, otherwise engaged.

"If Robert were to find out how I feel about you . . ." says Heather, putting a cigarette to her mouth with one hand and using the other on me.

I try to keep my mind on what she is saying and not what she is doing to me—it isn't easy. "They say he's extremely jealous."

She considers that for a moment. "'Proprietorial' might be a better description. Easily hurt too—you'd be surprised."

I am. It doesn't sound much like the Robert Brookfield of the rumours.

"But enough about him." She turns her head away, breathes out a stream of smoke, and stubs out her cigarette. Then she rolls towards me. "Do you like it when I do this, Kathryn?"

She laughs as the noise in the back of my throat makes it perfectly clear that I do . . .

Later, after I have made love to her in return, I close my eyes, sleepy after our exertions. The mattress bounces as she sits up. Strange how making love always seems to energize her. I force open my heavy eyelids and watch her pull on her clothes—something smart and expensive, as usual.

"Are you going? Already?" I ask drowsily.

She leans across and kisses me, her mouth tasting as always of cigarettes. "I'm going to paint for a few hours. Go to sleep."

DOG

Mistress is delighted with her "work," and so is Master.

"It's developing really well, Heather," he tells her. "It may turn out to be one of your best yet. Looks like you picked an excellent 'muse' this time."

Mistress smells happy, excited. It's hard to remember that just a short while ago she was in the depths of misery. My tail thumps loudly on the floor.

"It's not bad, is it? I'm thinking of calling it 'Night Petals in Scarlet and Gold.' What do you think?"

He sips his drink and tilts his head to one side, gazing at the wall.

I stare at it too, at the red stripes and whorls, the blotches and streaks of gold, wishing I could see it through their eyes. But it's no use. It means nothing to me. Perhaps if Mistress painted things like cats and dogs, trees and slippers, bones and baskets . . . I whimper softly, but she glances at me and puts a finger to her lips.

"Night Petals," he muses. "A hint of the exotic, the erotic . . . I like that." He looks at her. "Is there much left to do?"

She shakes her head.

"Because I need a definite date for GalleryNet. Their director saw that interview you did for your little ArtNet 'friend,' and he's been pestering me for details of this new piece ever since. Says he's already provisionally cleared a slot in his exhibition pages for it. He's offering a premium price."

She shrugs. "Two days at the most."

He nods and turns away. Then he stops and looks back at her. "When the painting's finished . . . you will leave her, won't you?" I can smell anxiety.

"Of course," says Mistress. "Don't I always?"

KAT

"Look. What does it matter what anyone else thinks? As long as you are happy with your work . . ."

Heather looks scornfully at me. "Don't be so naive, Kathryn. Of course it matters. Critics can make or break an artist. And Roarke has got it in for me . . ."

I frown at her, puzzled. "Why?"

Her eyes are evasive. "It doesn't matter."

This is not how or where we usually spend our afternoons. But the previous tenant perversely refused to install a vid-screen in my flat, and I can't afford the equipment and connection fee yet. Heather's studio has a huge state-of-the-art vid-screen.

I stare at the pages of the ArtCrit Website that it is currently displaying. A miniature version of "Night Petals In Scarlet and Gold" has pride of place. She released it to the GalleryNet yesterday afternoon, and since then has been fidgety. I don't know why she's so worried. Most of the critics seem to like it:

"A brilliant return to form for Brookfield . . ."

"'Night Petals in Scarlet and Gold' is a potent abstract metaphor for our times . . ."

Only Roarke hasn't turned in his copy to the Website yet. Apparently, his fame is such that he can take his time, keep an artist sweating. Heather has bitten her fingernails nearly down to the quick.

At least she's sat down at last. Her constant pacing was making me dizzy, not to mention wearing out the carpet.

"Maybe if you stroked Boy, it would calm you down?" I suggest.

Black floppy ears prick up eagerly, and for a moment I'm tempted to cross to Boy's basket and stroke him myself, but he's a one mistress dog.

"For God's sake stop fussing, will you?" snaps Heather.

I sigh. This is a side of her I haven't seen before, and one I could do without. But I suppose it comes with the territory—all artists feel insecure when it comes to their work. It certainly bugs the hell out of me if an editor meddles with my final cut.

I stand behind her chair and start to knead her shoulders, feeling for the knots of tension and digging my thumbs in. She gives a grunt, part pain, part relief, and leans against me, her blonde head resting heavily against my midriff.

"Thanks," she mutters, probably as much of an apology as I'm going to get. Her gaze never leaves the screen for an instant.

A flicker of movement—more text is scrolling up, followed by the byline: Maurice A. Roarke. Heather's shoulders tense, and she inhales sharply.

As I read Roarke's words, Heather starts to moan, so low at first I can barely hear it but Boy's body is stiff with tension.

"Brookfield's latest work is self-assured, certainly—from an experienced artist what else can one expect?—but it is also empty and glib, vain posturing disguised as metaphor. It adds nothing what-soever to the canon. It is sad indeed to see a once considerable artist resting on her artistic laurels . . ."

Heather's moaning rises to a loud, high-pitched keening, and I stop reading, shaken by the sound. I hug her round the shoulders, but she stands up abruptly, shaking me off.

Already her anguish has turned into something different. Her cheeks are flushed an angry red, her eyes flash dangerously. "That bastard!"

"What does one man know," I soothe. "Everyone else likes it . . ."

"That bastard!" Her gaze flicks round the studio. I turn to watch as she darts towards a large vase made of heavy crystal and upends it, raining stale water and yellow tulips onto the carpet. In one easy motion she flings it straight at the vid-screen.

The explosion sends shards of plastic and glass everywhere, and I duck, shielding my eyes with my right forearm, feeling something sting my hand. The loud bang leaves my hearing muffled for a moment, then Heather's shouting—obscenities now—and Boy's excited barking regain their clarity.

Maybe she'll calm down now she's smashed the vid-screen, I think. But she starts to sweep her arm across her worktops and shelves, sending ashtrays and sketchbooks, pencils and printouts flying. There is an aura of madness about her, and I realize she is totally out of control.

"For God's sake, Heather!" I crouch behind a chair, rubbing the cut on my hand, then glance towards the studio door seeking a way out. I'm surprised to find it is open and Robert Brookfield is standing there.

He beckons to me. While Heather's attention is still elsewhere, I run towards him.

"Roarke's review?" he asks, as I squeeze past.

I nod, breathlessly.

"I thought this might happen." He seems to be talking to himself.

I peer over his shoulder and watch aghast as Heather, her mouth a rictus, picks up a still intact, solid glass ash tray and advances on Boy. The Labrador is cowering in his basket, shivering as though he has an ague.

"The dog!" I say. "We must get him out of there."

Robert's eyes are cold. "This is no longer your concern, Ms Morrison," he says. "Please leave."

I stare at him, aware my mouth is open. Then a canine yelp draws my gaze back to the shambolic studio. Heather is holding the ash tray high above her head; in the sunshine streaming through the blinds, glass glistens wet and crimson, and the wall behind Boy's basket is spattered with what looks like red paint . . .

I try to push past Robert, but his arm is rigid, blocking the way.

"Let me through. Don't you see? She's killing Boy!"

But he refuses to move. "No, Ms Morrison. Don't you see? That's what he's for. Now, for the last time, please go . . . Oh, and don't bother to come back. Heather doesn't need you anymore." There is a glint of something I can't quite interpret—relief, satisfaction?—in his eyes.

After a long moment, numbly, I turn and walk away.

DOG

At least the pain has almost gone now. I can see again, and hear too. And my sense of smell is getting stronger each day. I can't walk yet though, and my memories of a week ago are faint.

Something happened, but I'm not sure what. Something involving Mistress—something I would rather forget. Instead, I think about rabbits and kittens, walkies and bones . . .

Master came to visit me this morning. Mistress has been away, on holiday, he said, but she is back now and missing me. He was pleased with my progress, said the nano—or was it nanny?—machines inside me are repairing me even faster than last time . . .

Soon I will be able to go home. My tail thumps the floor; the noise brings the girl in the white coat who is looking after me. She places a bowl of my favourite food where I can reach it, then pushes back a lock of her long black head fur with one skinny wrist.

"Who's a good boy, then?" she says. "Eat up."

I crunch some dog biscuits between my teeth and swallow the mush. "Mistress is my mother and pack leader," I tell her happily, though I know she can't understand me. "I would follow her anywhere."

The girl nods encouragingly and watches me eat.

AFTERWORD

I wanted to try something I hadn't done before—tell a story from a dog's point of view and keep the reader guessing about what was really going on until the end. As for the plot, I had been reading about nano technology and genetic enhancements. But you can only enhance a dog's intelligence so far, and the thing about pets is that they love you no matter how badly you treat them . . .

THE CREATURE IN THE CUT

"WHAT'S UP?" CALLED Rose, as her husband came striding towards the narrowboat, his normally amiable face grim.

He leaped across the gap between the lock and the *Friendship*, and joined her by the tiller. "Alf says the Echo's blocked."

She glanced to where the lock-keeper, in his battered hat, waistcoat, knee-breeches, and gaiters, was walking towards the lock gates. "What happened? Did the roof cave in?" And if so, how were they going to get their cargo delivered on time?

"Alf doesn't think so." Mike grimaced. "But something's up. The *Elizabeth* was the last boat through, and she came out half wrecked, eight hours after she should have, and not under her own steam either."

Rose's brows drew together. There was no towpath inside the half-mile long Echo tunnel, and the rock bottom was too smooth for any shafting pole to gain purchase. Crews had to lie on their backs on the wing-like legging boards and walk the seventy-foot-long narrowboats through, boot after boot, along slimy walls. "What do you mean?"

"The current from the lock must have flushed her through."

"Isn't the *Elizabeth* the Tooleys' boat?" Jenny was standing on the lock side, Woof prancing at her heels.

"Yes." Mike gave their eight-year-old daughter a pointed look. "I thought you were keeping an eye on Hilda."

Jenny pouted but wandered back to the ageing mule, which was investigating the contents of the nosebag Mike had made from an old tin bowl and some straps and buckles.

Mike lowered his voice and continued. "Bill Tooley's dead, Rose. Ron too."

Her hand flew to her mouth. "Poor Stella!" The other woman would have walked her boathorse, Cobber, over the top while her husband and son legged the *Elizabeth* through. Rose could imagine her arriving at the other end of the tunnel and waiting for her family's boat to emerge. And when at last it did . . . "Were the bodies," she swallowed, "badly mangled?"

"There was no sign of any bodies, only bloodstains all over the legging boards."

She gripped his arm. "Then they could still be in the tunnel, Mike! Injured."

He shook his head. "Jack and Tom Littlemore legged the *Endeavour* in and found nothing. Mind you, they only went part way through." He ran a hand through his curly black hair and avoided her gaze. "Jack claimed he could hear something splashing and wheezing in there. Some kind of . . . creature. He reversed out again sharpish."

"Are you serious?"

Brown eyes met hers. "Ever known the Littlemores to joke about something like that?"

She shook her head. "But Alf Gamble might."

They both glanced to where Alf was preparing to turn the windlass. The old lock-keeper gestured enquiringly, and Rose nodded.

"Jenny," she called. "We're going through now, love. Take Hilda on down the Cut a little way, will you."

"OK, Mum." Jenny began to undo Hilda's tether.

Rose turned back to her husband. "Alf must have got it wrong about the Tooleys."

"Maybe. But he wouldn't lie about the tunnel being blocked."

She bit her lip. "What are we going to do?" The lock gates creaked open and the water level began to drop, taking the *Friendship* with it.

"Not a lot we *can* do." Mike glanced over the side to check their progress. "Except moor alongside the others waiting to go through and find out the facts." He frowned. "If the Echo really *is* blocked, we'll have to unload the timber and hire someone to take it by road."

Rose rested her hand on the tiller and steadied the boat as it floated out of the lock. "That's going to cost." Already they were losing momentum, and she steered towards the bank.

"At least our cargo isn't perishable," said Mike.

Rose turned and saw Jenny skipping along the towpath towards them. At her side walked the mule, still munching, and behind them bounded Woof.

Mike leaped onto the bank, caught the rope Rose threw him, and waited for the mule to arrive. While he reattached the towrope to

Hilda's harness, Jenny scrambled on board. Her dog curled up under the three-legged stool Rose kept beside the tiller.

"Ready?" called Mike, straightening. Rose nodded.

He slapped Hilda's rump, and she planted her hooves, leaned into her collar, and staggered forward a few steps. The sagging towrope snapped taut, and the *Friendship* began to move, sluggishly at first, but gathering speed as Hilda settled into her stride.

Rose steered away from the bank, forcing herself to think about anything except what might have happened to the Tooleys. It was a sunny day, and the Cut was calm as a millpond. Mike whistled as he trudged beside Hilda's head, and somewhere in the hedgerow a blackbird trilled. The column of black smoke to the north had diminished to a wisp of faint grey—whatever had been on fire for the last two days must be out.

There were no bridges on this stretch of the canal; in fact it was plain sailing to the Echo. She checked her watch. *Time to get that rabbit stew in the oven.* "Take over for a bit, will you, love?"

Jenny hopped up onto the stool and accepted the tiller from her mother. And with a "Call me when we get there," Rose ducked down the step into the cabin.

"WHERE IS STELLA now?" Rose replaced her teacup in its saucer.

Marge Beauchamp stubbed out her cigarette before answering. "Gone to stay with her sister, poor thing."

The two boatwomen were sitting in the smoke-filled cabin of the Beauchamps' *Gertrude*, moored with the other narrowboats at the mouth of the Echo. Their men had gone to The Boatman's Arms, which was only a hundred yards from the Cut. As for their children, Marge's two were grown up and no longer travelled with her, while Jenny was on the *Friendship*, practising her reading by poring over an old newspaper she had found blowing on the towpath.

Thoughts of Stella's overwhelming loss made Rose wince. "I don't know what I'd do if I lost Mike or Jenny." *Losing Alby was hard enough.*

"Me neither." Marge made a face. "Though Bert can be a trial at times."

Rose laughed. "Can't they all?" She sobered. "So no one's been through since the Littlemores tried?"

"No." The other woman fingered a doily she had made; she was renowned for her crocheting. "Everyone's pretending it's out of respect, but the truth is, Rose, they're scared."

"Do you believe what Jack Littlemore said then . . . about there being a creature?"

"It's not just what he said, Rose." Marge looked up. "They found a trail leading to the far end of the tunnel."

"What kind of trail?"

"Crushed grass and that. Like something big dragged itself that way." Her friend looked troubled. "And then there's the *Elizabeth*. Me and Bert walked over the top to take a look at what's left of her." Her gaze flicked towards Rose then away again. "It certainly looks like something attacked her."

Rose frowned. "Shouldn't we tell the Authority? Let them sort it out?"

Marge snorted. "Can't see that happening, can you?"

She sighed. Boatmen tried to avoid contacting the Authority about anything. Once invited in, it wasn't always easy to get rid of them, and red tape could tie up a narrowboat, or more importantly its cargo, for weeks.

"Which reminds me," said Marge, glancing at her, "have you decided whether to send Jenny to the new school at Marshbury yet?"

The Authority had converted a barge and moored it at Marshbury wharf. For boat children only, there'd be no bullying and derision from classmates "on the bank," and boarding during term time meant no missing of vital lessons. It would be much better for Jenny than the "lesson here, lesson there" education she was getting from the various schools along the Cut—luckily her daughter soaked up facts like a sponge.

"She wants to go. But Mike says it's a waste of time and anyway, Jenny's too useful a pair of hands about the boat." She mimicked her husband. "'What was good enough for us, Rose, is good enough for her.'"

"He's got a point."

Rose looked at her friend. Like Rose, Marge could barely read or write, and though she could count, she had trouble with big numbers. "I can't swim," she said pointedly, "but I've made sure Jenny can." *If only I'd done the same for Alby.*

"Maybe Mike just doesn't want to be parted from her, especially after . . ." The words "losing his son" hung unspoken between them.

"Maybe," said Rose. "But it's Jenny I'm thinking of."

Rose wished the Authority had made attendance at the new school compulsory. She would never dream of approaching an official behind Mike's back, but if one were to approach her . . . She still had her doubts, of course. Education was a double-edged sword. In the long run, Jenny might decide she preferred life on the bank to life on the boat, grow to regard her illiterate parents as an embarrassment—

Marge grunted. "Anyway, I'm sure Bert and the others will come up with some way to deal with the creature in the tunnel." She reached for the teapot. "Another cuppa?"

Rose nodded and watched her pour. "Let's hope it still makes sense when they sober up."

"NASTY BUSINESS." MIKE kept his voice low so as not to wake their daughter, who was sleeping on the other side of the curtain.

"What have you decided?" Rose raised herself on one elbow and looked at him.

He sat on the edge of the fold-down cross bed and unlaced his boots. "To pour lamp oil down the airshafts and set light to it." He unbuttoned his trousers and stepped out of them, then stripped off his waistcoat and shirt. She admired the play of lamplight on his muscles. "That ought to scare it out."

"Was that your idea?" Mike's grin was smug as he clambered into bed next to her. "Thought so." She clasped his arm. "Jenny's sound asleep," she whispered. "I don't think anything will disturb her."

Her husband kissed her. His mouth tasted of beer, but it wasn't unpleasant. "Let's find out."

"A FINE DAY for it," came a shout from the *Perseverance*. Laura Ward was pegging her washing on a line strung from bow to stern.

Rose waved at her, sighing as she couldn't help contrasting the younger woman's trim figure against her own broadening hips. It was indeed a fine day, she thought, glancing up at the cloudless sky then towards the towpath where Mike and the other boatmen, including thirteen-year-old Tom Littlemore, were in a huddle, clutching jerricans of lamp oil.

Hard to remember that only two days ago, not far from here, Bill and Ron Tooley died, and the thing that killed them is still lurking in the tunnel.

Jenny looked up from scratching Woof's belly. "Can I go with them?"

Rose gave a grudging nod. It should be safe enough on top of the Echo. "But I'll come with you." She could do with stretching her legs. "And put Woof on a lead. We don't want him getting under people's feet."

"Thanks, Mum."

The path over the top had been well trodden by boatmen and horses over the years and after the initial pull was relatively easy going. Fifty yards in, the four men left the path and headed to the tunnel's crest and the first of the airshafts sunk to keep the air sweet. Rose and her daughter followed, Woof straining against the rope knotted to his collar.

"We don't know how far in this thing is," Mike was saying, as he set down his jerrican next to a round hole, two feet across and protected by a low metal rim. "So we'll start here and work our way along."

Tom searched around for a pebble and chucked it down the shaft. Seconds later, Rose heard a distant echoey splash.

Jack Littlemore glared at his freckle-faced son. "Don't do that!"

"Why not, Dad? We want to scare it out, don't we, not kill it where it is?"

"He's got a point," said Dave Ward, who was badly in need of a haircut. "Last thing we want is its carcass blocking the tunnel. We'd have to go in and clear it."

"Look, Mum." Rose turned and saw that her daughter was pointing at something. "That must be the trail Mrs Beauchamp told you about."

From up here they had quite a good view. There was the Cut continuing on beyond the Echo, heading east towards Marshbury. And there was what Marge must have been referring to, a wavering line of crushed vegetation heading for the far end of the tunnel.

Whatever made it was large . . . and heavy.

"It seems to be coming from where the column of smoke was, doesn't it?"

"Yes, love. It does."

Mike unscrewed the cap, tilted the heavy can, and poured a steady stream of lamp oil down the airshaft. "Got that match, Bert?"

Marge's husband struck a match on the sole of his boot, then tossed it in. Rose grabbed her daughter's hand and tugged her back a few yards. Seconds later came a distant dull *whoomp*.

"Take that!" shouted a grinning Dave. He peered down the hole, then retreated, coughing. The air above the shaft shimmered and Rose caught an acrid whiff of burning.

Bert pushed his spectacles back up his nose. "Did we get it?"

Jack Littlemore scratched his jaw. "Doubt it, or we'd have heard something."

"Whatever it is might be mute," said Jack's son.

Mike shook his head. "Most animals make *some* kind of noise when they're injured." He picked up his can and strode towards the next airshaft. The others exchanged a glance, shrugged, then followed.

"You all right?" Rose asked her unusually silent daughter as they trudged.

"I was thinking about a map I saw once at school, Mum. It looked just like this—" Jenny's expansive gesture encompassed her surroundings, "—only from high up. A long blue line was supposed to be the Cut, and little red blobs were Marshbury and Woodton."

"Useful things, maps." *Less so when you can't read the names on them.*

Jenny nodded and smiled. "Anyway, I was just remembering. There was this blue star . . . over there." She pointed to where the smoke had arisen. "It said 'power station.' What's one of them, Mum?"

Rose thought of windmills and watermills. "Where they turn something into 'lectric, I expect."

"That's what lights the houses of people who live on the bank, right?"

"Right." She walked on a few more paces, remembering the clean, bright lights, so different from the *Friendship*'s smelly lamps. "The rich ones, anyway."

Woof yelped as a bee emerged from the foxglove bell he had been nosing. Jenny soothed him then turned back to her mother. "There was something in that newspaper I found about the power station. The science men are sper . . . exper . . ." She broke off, looking frustrated.

"Trying things out?"

Jenny gave her a relieved smile. "That's it. They've found a way to produce power out of thin air."

Rose remembered once seeing a conjuror pull a rabbit out of a hat. "That's impossible, love."

The men had stopped at the next airshaft and were pouring oil down it. This time it was Jack Littlemore who lit the match and dropped it. A loud *whoompf* was followed by a cheer. Mike shushed the others and listened intently. So did Rose but she heard no sound except the breeze, the chirping of sparrows in a gorse bush, and a distant crackle of flames that soon faded. The men exchanged disappointed glances and moved on.

"But, Mum, it was in the paper so it must be true."

Rose took Jenny's hand and started after Mike. "You can't get something for nothing, love. Stands to reason." She glanced at her daughter and sighed. Jenny had adopted an expression that reminded Rose of their mule at her most obstinate. "All right. Did they say *how* they are getting power from thin air?"

"They make a rip and suck stuff through it from another di . . . dim—" Jenny frowned. "Another place."

Rose was doubtful, but she could tell from her daughter's expression that she was serious. "Well I never! Whatever will they think of next?"

They had reached the next airshaft, and Bert was saying, as he pushed up his spectacles, "It might not even be *in* the tunnel any more. Could've fled somewhere else last night."

"There'd be another set of tracks." Mike gestured to the trail of crushed vegetation.

"Not if it went back the way it came," said Tom.

Jack looked at his son. "Why would it do that?"

Tom rubbed a ginger eyebrow. "How should I know?"

"Let's just get on, shall we?" interrupted Mike.

Jenny leaned closer to her mother. "Does Dad know what he's doing?" she whispered.

"As much as anyone else does," Rose whispered back.

But at the next airshaft, the expedition's luck suddenly changed. Jack poured the last of his jerrican's contents down the hole, and Dave pushed his hair out of his eyes and dropped a match. Almost instantly there came a noise unlike anything Rose had ever heard, a high-pitched scream, almost at the limits of her hearing. It jangled her nerves. And she wasn't the only one. Jenny's grip on her hand became painful.

"If that doesn't make it run, nothing will," said Mike, with a look of grim satisfaction.

The blood drained from Jack Littlemore's face as a thought occurred to him. "Oh no! Suppose it doubles back?" The others blinked at that then looked horrified.

"Mum!" croaked his son.

"We can't think about that now," said Mike, throwing Rose and Jenny a glance full of guilty relief that they had come with him. "We have to finish what we started. There are only a few airshafts left."

After a long tense moment, the others nodded.

"MAYBE IT'S AFRAID of daylight." Rose spooned bacon stew into bowls and handed them to Mike and Jenny. Woof cocked his shaggy head to one side, his expression pathetic. "You've already had yours." After spooning out stew for herself, she took her seat at the little table.

The men had poured oil down every single one of the Echo's airshafts, but the creature hadn't emerged . . . from either entrance. In fact after that initial weird screaming, they had heard nothing further. It must be intelligent enough to realise it would be safe between the airshafts.

Mike rubbed singed eyebrows. "We'd better moor further from the entrance and keep a watch tonight."

"OK," said Rose

But the creature didn't come out that night. Or the next.

"CARROT AND STICK." Rose spat on the iron, which gave a satisfying sizzle. She set to work on her husband's clean shirt.

Mike looked at her. "What?"

"A stick never makes Hilda move. But a carrot works wonders."

He snorted. "If the creature were hungry, it would have come out and eaten us by now."

Rose turned the shirt and started on the other sleeve. "Sometimes you have to put food right under an animal's nose. Especially if it's scared or hurt."

"You want a volunteer to leg a boat in and wait for it to take a bite?" Mike's brows rose.

"Who said anything about volunteers?" She ironed the collar. "We'll use Hilda as bait."

"And how's a mule supposed to leg a narrowboat in?"

Rose rolled her eyes, though the image of Hilda on her back, legging the *Friendship* through with her hooves, amused her. "We build a raft and tether Hilda on it, then put it in the tunnel entrance. If Alf Gamble opens the lock gates, there should be enough water coming down the Cut to float the raft inside." She folded up the shirt and reached for the next item in her laundry basket: Jenny's skirt. "When the thing in the tunnel goes after her, we haul the raft out and it follows."

Mike frowned. "Bit risky for Hilda, isn't it?"

She placed the iron on the range to reheat. "Have you got a better idea?"

Her husband's silence spoke volumes.

ROSE FINISHED BUCKLING the nose tin on Hilda then led the blindfolded mule onto the makeshift raft—four cabin hatch doors nailed and roped together, and a rickety rail erected round three of the sides. It bobbed under her feet.

"Are you sure about this?" she heard Bert Beauchamp ask her husband. "If the creature eats the mule, you'll have to buy yourself another."

Mike shrugged. "Worst comes to worst, maybe Stella will let me have Cobber cheap. A boathorse ain't much good without a boat."

Rose finished tying Hilda's tether to the railing, removed the blindfold, and stepped carefully back onto the bank. The mule looked about her, shifting uneasily until the bobbing stopped. Rose held her breath, but released it when Hilda began to munch the contents of her nose tin.

Mike pushed the raft further out into the canal with a shaft pole, while Jack Littlemore paid out several feet of the towrope they had attached to it.

A small hand slipped itself into Rose's. "Will she be all right, Mum?" asked Jenny. Woof flopped on the bank at her feet and settled his chin on her sandal.

"Hope so, love." Rose glanced at Mike. "What time did you ask Alf to open the lock gate?"

He pulled out his pocket watch. "Five minutes ago." He re-pocketed it and turned to Jack. "Ready?" The big man nodded.

For a few moments more the raft and its placidly chewing passenger remained stationary, then the extra water coming down from the lock reached them, and the raft began to move. Steadily Jack paid out more rope, the pile of coils beside his boots diminishing. Hilda's hooves clattered as she shifted, and she let out a muffled, indignant bray.

"Easy, girl," called Mike. "Easy."

Jenny's grip on Rose's hand tightened. "Suppose she tries to swim for it, Mum."

"She won't, love. Remember last summer when your dad had to pull her out?" A cobblestone shied by a townie had startled the mule off the towpath. "Ever since then, she's hated the water." Which wasn't to say, of course, that if Hilda were sufficiently panicked . . .

As the raft picked up speed, the mule spread her legs and braced herself. The craft rocked and yawed, and if the towrope hadn't damped its progress, it would probably be going in circles. As it disappeared inside the tunnel, its passenger let out one last despairing bray. Rose winced and hoped she hadn't sent Hilda to her death.

"Now we wait," said Mike.

NIGHT HAD FALLEN in earnest, bringing a chill with it. Rose yawned and moved closer to the campfire. In the distance a fox barked. She envied Jenny, snug in her bed on board the *Friendship*.

"Maybe nothing will happen tonight," said Polly Littlemore, fiddling with one of the hoop earrings she always wore. "Maybe the creature has already fled, or died of its wounds, or drowned, or something."

Jack grunted and looked at his wife. "If so, we'll all have wasted our time."

And Hilda will have spent a lonely, cold night in the tunnel for nothing, thought Rose.

Mike lit a cigarette and offered her one. She shook her head. Close by, an owl hooted. Then came an echoey muffled braying.

"Hear that?" Her husband frowned. "She sounds spooked."

There was certainly a fearful note to Hilda's braying that Rose had never heard before. The braying came again, and the hairs on the back of Rose's neck lifted at the note of terror in it.

"That does it!" Mike threw the barely smoked cigarette in the fire and stood up.

He grabbed one of the lanterns and left the warm circle of the campfire, hurrying along the bank to where he had earlier jammed a windlass handle into the earth. Rose watched him untie the towrope knotted around the metal bar, then she got to her feet and went to help.

It was slow going, hauling in the raft. The rope was rough, even on hands as callused as hers, and its recent soaking had made it heavier. But as she and Mike hauled in tandem, coiling the dripping rope onto the bank beside them, and the craft attached to the other end began to gather momentum, it became easier.

After a moment's indecision, Bert, Dave, Jack, and his son grabbed windlass handles, shovels, and shaft poles and came to join them. The women stayed by the fire, talking in low voices and casting frequent anxious glances in their direction.

"Want me to take over?" Jack asked a panting Rose. She was glad to relinquish the rope into his capable hands.

She turned to look at the tunnel mouth, just as something emerged. It was hard to make it out in the moonlight, but the panicked braying from its passenger was unmistakable. She moved closer to the edge of the bank and squinted. Hilda's tail was swishing, and she kept craning her head round to look behind her.

"She's terrified," said Rose.

"Don't stop," Mike told Jack.

"Sorry." The big man resumed his hauling.

Water lapped over Rose's shoes and she looked down at it in surprise. Surely the raft's approach wasn't enough to cause such a wash? But what else could be its source? Alf wouldn't be opening the lock gates at this time of night, and anyway the current was going in the wrong direction. She blinked and focussed on the raft once more, and had her answer.

Something large was pushing through the water behind it. Only its top few inches were visible, but they were enough to send a shiver down Rose's spine. Were those gleaming things eyes? As for those writhing, lashing tentacles reaching for Hilda . . .

Bert Beauchamp voiced the thought uppermost in everyone's mind. "What the hell is *that*?"

It was hard to tell how big the creature was. *As large as our cabin?* wondered Rose, her heart pounding. *Larger?*

Its flesh was blotchy and slightly translucent, glistening in the moonlight. As she watched, a tentacle touched Hilda and sturdy back legs lashed out. Hooves caught it a glancing blow, and the creature emitted the high-pitched screech Rose had last heard from inside the tunnel. This time there was no rock to deaden the sound, and from the campfire came shocked exclamations as the women clapped their hands over their ears and huddled together, faces pale.

After a frozen moment, Mike and Jack began to pull faster, their grunts loud in the still night air. The lapping of water against wood grew louder, and seconds later, the raft rammed into the bank, its edge splintering. Rose rushed forward, but before she could free Hilda, the mule had snapped her overstressed tether. She lunged past Rose, knocking her aside with a solid shoulder.

"Rose!" yelled Mike as she fell. Hoofbeats disappeared along the towpath and faded into the distance.

She had turned to tell him that she was all right when his lips formed a surprised "O" and water soaked her from head to foot. Cursing, and clawing wet hair from her eyes, she turned. The creature had failed to pull itself onto the bank, but as she watched it began to try again.

"Get out of there!" yelled Mike, reaching for his lantern. But Rose was already on her feet and backing away from the thing as fast as she could.

A dark shape darted past her, barking.

"Woof!"

More by luck than judgement, Rose managed to snag the mongrel's collar, almost wrenching her arm from its socket in the process. She turned her attention back to the creature, which had now succeeded in heaving itself out of the water.

Rose's terror vied with her curiosity. The creature was bigger even than the track of crushed vegetation had led her to believe and much more grotesque—all those eyes and tentacles and that maw-like hole in its midsection. Those things dangling from its back were much too insubstantial to be wings, surely, but what else could they be? She clamped down on a surge of nausea and remembered a squashed jellyfish she had seen once during a rare day trip to the seaside. *That was out of its natural element too.*

Woof barked and intensified his struggle to break free.

Light arced towards the creature, then came a tinkle of breaking glass and the oil from the thrown lantern caught fire. Flames spread rapidly over the splotchy surface, and the creature screeched. Rose gasped as Mike threw himself backwards and a lashing tentacle missed him by inches. Before it could strike again, there was a loud *clang*—Dave's shovel had crushed the tentacle to a pulp. Jack tugged free the windlass handle that had anchored the towrope and took two steps forward.

"Mum!"

A nightdress-clad Jenny was hurrying towards Rose. Her stomach lurched. What was her daughter doing out of bed? "Get back to the boat!"

"Woof's missing."

"He's with me. Back. Now!"

A sickening sucking noise brought Rose's head round, and she saw Jack Littlemore withdrawing the windlass handle from a ruined eye and preparing to spear another one. He ducked and a tentacle whooshed over his head. Bert wasn't so lucky. One minute he was standing on the bank, whacking away with his shovel, the next he had disappeared.

Rose gaped at the space he had occupied a moment ago, then frantic cries and splashing noises drew her attention to the canal.

"Help!" Bert was staring short-sightedly up at her; he must have lost his glasses in the Cut. "I can't swim."

Neither can I. As she stood, frozen, a slim figure dashed past her and dived in.

"Jenny!"

Where there had been one head bobbing in the water now there were two. But the smaller figure's attempts to support the larger one didn't seem to be working. Bert's fist almost caught Jenny a blow on her chin.

"Stop fighting her, Bert!" ordered Rose. But the boatman was too panicky to take in what she was saying.

Rose thought fast. She released her grip on Woof's collar and picked up the shovel Bert had dropped. "Grab hold of this." Leaning out as far as she dared, she reversed the shovel and extended the handle towards her daughter. But Jenny was too far out and too busy trying to stop a thrashing Bert from sinking them both.

She heard a loud splash then Woof swam into view, tail streaming out behind as he arrowed straight towards his mistress. He grabbed the sleeve of Jenny's nightdress and began to tug, tearing the thin material and threatening to submerge both her and Bert.

"Stop it, Woof!" Jenny's voice was shrill with fear. "Let go!"

Rose added her pleas to Jenny's. At first the dog wouldn't obey but eventually he released his grip and trod water, still eager to help his mistress but succeeding only in getting in her way.

"Grab hold of Woof's collar," ordered Rose. "Let him tow you to the bank."

"I can't let go of Bert."

"You don't have to. Hook one arm round his neck or something."

"But—" Jenny's head vanished underwater and she reappeared spluttering.

"Just do it!" shouted Rose.

A thin arm flailed in Woof's direction but missed and doused him with water. He shook his head and sneezed.

"You nearly had him," encouraged Rose, trying to keep her voice steady though fear had her heart in a vicelike grip. *I can't lose another child to the Cut. I can't!* "Try again, Jenny."

For a moment she thought her daughter hadn't heard her, then Jenny's hand flailed and grabbed hold of the startled dog's collar. Woof barked, thinking it was a game, and tried to lick Jenny's nose

"Here, Woof," called Rose. "To me." His ears flicked in her direction. "Good dog." She slapped her thighs. "Come here."

Giving his mistress's nose a last playful lick, he turned and began to dogpaddle towards the bank. It was hard going, tugging the combined weight of Jenny and Bert, but slowly but surely he began to close the distance.

The grip on Rose's heart eased. "Almost there, Woof. Almost—" She leaned out over the canal and hooked her hand through Bert's trouser belt. "Got him! You can let go, love."

When at last Bert lay gasping on the bank, Rose helped her daughter out of the water and enveloped her shivering, drenched frame in a hug.

"Thanks, Mum," said Jenny. "It's a lot colder than it looks."

"Yes, thanks," panted a sheepish Bert, as beside them Woof shook himself dry.

Somewhere, a fox barked, and Rose belatedly remembered what

had been going on before Bert fell in. *Things shouldn't be this quiet.* She turned, dreading what she might find.

The creature now lay on its side, eyes pulped, wings torn and bloodied, a tentacle waving feebly, maw slack and emitting painful wheezes. Facing it, still brandishing their windlass handles, shovels, and shaft poles, were the four boatmen. Woof trotted over to join them.

The wheezing stopped and the last of the tentacles flopped and lay still.

"Is it dead?" called Rose.

Mike shoved the toe of his boot into the creature's side. No reaction. "Looks like it."

Woof nosed it, gave a single dismissive bark, and wandered back to Jenny's side.

The ragged sound of clapping made Rose glance to where the women were still gathered round the campfire.

Surely killing it shouldn't have been that easy? But she was too exhausted to think about that right now. She turned back to her shivering daughter. "Let's get you dry before you catch your death."

"What *was* it, Mum?"

"I have no idea."

THE FOUR WOMEN stared down at the carcass.

"Ugly brute, ain't it?" Polly Littlemore fiddled with an earring. "And it stinks."

It was decomposing faster than it should. *But then*, thought Rose, *who's to say what it should and shouldn't do?* She squatted for a closer look. In daylight it was, if anything, even more grotesque.

"Those poor Tooleys!" Marge Beauchamp took a pull on her cigarette. "Imagine coming face to face with *that*."

"It was probably quick," murmured Rose. "And they wouldn't have been able to see it."

"Hope so."

Woof trotted over, sniffed a rotting tentacle, sneezed at the ripe, sweet-sour stench, and wandered off to harass a water rat.

"Where's Mike?" asked Laura Ward, looking round.

"Searching for Hilda," said Rose absently.

"She won't have gone far," said Marge. "She'll be wanting her nose tin refilled."

Rose glanced towards the tunnel mouth. Just inside it floated the *Endeavour*. She had sprouted legging boards, and Jack and Tom Littlemore, Bert Beauchamp, and Dave Ward were settling themselves on them, preparing to leg her through.

Bert was wearing a cracked pair of old spectacles Marge had unearthed. He hailed his wife and she waved to show she'd heard him. "Looks like Bert's ready for the off."

As Marge spoke, four pairs of heavy work boots made contact with the tunnel wall and the *Endeavour* began to inch its way inside, pulling the *Gertrude* and the *Perseverance*, linked by towropes, behind her.

"Sorry we can't wait, Rose." Laura looked guilty. "But we can't afford any more delay."

Rose shrugged. Who could? It didn't matter. Pooling manpower would have made getting through the Echo easier, but she and Mike had legged the *Friendship* through on their own before.

"Maybe we'll see you in Marshbury?" said Polly.

"Maybe."

Already the clatter of boots was fainter and had taken on an echoing quality. The stern of the *Endeavour* disappeared into the tunnel then it was the *Gertrude*'s turn to enter.

"Better get a move on or they'll reach the other end before us," said Marge. "Bye, Rose."

"Bye."

The three women hurried to where their boathorses and mules were cropping the grass. Rose watched them start along the path that would lead them over the top, then resumed her perusal of the creature.

Hauling such bulk around must have taken huge amounts of effort. And what about those feeble-looking wings? No wonder it had made for the Cut—the water would have provided it with some support. She frowned. The signs of last night's battle were all too obvious, but there seemed to be lots of older burns, partially healed, too. Some could be due to the boatmen's attempts to burn it out of the tunnel, but the rest . . .

"What are you doing, Mum?"

She glanced up at Jenny and smiled. "Wondering."

"About what?"

"What it is. Where it came from. Why it was so easy to kill." *Relatively speaking.*

Her daughter regarded her with bright eyes. "It came from the power station, didn't it?"

Smart as a whip, our Jenny. "I think it must have."

"Remember the smoke we saw? Maybe it got hurt in the fire." Jenny leaned down to pet Woof, who had finished with the rat and was now snuffling at his mistress's socks.

"That's what I was thinking."

"But how did it get there in the first place, Mum?"

Rose straightened. "You know how sometimes you open the cabin hatch door and Woof comes flying through it?" She had lost count of the number of times the exuberant dog had almost knocked her over.

Jenny blinked at her. "It came from thin air, with the power?"

Rose nodded. "And maybe in the process it smashed their machinery and *that* started the fire." She thought for a moment. "But no one knows about it yet." *If they did, the Authority's officials would be everywhere, asking questions.* "Maybe the fire killed all the scientists and destroyed the evidence."

"But *we* know, Mum," said Jenny. "Shouldn't we tell someone?"

The thought of contacting the Authority was daunting—Rose could just imagine their scepticism—but if she didn't, they'd rebuild the power station, and who knew what would come through from the other dimension next?

"While you're at it," continued Jenny, her eyes bright, "you could talk to them about my going to Marshbury school."

The hopeful note in her daughter's voice decided Rose. "I could," she agreed. "And I will. Your dad isn't going to like it though."

"Why not?"

Rose smiled. "That's just the way Dads are." She brushed an errant lock of hair out of Jenny's eyes. "Will you help me explain to him about the power station?"

"All right."

A distant bray brought Rose's head round. Mike was striding along the towpath towards them; beside him trotted a chastened Hilda.

"Found her in a field half a mile away with some donkeys," he called, when he was within earshot. He glanced to where the stern of the *Perseverance* was just vanishing inside the tunnel. "They decided not to wait for us, then?"

She nodded. "Just as well. There's something else we have to do before we get moving."

"Oh?" Mike came to a halt in front of her and raised a dark eyebrow. "What?"

Rose hesitated. A small hand slipped into hers and gave her an encouraging squeeze. She smiled at her daughter, took a deep breath, and met her husband's gaze. "You know that creature in the Cut? Well, we think it wasn't from around here . . ."

AFTERWORD

I never know what I'm going to find on my library's non-fiction book-shelves. Quite by chance I came upon Ramlin Rose: The Boatwoman's Story *by Sheila Stewart, a slim book about the women who worked the narrowboats on England's canals during the first half of the 20th century. Stewart's book was full of colour, dialect, and incident and after reading it I decided to write a story about a family on a narrowboat.*

DEMONSBANE

THE BOUNCER'S GAZE was stubborn. "Sorry, mate."

"But Regan *told* me to come!" Brad remembered the card and produced it. "She gave me this."

The bald-headed man studied the Demonsbane business card and flipped it over. Brad knew what the scrawled message on the back said: "He's with me. Regan."

Brad had been standing in the crowded College bar before the gig started, trying to order a beer, when someone elbowed him in the back and shouted, "Gangway! Thirsty rock band to supply."

The elbower had proved to be a diminutive woman in a tie-dyed purple T-shirt and flowing skirt, her raven hair so long it almost reached her waist. When she looked up at him and winked, Brad's protest had died in his throat. Even Holly had never made him feel the way this woman did with just a glance, as if electricity were zipping through his veins.

On her return trip, clutching a tray loaded with bottles and glasses, the roadie had paused next to him and raised an eyebrow. "Like what you see?"

He blushed—he had been staring, he supposed—but she simply grinned, revealing even white teeth, and said, "Come backstage afterwards. Ask for Regan." She balanced the tray with one hand, and scrabbled in the pocket of her skirt with the other.

As she walked away, Brad examined the card she had given him and resolved to do just that.

"Looks okay, mate," said the bouncer at last. "Regan's room is that one." He indicated the dressing room door farthest away.

"Thanks."

Brad made his way between impatient autograph-hunters and stoned hangers-on towards the door, knocked, and waited nervously. No reply. He knocked again. Eventually he grew tired of waiting, opened the door, and walked in. Then he stopped, stunned.

Regan was standing in front of a huge wolf, her hand resting on its left shoulder. As both woman and animal turned to regard the intruder, the wolf's ears came erect. Its fur was a deep matte-silver-grey, and it gazed at Brad through keen amber eyes.

Brad became aware that the roadie was gesturing at him, then his vision clouded, and his legs went out from under him . . .

"ARE YOU ALL right?" Regan was stooping over him, her strange pendant—a misshapen, semi-precious stone of some kind—swinging.

"Wha—?" Brad struggled to sit up. What was he doing on the floor? Memory came flooding back and his stomach clenched as he scanned the small dressing room. Someone had scrawled an obscene, anatomically incorrect doodle on the wall next to the sink. "What happened to the wolf?"

"You must have been dreaming. Fainting can make you do that, you know."

"I never faint."

"Then what are you doing on the floor, sweetheart?"

What indeed? Brad frowned.

"Too much beer on an empty stomach, I expect." Regan held out a hand. "Up you come."

He took it, hauled himself to his feet, and, while he struggled to make sense of what had happened, brushed the dirt off his jeans.

"You know my name," she said. "What's yours?"

"Brad."

"Okay, Brad. Glad you could make it. If you're feeling better, why don't I introduce you to the band?"

"Uh, sure."

REGAN LED BRAD into the much larger dressing room next door, where the smell of body odour, beer, and cigarette smoke rocked him back on his heels.

Four of the five members of Demonsbane were sitting with their feet up on the table, towels draped round sweaty shoulders, half-empty beer bottles in their fists. The laughter and talk stopped dead, and every eye swivelled to regard Brad. His cheeks burned.

"Can we help you, mate?" growled the huge drummer.

"It's all right, Dave," said Regan. "He's with me. Name's Brad."

"Might have guessed." This from the tall blonde woman who had sung like an angel and whose name, Brad learned, was Jodi. "A student too!" She rolled her eyes.

Was it that obvious? Brad frowned.

Regan laughed. "Sit down before you fall down."

He felt a chair dig into the back of his knees and let himself slump onto it. "Sorry." He was still feeling slightly faint. "Must be the heat."

"I'm Will." The skinny keyboard player shoved an opened bottle at Brad. "This'll cool you down."

"Thanks." He took a long swallow of beer, feeling the welcome chill travel down his gullet.

A woman with short black hair and glasses nodded at him. "Hi, I'm Ella. On bass guitar."

"Hi."

The band members were half-naked, cooling down after the gig, and Brad couldn't help noticing the tattoos each wore at the top of a left arm. Must be a band thing, he decided. Jodi's was a black cat, that looked so real he could imagine it purring; Ella's an owl of some kind; Will's snake tattoo had vivid red-and-black markings on its back; and, just visible beneath the drummer's thick black body hair, was a snarling bear. He wondered if the missing member of the band—guitarist Johnny—also had a tattoo.

"Is Brad going to be recharging your batteries while we're here?" Dave asked Regan.

"Looks a bit young," said Jodi. "You sure he's up to it?"

"The young ones have the most stamina," said Regan.

The drummer opened another bottle of beer with his teeth. "You should know."

Letting the banter flow round him, Brad drank his beer and tracked Regan's movements as she folded dirty towels and picked up discarded T-shirts, retrieved stray picks and packets of guitar strings, stacked empty bottles in a crate and tapped cigarette ash into the waste bin.

When she had finished tidying, she gave him a smile that made his toes curl, then turned to the others. "Drink up. You have autographs to sign, and," she quirked an eyebrow, "groupies to satisfy. Be back at the hotel by eleven-thirty p.m. Jodi, Dave—pick up a Balti— enough for seven." She glanced at Brad. "You like Balti?"

"I ate earlier."

"No probs. Dave'll have what's left of yours." Laughter greeted her remark. "We'll eat in Ella's room."

"Oh no," groaned the bass guitarist. "It'll stink the place out."

Regan shrugged. "Tough. It's your turn."

Brad was puzzled. The way Regan was laying down the law, she was clearly much more than a roadie.

"And remember, we've got another gig here tomorrow night. So don't do anything that might get you run out of town."

Still grumbling, the members of Demonsbane left, and Brad and Regan were alone at last.

What happened next happened so quickly and naturally, Brad wondered if one of the band had slipped something in his beer. For he was not so experienced that he could have sex with a complete stranger without some apprehension or preparation.

But, in short order, the dressing room door was locked, his clothes (and Regan's) were discarded, and he was flat on his back on the table, being straddled by the small woman, and having a very pleasurable time indeed.

BRAD HELPED HIMSELF to some Tandoori Chicken Balti and gazed round Ella's hotel room, which was identical to the one he was sharing with Regan.

Guitarist Johnny, whose hair was long, shaggy, and prematurely grey, had joined the other members of Demonsbane and was taking some stick about his bum chord in the middle of "Elf Help." It was good-natured criticism, however. These people felt comfortable with one another, observed Brad. And most of the comfort stemmed from Regan.

She was far more than the roadie he had mistaken her for in the bar. She was Demonsbane's manager, songwriter, and guiding light, and their interest in and respect for her opinions was obvious. And since, for tonight at least, Brad belonged to her (something she signalled by placing a hand gently but firmly on his thigh while they ate) the others seemed happy to have him along too.

Being a sex object should feel shameful, he supposed, but it didn't. Especially since, unlike his "ex" (the insults Holly had flung his way when they broke up a month ago still stung), Regan appeared to have no complaints about his sexual prowess. He smirked and reached for another helping of mushrooms.

The conversation turned to the recent spate of art robberies—five so far, the latest involving the local Art Gallery. Its insurers had not been happy to learn that several prestigious paintings on loan from elsewhere had been stolen—then moved on to the outrageous antics of the rock bands Demonsbane had met on the gig circuit.

By the time they finished eating, it was nearly one a.m. and Brad's grip on the proceedings was beginning to slip. He gave in to the impulse and yawned.

"Bed for you, sweetheart," said Regan.

Johnny snickered, and received a quelling glance from the small woman.

"Remember where our room is?" Brad nodded. "I'll join you in a little while. Okay?"

Brad struggled to his feet. "Okay."

NEXT MORNING, BRAD woke to a feeling of lethargy and sheets that smelled of sex. He squinted at his surroundings. On the dressing table was Regan's makeup bag and hairbrush, and in the corner was her suitcase. The door opened, and Regan herself came in bearing a tray. She glowed with vitality.

She placed the tray on the bed in front of him and tousled his hair. "I called room service, sweetheart. Eat up."

He stared at cornflakes, toast and orange juice, bacon, eggs, sausage and tomato, at the coffee with a swirl of cream, and wondered if he would be able to manage all of it. One bite made him realise he could. He ate like a ravening wolf.

She grinned. "We're going to be busy today. Can you look after yourself until tonight's gig?"

"I have lectures all day. And I'm a big boy, Regan!"

She gave him a knowing look. "That you are." She stood up. "I'll see you tonight then."

THE DEMONSBANE GIG was a huge success—word had spread since last night's concert—and afterwards, the band (accompanied by a few fans whose dogged persistence they felt was worth rewarding) held a boozy celebration in a nightclub round the corner from the hotel.

Around two a.m. Brad and Regan returned to Regan's room, where a bout of vigorous coupling left him feeling happy but drained, and he sank into a deep sleep.

He wasn't sure what woke him. One minute he was dreaming—erotically charged dreams of Regan—and the next he was blinking into darkness. Not quite darkness, he amended. There was a strange sharp scent, rather like ozone, and flickering light was coming from the open door to the other room.

He reached for Regan, but found only the cooling imprint of her body. She must be watching TV. He sat up and stretched. Flinging back the duvet, he slipped out of bed and padded across the worn carpet, stubbing his toe in the process. He hopped the last few steps through the open door and came to a halt, mouth open, words frozen in his throat.

The flickering light wasn't coming from the TV set but from some . . . "thing" was the only word Brad's startled brain could supply. It was like a column of twisting, coiled blackness shot through with sparks, yet at the same time there was a suggestion of eyes and of wings, clawed wings. Facing it, one arm outstretched, her face as pale as a ghost, sweat beading her forehead, was Regan.

Her gaze flicked in his direction. Then she closed her eyes and began to mutter something that sounded like an incantation. One hand, Brad saw, was holding the strange pendant she wore even in bed.

The column of darkness churned, as though in discomfort, and let out a bellow of protest. Then there was a soft implosion, like a soap bubble bursting, and the thing was gone.

Regan fell to her knees, gasping, and Brad rushed to her side. "What the hell *was* that? Did it hurt you? Shall I call the police—?"

She held up one hand. "Just let me get my breath back."

He frowned but did as she asked, watching her impatiently. Already her colour was better. He fetched a towel from the bathroom and handed it to her. She smiled and wiped away the sweat.

"So," he said at last, "are you going to tell me what's going on? And don't tell me I was dreaming, because I know I wasn't."

Regan struggled to her feet. He helped her back to the other room, where she eased herself into bed.

"You're right," she told him. He crawled in beside her, propped himself up on one elbow, and looked at her. "It's time I told you." She paused before continuing. "That 'thing' was a demon."

"A demon." His voice was flat with disbelief, and she threw him an exasperated look.

"You wanted to know, sweetheart; I'm telling you. Okay?"

He decided to play along for now. "How did it get here?"

"Someone must have summoned it. It completed its task then had some time to kill . . . literally. So it came after me."

She was serious! Panic began to well up inside him, and he stifled it quickly. Now was not the time for hysteria. "Why *you*? Did the summoner target you?"

"Unlikely. Word gets around, even in the demon realm. It knows I'm a threat so, when it sensed my presence nearby, it took a chance, tried to get me while I was sleeping." She caressed the pendant and smiled like the cat that ate the canary. "But my wards woke me. All I had to do then was hold it at bay until its visiting time ran out."

"Who would summon such a thing? And why?"

"You sure ask a lot of questions! . . . Someone who doesn't know what he's doing." Regan sighed. "It's always the same. Guy gets greedy—for power, wealth, health, sex . . . whatever—and summons a demon to do his dirty work."

He blinked at her.

"Don't look so surprised. The summoning spell's easy enough to get hold of, if you know where to look. There's a catch, of course. There always is. Quite a large one in this case."

"Oh?"

"Demons can't be housetrained, controlled. Oh, they let you think they can—devious little shits! But they have their own agendas. All the time they're doing their master's bidding, they're also waiting and scheming . . ."

"For what?"

"A way to cross into our world permanently, with no one giving them orders."

"Why would they want that?"

"Why do you think, sweetheart? Demons get their kicks draining the life force from humans." She grimaced. "Tastes like fried chicken, apparently."

He fought a sudden feeling of nausea. "Back up a minute, Regan. I thought you said that demons can only come to our world for a limited time."

"That's true, unless the summoner dies while they're here. And if he stays in his protective circle, he's safe. But one slip and he's toast." Her gaze became distant. "And he always does slip, in the end. My job is to get to the poor bastard first. Sometimes I'm too late. Sometimes he's just too greedy, or too hooked on the rush of controlling a demon to take my advice."

Brad leaned back against the headboard. Either the woman in bed with him was a raving loony, or she was telling the truth. But he had seen that thing with his own eyes. The panic threatened to surface once more.

"Take a few breaths, sweetheart. Works wonders on the nerves."

That she had noticed the state he was in annoyed him for some reason. "I'm fine," he snapped.

"Hey, nothing to be ashamed of. Changing your worldview can knock the stuffing out of you. We've all been through it. You'll adjust."

"I'm not sure I want to, Regan."

She shrugged. "You wanted to know."

"I know I did, okay?" He got his temper under control with an effort. "So. It was a demon." Even saying the word gave him the heebie-jeebies. "What did you do, send it back to its own world?"

She nodded.

Brad was suddenly afraid of her. "What exactly *are* you?"

She smiled. "You can call me a wizard."

"Wizards are male."

"They're magic users," she corrected. "And right now this one needs you to do something for her."

His gaze was wary. "Yes?"

"It's not something you'll find difficult, I hope. I want you to have sex with me."

Brad's jaw dropped. "Now?"

She nodded.

He remembered a remark about batteries made earlier by one of the band. A piece in the jigsaw clicked into place. She looked deep into his eyes, and he felt the beginnings of arousal. He must be mad to be even considering this. She was either totally round the bend, or she could turn him into a toad. But his hormones seemed to have a will of their own, and the prickle of fear was only arousing him more.

"Wizards use all kinds of emotions to fuel their magic," she told Brad. "Hate, love . . . I happen to use sex." She kissed him, a hot, hungry, open-mouthed kiss that left him breathless. "It's not so bad, is it?"

BRAD WAS THE last one up the next morning, and joined the others in the hotel dining room for breakfast. As he sat down, a silence fell over the group. They glanced at him, then back at Regan, then at him again.

"I guess you know I know, huh?" he said.

Ella blinked at him, her eyes large through her spectacle lenses, while Johnny merely raised one shaggy eyebrow. Jodi and Dave exchanged a significant glance.

Regan buttered herself another slice of toast. "He doesn't know *everything*," she corrected. "Time to fill in the blanks." She reached for a sachet of orange marmalade.

Will raised his coffee cup in ironic salute. "Welcome to the crazy world of Demonsbane."

"It's to do with the tattoos, isn't it?" Brad had spent a good deal of time thinking, while Regan slept peacefully beside him. "Johnny's must be of a wolf."

Raised eyebrows met that remark.

"Brad saw me briefing the wolf before he went out the other night," said Regan. "He put two and two together."

"You forgot to put wards on the dressing room door?" Dave looked startled.

She tapped the side of her nose. "Who says I forgot?"

Brad blinked. "You mean that was some kind of test?"

"Figured it couldn't hurt to see how you reacted to weird stuff. You didn't run away screaming. Always a good sign." Regan cocked her head to one side and regarded him. "Forgive me?"

He grunted.

"So show him, Johnny," she ordered.

He watched as the guitarist undid the top buttons of his shirt then eased it down over the top of his left arm, revealing a grey wolf with amber eyes. The tattoo had clearly been done by the same artist as the others.

"Hey, people," said Jodi. "We're getting funny looks."

Regan glanced round the dining room, her challenging gaze causing the other hotel guests to look away. "No problem," she said. "We're just comparing notes about last night. Got drunk, got laid, got a tattoo . . ." She gave a mock sigh. "A rock star's life—ho hum." She grinned at the band members and they grinned back.

"Seen enough?" asked Johnny. Brad nodded, and the guitarist covered himself up again.

"So, are you all wizards too?" Brad glanced at the band members.

Ella snorted. "Puhlease! I leave that sort of thing to Regan, thank you very much."

"Nope. We're shapeshifters," said Jodi.

First demons, then a wizard, and now shapeshifters. He pinched his forearm. *Ow!* "All of you?"

"Except Regan." Will nodded at the small woman.

"What triggers the shift? A full moon?"

Catcalls greeted Brad's remark, but Regan took pity on him. It was she who triggered the shift to animal form, she explained, via the tattoos, which she had designed and executed herself (his already high estimation of her abilities shot up). She could also maintain a telepathic link, see what the shapeshifter saw, sense what it sensed, and more importantly, interpret what it couldn't.

"And all that takes energy," she continued matter-of-factly. "Which is where you come in."

Even though he had begun to suspect as much, it still hurt. He was aware of the band members' gazes, part curiosity, part sympathy. "Why me?"

"A handsome, healthy young guy with the hots for me?" Regan shrugged. "Why not you?"

He could almost picture Holly laughing at him. "But I still don't understand," he said at last. "Why does a wizard need shapeshifters to help her?"

"My powers are limited. I can't climb up the side of a cliff, or fly, or crawl down a sewer . . ."

And they can! He eyed the band members. "What's in it for them?"

"What do you think?" Johnny spoke on behalf of everyone. "Before we met Regan, we could only *dream* of being rock stars. She's going to make it happen."

THE BREAKFAST PLATES had been pushed to one side and a map of the city was spread over the white damask tablecloth. Beside it was a copy of that morning's local paper—a small article had been circled.

Brad checked his watch. He should be in College right now, but at Regan's urging, he had phoned Rick and asked if he could borrow his notes from today's lectures. Rick had called him a randy sod but agreed. Now Brad wondered whether it wouldn't have been safer, not to mention wiser, to go to lectures after all. Who knew what weirdness Regan had lined up?

"As I suspected, given my unexpected visitor," Regan had filled in the others about the demon, "there was another art theft last night. A private gallery this time." She stabbed a finger at the map. "Johnny drew a blank last time—the trail was too old. But this time, it's fresh."

The band members glanced at one another. "Our anonymous art collector is getting greedy," commented Ella.

"And his pet demon is getting bolder," said Regan. "First sneaking off and snacking on the side, then coming after me. We have to end this now."

"We?"

Regan gave Brad a look. "It's what we do. I told you."

Something she had said was nagging at him. "Snacking?"

"The authorities have kept it quiet," growled Dave, "but Regan has a friend on the Force who's been giving her the heads up. At each of the crime scenes so far, a curator or guard has been killed."

Brad's palms felt clammy. "Like chicken," he murmured.

"What?" asked Johnny.

"Nothing."

Regan began to refold the map. "I'd say it's just about ready to turn on its master."

"Bye, bye, Mr. Art Collector," said Jodi.

"He'll be no great loss." Regan's voice was hard. "But if that demon of his gets loose . . ." She rose. "Let's get this show on the road."

WHILE THE OTHERS exchanged banter in the back, Brad sat up front with Regan, who was driving the Banemobile. Everyone except him seemed very relaxed considering they were tracking down a life-force-sucking demon. How many times had they done this before?

Regan parked the cramped minivan just around the corner from the Yew Tree Gallery, which was cordoned off with fluttering red-and-white police tape. And while Johnny, now in wolf form, slunk down the alleyway next to the two-storey building, Regan gestured and muttered what sounded to Brad like pure gibberish.

"Augmentation spell," she told him. "Demons leave no spoor, so we'll have to track the painting instead. It's old, though, and traces of oil paint will be faint even to a wolf's senses."

She closed her eyes, frowned briefly, then opened them again. "Johnny's picked up the trail."

"Cool!" said Will.

Regan beckoned to Jodi. "You drive. I need to concentrate on my link with Johnny."

"Sure." The blonde singer replaced Regan in the driver's seat, started the engine, then looked at Regan. "Which way?"

"First left."

As they followed the wolf, Regan kept up a running commentary for the others' benefit. Occasionally, she would send instructions along the link. "Not now," she instructed at one point. "Eat later."

Dave glanced at Brad. "Must have been distracted by a rubbish bin. It happens."

A little while later, the Banemobile pulled up outside the barred gates of a mansion and Regan reported that the wolf had lost the trail. "You'll have to pick it up, Ella. Johnny says it goes straight up the side of the house."

"No problem." As Ella stripped off her clothes and changed into owl form, Brad looked away. He had witnessed Johnny's transformation earlier and it had made him feel queasy. The human form shouldn't be able to do that, he had thought, wincing as bones and sinews, skin and hair, reshaped themselves.

Regan muttered something under her breath. Then came an owl's screech and the sound of wings flapping. They faded into the distance.

Brad glanced once more at the mansion situated in extensive manicured grounds, and realised where he was. "This is Edward Filmore's place!" Curious faces turned to his. "He's a well known local business man. His picture's always in the papers . . . giving money to good causes, etc."

"They're the worst." Jodi drummed her fingers on the steering wheel. "Later you discover they've been jamming coke up their nostrils and shagging school girls."

"Well, he's gone too far this time," said Will. "The demon will off him for sure."

"Of course, the summoner might not be Filmore himself," cautioned Regan. "A place this size—there are bound to be servants."

As she spoke, a huge grey wolf slipped between the gate's bars and loped towards the Banemobile. Regan gestured and muttered a few words. Moments later, Johnny was slipping into the clothes Dave handed him.

"Ella says she's picked up traces on a top floor window ledge," said Regan, opening her eyes.

"Is Filmore there?" asked Brad.

"I'm not sensing any life signs on that floor. But if he is, I'll deal with him." She stood up. "Right, let's go." She turned to the massive drummer. "Dave—can you get us through the bars, please?"

"Sure thing."

Brad looked at the others in consternation. "Hey. There are rules against breaking and entering—"

But Dave had already shucked his clothes, and was beginning his transformation into bear form . . .

IF I EVER go into the burglary business, thought Brad, I'll make sure I have a wizard and a band of shapeshifters with me.

Progress had been ridiculously easy. The bear had bent the bars of the gate as though they were pipe-cleaners, and Regan was able to anticipate the various alarm systems and magic eye beams with which Filmore had protected his property. As for the video cameras, she assured him the recorded images would be fogged beyond recovery.

When they encountered the gardener, and later on the maid, a few swift passes by Regan and they fell as though pole-axed. Brad sympathised. He knew how it felt to be on the receiving end of one of Regan's so-called fainting fits.

Hurriedly he closed the gap between himself and Regan. They entered the mansion by one of the side doors and were almost at the top of their second flight of stairs. Regan stopped in front of a lift door. It was too small for all of them at once, so Regan, Brad, and Jodi went first.

As the lift ascended, there was no sound except for their breathing.

Jodi adjusted the shoulder strap of the duffle bag she had brought with her. A bell pinged and the door opened to reveal an expensively furnished ante room.

"Welcome to the penthouse," said Jodi. The other two followed her out of the lift.

"Where's Ella?" asked Brad as the doors closed behind them and the lift begin its descent.

Regan got her bearings quickly. "Through here." She opened a door and they stepped into a corridor, which, judging by its length and the windows along one side, must run along the side of the entire upper storey.

Brad heard a faint tapping and turned to see what it was. A magnificent owl, its sandy plumage covered in grey markings and small white dots, was perched outside a slightly open window. It was pecking at the glass. "Ella!"

The window was stiff, but after a brief tussle Brad managed to open it fully. The huge bird stepped inside. It blinked at him, hissed, then hopped down onto the corridor floor. Regan muttered something, and a blurring of the owl outline warned Brad what was coming. He turned away.

When the transformation was complete, Jodi reached for the duffle bag, and the mystery of its contents was solved. She pulled out Ella's clothes and handed them to the shivering bass guitarist.

Regan extracted a spectacle case from her skirt pocket. "Here."

"Thanks." Ella put on her spectacles and blinked. Brad could see what had inspired Regan to give the bassist an owl tattoo.

"Right," said Regan. "Brad, you come with me. The rest of you wait here."

Brad traipsed along the corridor after Regan. "Where do I fit in?" he asked.

"Double entendres, sweetheart?"

He blushed.

"But you're right, actually. I may need a quick recharge." She winked.

He stared at her. "Are you serious?"

"Deadly. So, you gonna stand there gaping or help me fight this demon?"

Ignoring the numerous doors that opened off the corridor, she headed for the one at the far end marked "Gallery." Brad sighed and set off after her.

FILMORE'S PERSONAL GALLERY was lined with wonderful paintings from all schools, in all shapes and sizes. But Brad wasn't looking at them. His attention was split between the coiling column of blackness by the desk and the mangled mess of flesh and designer suit that had once been Edward Filmore. He gulped and looked at Regan, who had assumed her "living statue" pose.

Glowing eyes glared from the heart of the blackness, and the demon laughed . . . at least Brad thought it was a laugh.

"You're too late." The deep timbre of the voice shattered an expensive vase on Filmore's desk and showered flower stems and water everywhere. "I can stay here forever now."

Brad's stomach did a flip. The demon was much stronger than last time, and Regan had depleted her strength by fuelling three shape-shifts in a row. Already her arm was trembling and beads of sweat were trickling down her brow. She squeezed her eyes shut, muttered an incantation, then opened them again.

The deep laugh boomed round the study again. "You are weak, wizard. This time I will have you."

It surged towards Regan, only to be brought up short by an invisible barrier. Frustrated, it began to seek a way round the obstacle. It could only be a matter of time.

The small woman glanced at Brad. "Come here," she told him.

"What?" His eyes bulged.

"Quickly, or we're lost!"

The demon's attempts to cross the barrier were growing increasingly violent.

Brad edged towards Regan on trembling legs. If she wanted sex, he couldn't possibly oblige. He was terrified, close to shitting himself.

"Draw a circle around me." She nodded at Filmore's desk. "There's some chalk there."

He did as she requested, rolling back the ornate Chinese rug to reveal wooden floorboards with faint traces of old chalk on them. When the circle was complete, he looked at her.

"Now, inside the circle, a pentacle. Draw a pentacle."

"A five-pointed star?"

"Yes." Her voice cracked with strain. "Hurry!"

He drew a wobbly star. As he finished the last point, the demon gave a growl that sent chills down his spine. "Do you really think you can stop me?"

"Good," said Regan, ignoring it. "That's very good, sweetheart. Now," she widened her stance, "slide over here between my legs. Don't, whatever you do, rub out the chalk lines."

Brad did as she directed, scooting over until he was on his back, his groin directly beneath hers.

"Unzip your jeans."

Whether his jeans were unzipped or not seemed irrelevant—his balls seemed to be trying to crawl back inside his body for safety—but Brad did as he was told.

Regan released the pendant and gestured at him. Simultaneously, the demon surged towards her.

"That's all I can spare," she gasped. She clutched the pendant once more, and the barrier returned in force. The demon bellowed its frustration.

Brad, meanwhile, no longer cared much about anything. His groin felt as though it had been dipped in liquid fire and was sending warmth shooting through his entire nervous system. He became dimly aware that Regan was kneeling, positioning herself above him, then she sheathed him inside herself, and his brain turned to mush . . .

Later, he wondered if he should have died right there and then, for he would surely never surpass that feeling of bliss. As Regan slid herself up and down, all the while somehow managing to keep one hand on the pendant and one pointing at the demon, he lost himself in exquisite sensation, no longer aware of time or space . . .

The end, when it came, was sudden. Brad, who was groaning on the edge of orgasm, lost control and cried out. Simultaneously Regan shouted a string of gibberish.

Through cracked eyelids, a boneless Brad saw a flash of coruscating energy travel from Regan's fingertip. The air around the demon boiled, and it screamed—a cry full of anger, pain, and despair—then came the implosion.

Brad's ears popped, and something brushed over his face—papers sucked from Filmore's desk. A whistling sound, faint at first, increased to a shriek, and Regan's hair streamed as though caught in a gale.

"Hang on, Brad," she told him. "It's almost finished."

But he never saw the end. Whiteness seared the inside of Brad's eyelids. Then blackness claimed him . . .

"SO," SAID BRAD, putting down the newspaper with its lurid headlines about the butchered Edward Filmore. "You're moving on."

Regan didn't look up from her packing. "Afraid so, sweetheart. We've done all we can here. Got business to attend to elsewhere." She folded a Demonsbane T-shirt and stuffed it in her bag. "And you have your studying to do."

Brad sighed. He had known this moment would come, even so . . . "Another demon?"

Regan glanced up at him and smiled. "Not this time. Seems there was an A&R scout at the last gig. He liked the band. Wants us to talk to one of the execs at his record company."

He digested that. "I thought that was just your cover story."

"Uh uh," she said. "I keep my promises. Demonsbane has always been for real." She sat beside him on the bed and took one of his hands between hers. "You going to be all right, sweetheart?"

"I guess." He shrugged. "It takes a bit of getting used to, you know. Being a boy toy. Discovering that wizards, shapeshifters, and demons are real." He tried to smile. "Nearly scared the pants off me."

"Literally."

"Yeah. Yet I've never felt so alive in all my life."

She patted his hand. "That's why I picked you, Brad."

"Brad," he noticed wistfully, not "sweetheart" anymore. "Because I was naïve?"

"No," she said. "Because your life force is so strong. And I knew I'd need it—our last case left me feeling rather drained."

He gave her a wry glance. "If this has been you drained, Regan, I'd hate to meet you when you're fully charged!"

"No you wouldn't."

"No, I wouldn't," he agreed.

She cocked her head and regarded him. "You're better off without Holly, you know." Brad blinked. He was sure he had never mentioned his "ex" to Regan. "She wasn't your type anyway. There'll be someone else out there who is. Trust me."

At the moment he rather doubted that. Regan was a hard act to follow. But he managed a smile. "I hope so." A squeeze of his hand was his reward.

From outside the hotel came the sound of a minibus horn. "Gotta go." She flicked back her waist-length hair, then rose to her feet. "The band's waiting for me."

He followed her to the doorway, feeling like a puppy whose owner had just left him at the kennels. She turned and smiled.

"Thanks," she said simply. "Have a good life, Brad." She leaned forward and gave him a kiss, soft, almost chaste at first, but quickly becoming hard and passionate. When she pulled back, he was tingling from head to toe and still breathless.

"Something to remember me by," Regan told him with a wink. Then she stepped out of the door and out of his life forever.

AFTERWORD

Nene Adam's "Underworld Chronicles" (www.corrieweb.nl/library. htm) were the spark for this story. She has such fun with her tales of occult mystery and suspense that I felt inspired to try an occult tale of my own. And how better to give my wizard a contemporary twist than by making her "day job" manager of a rock band?

ABOUT THE AUTHOR

Barbara Davies published her first short story in 1994. Since then, more than forty of her stories have appeared in various magazines, including *Marion Zimmer Bradley's Fantasy Magazine*, *Rage Machine Magazine*, *Farthing*, *Electric Spec*, and *Here and Now*, and in several anthologies, including *Ideomancer Unbound* and *F/ SF Volume 1*. The readers of *Kimota* gave one of her stories their 1999 Best Story Award.

Barbara lives in Gloucestershire, England, where she reviews Fantasy fiction for *Starburst*. Her website is: www.barbaradavies.co.uk